CW01467174

CROSSROADS MAGIC

WHITE HAVEN WITCHES

BOOK SIX

TJ GREEN

.

Crossroads Magic

Mountolive Publishing

Copyright © 2020 TJ Green

All rights reserved

eBook 978-0-9951386-0-5

Paperback 978-0-9951386-2-9

Hardback 978-1-99-004786-2

Cover design by Fiona Jayde Media

Editing by Missed Period Editing

This is a work of fiction. Names, characters, businesses, places, events, locales, and incidents are either the products of the author's imagination or used in a fictitious manner. Any resemblance to actual persons, living or dead, or actual events is purely coincidental.

No portion of this book may be reproduced in any form without written permission from the publisher or author, except as permitted by U.S. copyright law.

Contents

One

A fire blazed brightly at the centre of the clearing, and figures weaved a dance around it as they passed candles between them. The light cast a warm, gentle glow on the faces of the participants, many of whom were laughing as they trod the well-known path in the centre of the woods.

It was midnight at Imbolc, and the entire Cornwall Coven was celebrating the festival together.

Avery was there with the White Haven witches, all of whom had travelled together to Rasmus's estate on the edge of Newquay. After the horrors of the vampire attacks before Christmas, they hadn't seen the coven since, so it was a chance to celebrate the festival and their victory over Lupescu, the Romanian vampire who had caused so much destruction only weeks before.

However, it was freezing cold. Imbolc fell on the second of February, and frost lay thick upon the ground. When the coven completed the circle, they stopped and turned to watch Genevieve, their High Priestess, raise her hands to the sky. She invoked the Goddess, giving thanks and asking for protection for the months to come, and then she turned to kiss Rasmus gently on each cheek, and handed him a besom broom. Rasmus accepted it with a small bow, and then walked around the circle, brushing it along the ground as he did so, symbolically chasing away the old in a cleansing ritual. Once completed, he gave it back to Genevieve, who invited the others to join in, and then there was a frenzied few minutes as they all grabbed their own brooms and repeated the ritual.

Avery laughed as she furiously swept the ground. It was an old rite, but fun, and the symbolic cleansing really did feel as if they were getting rid of the toxic time they had all experienced. *And at least the snow had gone*, she reflected, as she swept past Reuben and laughed even harder. He looked so out of place with a broom in his hands, but he participated with good grace, even though he had moaned about it on the way over.

When they all finally stopped, they were breathless and hot. Genevieve clapped her hands, her smile beatific, and called a halt to the proceedings. She said a few final words before lifting a chalice of wine from the altar next to her. "And now, it's time to eat and drink!" She gestured to the table on the far side of the clearing, filled with food, and with that the circle broke apart and they headed to fill their plates.

Avery fell into step next to Nate and Eve, the two witches who lived in St Ives on the north coast of Cornwall. Both were artistic and unconventional. Nate was dressed in scruffy combat trousers and an old flying jacket, and Eve had long dreads. "How have you been?" Avery asked them.

"Pretty good," Nate said. "Better than you, by the sound of things."

Avery shrugged. "At least I didn't get a head injury like Eve. Are you better now?" she asked her.

"I'm fine, thank you," Eve answered, with a rueful rub of her scalp. "It soon healed. It was scarier getting out of those tunnels surrounded by fire. I was more worried I'd burn us all. No more news of vampires though, I hope?"

They had all been worried that some vampires had escaped, but if they had, they'd been quiet, and there were no other disappearances or strange deaths that had been attributed to them. "No, fortunately, which is good because we now have a headstrong fey on our hands."

They arrived at the long table, and Avery filled her plate as Nate frowned. "Ah yes, the survivor from the Wild Hunt. I'm intrigued."

Avery laughed, or at least tried to laugh. "Her name is Shadow, and she's driving us mad, the Nephilim included. She's an absolute force of nature! She's using Dan, who works in my shop, as her own personal myth-ometer." She rolled her eyes. "He loves every minute of it. I guess it's good that someone does!"

Nate studied her for a moment. "Eve mentioned her to me, but what's Shadow trying to do? Get back to the Otherworld?"

"And treasure hunt at the same time. You know, find ancient artefacts and sell them for a high price."

"And will the Nephilim help her?"

"I think so. They're trying to find their way in our world, and to make money. They think this will be lucrative. And let's face it, they're supernatural creatures. They have a natural interest in this sort of thing."

Nate looked troubled, and Eve said, "Nate's worried, because he thinks she could find things that are best left hidden."

"You're probably right, Nate," Avery said, worry stirring within her again. "But there's little we can do to stop them. I think we'll just have to manage the consequences."

"But those consequences could be big," he pointed out. "Any black market for art, drugs, or guns will always attract the worst kind of people. A market for mythical objects won't be any different—except for maybe having supernatural buyers. She may even want to steal what's already been found for her own uses."

Avery had a sudden image of Shadow breaking into museums and raiding their displays. Nate was right. She could definitely see that happening.

"Although," Eve countered, "the Nephilim and Shadow are very capable of looking after themselves. If you ask me, anyone who takes them on would be an idiot."

Avery sighed. "True. An even better reason for us to remain on their good side."

Avery spent the next hour or two mingling with the other witches, glad of the chance to talk to Ulysses and Oswald, and then Jasper, Claudia, and a few others. The fire was now blazing, and they sat around it on old deck chairs and logs in an effort to keep warm. They were nearly ready to return to the warmth of Rasmus's house when Caspian arrived at her side. Caspian lived in Harecombe, the town next to White Haven, and like Avery was an elemental Air witch. His relationship with their coven had started badly, but over time things were improving.

"Avery," he murmured, his dark eyes appraising her. "How are you?"

"Pretty good," she replied. "How's your wound?" She was referring to the deep cut on his chest caused by a vampire.

He rubbed it absently. "Better now, thanks to Briar. It felt like it had poison in it for a while—maybe it had. Let's face it, we don't know much even now about vampires, do we?"

"No, and if I'm honest, I'd like to keep it that way." She remembered that Gabe was now working for Caspian. "How's it going with the Nephilim as security guards?"

"Good, but I'm not surprised. Gabe has a strong work ethic, and they're imposing. No one argues with them."

Avery was curious. "Your company doesn't work with occult goods, does it? Why did you want Gabe?"

"We hide enough of ourselves in everyday life, don't we? I thought it would be good to have honest conversations with as many people as possible. Life can be lonely otherwise." He held her gaze for a moment before returning back to the fire.

Avery knew Caspian seemed to have developed an interest in her, but she refused to be drawn in, instead deciding to tease him. "You need to find a girlfriend. You're a catch, surely, with your wealth and big house. I'd have thought you'd be battling them away."

"Is that all I am? Money?" he asked, his eyes narrowed.

Avery had been flippant, and certainly hadn't meant to cause offence, but this was a topic she wanted to steer clear of. "No, of course not. And anyone who is interested in only that clearly isn't worth your time."

"You don't care for money, do you?" he asked, watching her.

"Not particularly." Avery started to get annoyed. He was being a flirt, and she didn't like it. "And stop it, Caspian."

"Stop what?"

"You know what. I'm with Alex. I love Alex." As she said it, she glanced up and saw Alex across the fire, deep in conversation with Genevieve. As if he sensed her looking, he glanced her way and smiled, before turning away again.

Caspian stared at his feet. "I know."

Immediately, Avery felt terrible, which annoyed her even more. "Maybe you should turn your attention to someone who's free."

"But where's the fun in that?"

Now she knew he was baiting her. "I'll stop talking to you if you keep this up."

"Oh, please don't, we have so much fun!"

She was about to say something unpleasant, when she felt a tap on her shoulder, and she turned to see Reuben's large frame looming over her. "We're heading back to the house, and then home. Coming?"

"Sure," she said, grateful for the interruption, and swiftly rose to her feet. "See you soon, Caspian."

He nodded and turned back to the fire, and Avery fell into step beside her coven, feeling Alex's arm slide around her waist. Alex's strength was spirit-based, and he was able to banish demons and ghouls, and use his intuitiveness to scry, spirit-walk, and communicate with ghosts. He was also skilled with elemental Fire, and as an added bonus for Avery, he loved her, despite all her quirks.

Reuben and El, both tall and fair-haired, walked just a few steps ahead. Reuben was an elemental Water witch, who was still coming to grips with his powers after neglecting them for years. It had taken the death of his brother, Gil, to bring him back to magic. El was skilled with fire and metal work, wore lots of jewellery, and like Reuben, had several tattoos. Briar, the fifth member of their coven, was petite, with long dark hair, and a natural affinity for Earth magic and healing. She was a caring, gentle soul, who had just started a relationship with Hunter, the wolf-shifter who lived in Cumbria, and she was keeping very quiet about it.

Being with them brought Avery more pleasure than she could describe. She had resisted joining a coven for so long, but now these four amazing people were family. They completed her. She smiled and nestled against Alex, feeling a sudden flash of guilt about Caspian's behaviour, even though she hadn't done anything wrong.

"What's Caspian done?" he asked. It was as if he'd read her mind, and she loved him for it.

"Nothing, really. Just flirting, even though he knows it's useless."

A trace of annoyance flashed across Alex's face. "Doesn't stop him trying though, does it?"

Avery hugged him harder. "I ignore it, and so should you."

"I try. Don't worry, I'm not about to get violent."

He pulled her to a halt and kissed her, and Reuben grimaced as he glanced at them. "Oh, you two, get a room."

Alex flipped him off. "Sod off, Reuben."

Reuben just laughed, and El punched his arm. "Stop being naughty."

"You normally like it," he teased, as he increased his pace.

The house came into view, as did Rasmus, greeting them on the broad patio that stretched across the back of his old home. His place wasn't as old as Reuben's, and it was made of faded red brick rather than mellow stone, but it was eccentric, just like he was.

Avery broke away from Alex and went to his side, hugging him. "Thanks, Rasmus. It was great to finally be here and celebrate Imbolc with you. You have an amazing home."

Rasmus smiled, his old face dissolving into wrinkles. "Thank you, Avery. You're welcome anytime. Are you sure you don't want to stay? I have room."

When she'd first met him, Avery had thought him gruff and quite scary, but now she was incredibly fond of Rasmus, especially knowing now what she did of his past. "No, it won't take us long to get home. And besides, we all have to work in the morning." Newquay was on the north coast of Cornwall, and their trip to White Haven on the south coast would only take about 45 minutes.

Briar hugged Rasmus, too. "I'm sure after having to put up with us all, you'll be glad to have the place to yourself."

"I wouldn't offer if I didn't mean it," he remonstrated. He turned to Alex and gripped his proffered hand. "Alex, thank you. The White Haven witches have been a welcome addition to our coven."

"And we're glad to be part of it," Alex replied.

While the others talked, Avery looked back towards the trees, noting the feeling of peace and gentle magic that came from them. Rasmus's family and the Cornwall Coven had celebrated there for years, and the wood seemed to have absorbed the positive energy. A line of lanterns lit the way to the clearing, but the fire itself was lost to view. She was about to turn away when she felt a prickle run down her spine, as if she was being watched. She stared into the darkness and saw a figure standing a short distance away from the path, just at the edge of the wood. Avery blinked. She could have sworn the figure hadn't been there a second before. She stared on, waiting for whoever it was to come fully into view. It must be one of the other witches; although, it was odd that they wouldn't have followed the path. The undergrowth was thick in places.

The figure didn't move. Whoever it was just stood there, watching her. Avery could see a pale face, but it was impossible to tell if it was male or female. And then, as quickly as the person had appeared, the voyeur went. Avery squinted and blinked again. *Was she seeing things?*

"Are you okay?" Briar said to her, following her eye line. "What are you looking at?"

"I could have sworn I saw someone at the edge of the trees, but they've just vanished!"

Briar frowned. "It's dark, and the lanterns throw uneven light, or maybe it was one of the witches enjoying the solitude."

"Maybe." Avery finally turned away. "And it's late and I'm probably overtired."

But as they said their goodbyes and finally left, Avery couldn't help but look over her shoulder again, convinced that someone had been silently watching them all.

Two

T he sound of shouting, and the honking of horns broke the silence in
Happenstance Books on Monday morning, and Avery groaned.

She hadn't slept well because her mind had buzzed with memories of
their rites, and she sat behind the counter, nursing a hot coffee and a
chocolate biscuit.

Dan headed to the shop window, grinning. "Yes, the circus has arrived!"

"What circus?"

"The Crossroads Circus!" He looked at her incredulous, as behind him
a high-sided van drove down the road, large letters spelling the Crossroads
Circus painted on the side. Behind it were a couple of outlandishly dressed
performers, who ran up and down the street shouting loudly as they darted
into shops with flyers, and handed them out to pedestrians.

A young woman burst into Happenstance Books, her hair a bright
green, and wearing a skin tight green Lycra costume covered in leaves.
She thrust some flyers into Dan's hands, and said, "The circus opens on
Saturday! Come and see myths become real!" And then she left in a whirl
of energy, leaving Dan looking after her appreciatively.

Avery groaned again. "What *is* the Crossroads Circus, and why should
I be excited about it?"

Dan smacked his forehead with the palm of his hand. "Are you kidding?
You must have heard of it!"

"Er, no," Avery admitted as she racked her brains trying to remember if
she had. "Aren't you a bit old for one?"

"No one's too old for a circus, especially this one!" He placed the flyer in front of her and pointed at the text. "Look - *The Crossroads Circus brings the old myths to life! The Green Man, the Raven King, giants, dryads, King Arthur, dragons, and much, much more!*"

Avery was still perplexed. "Seriously, I have not heard about this."

Dan grabbed the local paper that was folded on the counter top, flicked through the pages and then placed it in front of Avery. The headline announced, "*The Crossroads Circus is coming to the supernatural home of Cornwall!*"

She almost spit her drink out. "Where's the supernatural home of Cornwall? Is that supposed to be here? White Haven?"

"Where else, my dear witch, descendant of the famous Helena, who most likely orchestrated the Walk of the Spirits?" he answered with a smirk. "We're on the map now."

Avery skim read the rest of the article, which described how England's most famous circus of myth and magic had worked its way down the country wowing visitors and building an impressive reputation.

She looked at him, slack jawed. "Well, I guess that does sound impressive. I must admit I've been avoiding the news lately. I've been trying to avoid all that speculation about the deaths, bones, and vampires." As much as she wanted it to, the news would not stop reporting on the police finding the hidden caves beneath West Haven, and the link to the House of Spirits, even though it had happened well over a month before.

"Ah, fair enough. Well it's a big thing. Everyone's saying it's the best circus ever - maybe barring Cirque Du Soleil. The theme is mythical figures and magical creatures, and that's what all the performances are based around – hence Crossroads." Crossroads had a reputation in myth as a place where boundaries between worlds weakened allowing in the strange and otherworldly.

"Are you going to go?"

"I think so. It might even distract our new friend."

"Shadow? You'll think she'll like a circus?"

"Why not?" Dan picked up the paper, and examined the article again. "I think it sounds great. I'll offer to go with her, keep her company." Dan was about to finish his master's in something to do with folklore, Avery could never remember exactly what, but he took an avid interest in magic, myths and legends. He also took an avid interest in Shadow. He was trying to look relaxed and nonchalant, but Avery knew him only too well.

"Yes, I'm sure you'll love that." She dropped her voice, even though the shop had no customers, and looked at him worriedly. "Dan, she's *fey*! Please don't forget that!"

He gave a very undignified roll of the eyes. "How can I forget that? She reminds me of the fact every time we talk. And, so what! There's nothing wrong with some cross-species' lovin'."

"Hasn't Nixie put you off?"

He frowned. "Nixie was a mermaid who hid her true nature and tried to drag me to the depths of the ocean. I know exactly what Shadow is!"

"But we don't know anything about her. She's fey. She might look like us, but she isn't." Her voice softened. "I just don't want you to get hurt. And I definitely don't want you being sucked to the Otherworld accidentally, if –" Avery wagged a finger, "she ever discovers how to get back, which is seriously unlikely. And, if she starts to try and sell mythical objects, that could involve some very dodgy people. In fact, that's probably a bigger risk to your health!"

Dan's shoulders sagged. "Yeah, I know. It's something I've tried to warn her about, actually, but she's seems to like the risk." He leaned forward. "I think she's finding life a little boring so far. That's why I think this circus is a good thing. February is cold and drab otherwise."

Avery leaned against the shelf behind her, sipping her drink. "I'm enjoying boring. It makes a nice change."

They were interrupted by Sally who joined them from the back room, where she'd been doing the accounts. She looked between them. "What are you two in deep discussion about?"

Dan showed her the newspaper. "We're just debating Shadow's interest in this."

Sally skimmed the page, and laughed. "It's here already. Cool! I'll take the kids. It sounds amazing. And I think we should set up a table of themed books - circuses, carnivals, and crossroads stuff." She looked very pleased with herself, and her eyes darted around the room as she looked for the best place to set it up.

"Dan thinks it will distract Shadow from her quest, but I seriously doubt that. She's obsessive about the Otherworld and portals." Avery tried to shrug off her worry. "But maybe I'm just sleep deprived and it's making me paranoid."

Dan squirmed. "Maybe not completely paranoid. You should know that she's planning to check out some old sites around Cornwall, just for starters."

"Like what?"

"Castle an Dinas, the old iron age hill fort. It's linked to King Arthur, like lots of places across Cornwall and the UK, including Tintagel, King Arthur's birthplace if you believe the legends. His history crosses over with the Otherworld — you know, the Green Knight, Excalibur, Avalon, the Lady of the Lake, she thinks that places linked to him will perhaps have links to her world."

Sally folded her arms across her chest and narrowed her eyes. "So, I presume she'll check out Glastonbury, the Tor, and Stonehenge too."

"Yep. And a few other places. I offered to take her to a few, but she's thinking on it." He looked miffed. "I think she wants to go with Gabe."

Avery tried to console him. "Maybe that's a good idea, but at least she comes to you for research."

"What myths does the Crossroads Circus focus on?" Sally asked.

"It mentions a few on this," Dan said, passing her the flyer. "But I know the Green Man plays a major part, as does the Raven King. That's who the

Ring Master appears as."

"Sounds great," Avery conceded. "Something to cheer us up after vampires. I'll have to take Alex, although I'm not entirely sure he's a circus fan. No live animals I hope?"

"None. Just the mythical kind."

"Well, that's alright then."

✝ ✝ ✝

During her lunch break, Avery decided to head to El's jewellery shop, the Silver Bough. She was curious to see if Shadow had mentioned any of her planned search to her as she knew El saw more of her, and she wanted to know if she'd heard about the circus, too.

She strolled down the streets, huddled within her coat. It was a grey day, the sky low with heavy, sullen clouds, and it was cold. The wind carried the smell of the sea, and as she rounded a corner it came into view between a gap in some buildings, and she paused to watch it. The heavy swells beyond the harbour were as grey as the sky. The fishing boats were out, and she was glad she wasn't with them.

Avery picked up her pace, nodding greetings to a few locals as she passed. The town had finally emptied of all their visitors, but that wouldn't last now that the circus was here, which was a shame because it was nice while it lasted. The tourists would return, and the place would be full of the performers from the circus too; that would be different.

As Avery made the final turn onto the main street that ran down to the harbour, she ran straight into a familiar figure. Rupert, the owner of the House of Spirits. She hadn't seen him since before Christmas.

Rupert stepped back, giving her space, and looked down at her. He wasn't a tall man, but he was imposing and ever so slightly sinister, an impression exacerbated by his hooded eyes that seemed to pin her to the spot. "Avery, I'm glad to see you. I've been meaning to thank you for those books." He was referring to the books that had been sold from his house to Happenstance Books, and that Avery had willingly returned.

"Hi Rupert, it's fine. I hope they were interesting." There was nothing unusual about them that Avery could find, other of course than the one with the witch-mark on it, but she doubted Rupert could see that.

"They're excellent. I've placed them in pride of place on the book case in the main living room."

"The one with Madame Charron's painting in it? That's a good place." It wasn't until she'd said it that Avery had the horrible realisation that Rupert didn't know she'd been back to the house with the other witches while he and Charlotte had been away. *Crap.*

He frowned. "You know about the painting? How?"

She lied quickly, startling herself with its smoothness. "Cassie told me. She loved it, and she knew I would want to hear about it." She met his eyes, smiling lightly.

"Of course, Cassie," he murmured, doubt lurking behind his eyes. "The house is looking a bit different now. We've started to do some of it up. Not too much of course, we want to keep its character."

"Did you ever find a ghost?"

Again, he narrowed his eyes, and then his chest swelled as a gleam of excitement fired. "No, but you might have heard the police visited us — it was on the news. They found a passage beneath our house—that actually *starts* in our house! It leads to caves and piles of bones."

Of course she knew, she wanted to shout, *they'd* found the passage and tipped the police off, but she held her tongue. Rupert knew none of it. However, it had been all over the papers. "Of course, I've been reading about it. Didn't you have Sarah Rutherford visit you as well, from the news?"

He smiled, but she didn't like it. There was something challenging about him. "Yes, we've had lots of interest. We've decided to run small tours of the house, a sort of paranormal experience."

Of course you have. "Well, it is in keeping with the theme of the town I guess."

"You weren't entirely honest with me though were you, Avery?" he said.

"In what way?"

"Your ancestor? Helena, the witch who was burned at the stake. You never said."

She laughed outright whilst simultaneously wanting to punch him. "It's not a secret, Rupert! But equally it's not something I announce to everyone as I introduce myself. That would be a little odd, don't you think?"

He persisted, almost glaring at her. "You knew I had an interest in the occult."

"So does everyone in White Haven. Anyway, I must get on. I'm meeting someone. I'll see you again sometime," she said, forcing herself to be polite as she pushed past him and headed down the street. She could feel his eyes on her back, watching her leave, and she resisted the urge to hex him.

By the time she entered El's shop she was seething. Zoey, the Immaculate Guardian of the Shop, was, as usual, looking, well, immaculate. Her dark hair was cut into a blunt bob, and this time the tips ended with deep purple dye. Her eye makeup and nail polish matched, and as usual she made Avery feel woefully underdressed.

"You look furious," Zoey noted as she lifted the counter to let her through to El's workroom.

"Stupid Rupert from the House of Spirits is a ginormous ass," Avery told her.

"Oh him. Yes, he is."

Avery stopped, surprised. "You know him?"

"Everyone's getting to know him. He likes to visit announcing his paranormal house tours." She put the counter back down behind Avery. "Don't worry; he's annoying the crap out of all of us."

She turned away as a customer entered, and Avery passed through the door to see El bent over the counter, a small soldering iron in her hand. She was perched on a stool next to the bench, her white blond hair piled on her head, wearing a pair of scruffy jeans and a jumper, and the most enormous goggles over her eyes. She was concentrating on soldering an intricate piece of jewellery, and Avery hesitated to disturb her. And then she noticed the buds in her ears, and realised she couldn't hear her anyway.

Rather than startle her, she moved around to the side so she appeared in El's peripheral vision. While El was concentrating, she looked around the room, noting the rings, earrings, nose rings, belly-button bars, and necklaces in various stages of completion along the bench. She was obviously working on a new range, because these looked slightly different to the designs she'd seen before. Tiny black gemstones littered the bench that Avery was sure were jet; it was commonly known as a protection and purification stone. To the side of the bench was El's oldest family grimoire, the one she had found in the cellar of Hawk House. A hum of magic floated from it, and she realised that El was working a spell into the object.

Avery's gaze drifted around the room, taking in the huge cabinet with the glassed front. It contained hundreds of jars of different gemstones, and they sparkled in the light, making Avery want to pick them up and run her fingers through them. There was also an organised collection of tools, many of them tiny, and an array of magnifying glasses. It was stupid to only realise now, but watching El, Avery realised how intricate and skilled her work was.

After another few moments, El looked up and Avery waved, gesturing her not to rush, and she sat in the chair in the corner, but it was only another moment before El turned the soldering iron off, and pulled her buds from her ears.

"Sorry, Avery, didn't see you there for a minute, and then I just became aware of someone hovering. I thought it was Zoey." She looked at her watch. "No wonder I'm starving! Look at the time." She pushed the goggles on to the top of her head, and smoothed her hair.

"What are you making?" Avery asked, rising to her feet and moving to the bench for a better look.

"A Crossroads Collection to coincide with our visitors. I thought it was too good an opportunity to pass up."

"You've heard about the new arrivals then? I hadn't."

El laughed. "Avery! Where have you been? They've been in all the news recently, and everyone's saying how inventive they are. That they're breathing life into old tales! We should go."

"I was just talking to Dan and Sally about it actually. I'm game. I just hope there won't be some dodgy woman pretending to look into a crystal ball, and asking me to cross her palm with silver."

El laughed even harder. "I think it's going to be a little bit more inventive than that. And it's set in the castle! What a back drop that will be." She rose from her seat and headed to the percolator sitting on the end of the bench top. "Want one? It's strong."

"Yes please."

El poured them both a cup, and then headed to the fridge in the corner and pulled out a large round cake that already had half missing. "Do you want some?"

"Go on then," Avery said, hearing her stomach growl.

"There was more," El explained, "but Reuben popped in." She didn't need to say anything else. Reuben ate like he had hollow legs, and he never put on a pound.

"Don't tell me he's surfing in this weather."

"Of course he is. It's like breathing to him." El placed a large slice on a chipped plate and pushed it in front of Avery, and then took a large bite of her own. In between chews, she asked, "Is there a reason for this visit? Not that there has to be, obviously."

"I wanted to stretch my legs, but yes, just wondering if you've heard about Shadow's plans."

El nodded. "Of course. I even offered to help. I figure, the more she has to try, the less frustrated she'll feel."

Avery licked her fingers. This really was a great cake, sticky orange if she wasn't mistaken. "I guess you're right. It's better than us blocking her at every turn."

"We can't do that. Remember what I said last night. This is part of my management strategy. Although it's inevitable that she'll do her own stubborn thing eventually."

"Dan thinks the circus will distract her. I think she's just distracting Dan."

"Yeah, but he enjoys it. You coming around later anyway? Newton phoned and said he wants to talk. I thought he'd already phoned you actually."

"I haven't heard from him, but this morning I have been very distracted." Avery pulled her phone from her bag and checked her messages. There was nothing. "I think I've upset Newton."

"No, you haven't." El stood and brushed crumbs off herself. "He's probably just smarting a little after finding Briar has hooked up with Hunter. You do give him heaps about his *issue*."

Avery felt guilty. Yes, she had told him off several times, but hadn't wanted to upset him, not really. "Maybe I should apologise."

"Maybe. He's just confused, and that's okay. And Briar's happy." El sniggered. "She has a glow."

"And then some," Avery agreed. Getting together with Hunter had certainly lifted her spirits.

El looked even naughtier. "What do you think shifter sex is like? I reckon he'd be very hot in the sheets. He smoulders every time he looks at her."

Avery shrieked. "El! I don't want to think about that!" Although it had crossed her mind, briefly, before she banished it forever. And now it was back in her head again.

"Well I'm going to ask her."

"We don't ask you what sex is like with Reuben!"

"You could!" El raised a wicked eyebrow. "But I wouldn't tell. Just know that it's good. *Very* good."

"That's it, I'm out of here!" Avery said, laughing. "Are we meeting at yours then?"

"Yep, and Reuben's bringing curry. Aim for seven."

✝ ✝ ✝

After work, Avery headed to The Wayward Son and had a drink at the bar, before she and Alex headed to El's place where they'd arranged to meet Newton.

They walked briskly through the chilly streets, and Alex hugged Avery to his side. "Any idea what Newton wants with us?" he asked.

"None, but it will be good to see him. He's been so busy lately."

"Which is our fault. We must have given him a massive headache. Imagine having to legitimately investigate that?" He was of course referring to the mass of bones found in the cave system beneath West Haven.

"Those bones need to be identified," Avery pointed out. "And Newton will want to do it."

They entered the lobby of the building where El lived, a converted warehouse next to the harbour, and used the lift to reach her flat on the fourth floor. They were greeted by a welcome blast of central heating, which thawed Avery's chilled extremities.

They were the last to arrive. Briar and Newton were already there, chatting quietly next to the fire. Despite their differences recently, both seemed civil. Newton was in his mid-thirties, dark-haired, and grey-eyed, and a descendant of another old family in White Haven. He struggled with magic and the paranormal, but he was a good friend regardless, and firmly part of their world. For a while it seemed something may happen between him and Briar, but not anymore.

The smell of curry filled the air, and Reuben was already placing out containers of food down the centre of the dining table, which sat in the open-plan living area. He looked up and grinned. "Good timing. I couldn't have guaranteed much would have been left if you hadn't arrived soon."

"There's enough there to feed a small army, so I'm sure you couldn't have eaten it all," Alex observed, as he and Avery shed their coats and joined him.

El strode to the table with a bottle of red wine in her hand, and poured Avery and herself a glass. "But you know he'd have tried!" She called over to Briar and Newton, "Come and sit, you two. I'm starving."

They sat around the table, filling their plates as they exchanged pleasantries, until Avery eventually asked, "Are you making much headway with the bones?"

Newton shook his head regretfully. "No. The forensic pathologists have just started, really. They have to organise the bones before they even start analysing them. This is going to take months, and that's a conservative estimate. Meanwhile, we're looking at missing persons files going back years, and then we're collecting DNA samples from relatives who are still alive." He shook his head. "It's something I've never done before on this scale, so there are a few people involved."

Briar smiled. "Well done. That's quite an achievement."

"Or an absolute nightmare, depending on the moment," he confessed. He looked tired, Avery noticed, now that she was sitting closer to him. He wasn't as cleanly shaven as usual, and dark shadows circled his eyes.

Avery shifted in her seat and faced him. "Has something happened?"

Newton looked up, his eyes haunted. "Well, the word *vampire* won't go away, and my superiors have decided it's something we can't ignore." He shuffled uncomfortably. "I know that I've joked about this, but they really do want me to investigate any deaths that look remotely paranormal. This latest debacle has forced their hand."

They all paused, forks lifted halfway to lips, but Alex spoke first. "Is that a good or a bad thing?"

He sighed. "I don't know. If you guys are remotely involved, it could be bad, but obviously I'll try and keep you out of it."

"But we're never involved in deaths," El pointed out, indignant. "We're the good guys."

"Well, I know that, but they don't. And frankly, it's hard to explain away magic without me sounding like a fruit loop."

The witches looked at each other furtively, and Avery said, "Thank you. We want to be kept out of things as much as possible."

Reuben waved his fork. "Do you mean they really believe the deaths were caused by vampires, and it wasn't someone playing a sick prank?"

Newton exhaled heavily. "Initially it was thought to be a joke, and for a while people laughed it off, but not anymore. With the marks on the victims' necks, the blood loss, and what happened at the Coroner's office, everyone had to take it seriously. My superiors consulted with some bigger town divisions, and what they heard made them reconsider their position." He looked at Avery. "What James said to you was pretty much what the police said, you know, about vampire activity being more easily disguised in a big city environment. So, yes, they are being considered as a probable perpetrator in these deaths. And the presence of ashes as remains supports that theory."

Avery looked down at her plate as she remembered when they burned Lupescu, and when the sunlight spell destroyed the vampires in the main cave. All of a sudden, her appetite retreated. They may have been vampires, but it was a horrible thing to have done.

Newton continued, "That leaves us in an unusual situation in that we've had a few big city activities we wouldn't normally see in little ol' Cornwall, and that has raised suspicion. At least no one knows we have seven Nephilim and a fey living here as well."

Alex frowned. "Does this mean there are other paranormal activities going on out there that we don't know about?"

Newton's grey eyes darkened. "Outside of Cornwall? Yes, without a doubt. Which leads to my next subject. The Crossroads Circus is coming to town, and I need a favour." His eyes scanned them, gauging their reaction.

El groaned. "Don't let it be bad! I'm making a Crossroads Collection."

Avery's stomach sank. "What's wrong with the circus? We were talking about that today."

His lips pressed into a thin line. "I don't know yet. That's what I want you to find out."

Reuben leaned forward. "Something must have happened."

"We've been advised that strange occurrences seem to follow the circus. It could just be a coincidence, or—" he spread his hands wide. "It might actually be something. You're the best people I know to find out."

Alex glanced at Avery before he spoke. "But how do you get around asking us? I mean, what happens if we find something? I presume we don't come into it?"

"Absolutely not," Newton said, shaking his head vehemently. "You just tell me what you find, as you've done before. And of course, we'll be keeping a close eye on them anyway."

"Your friend, Officer Moore, has seen us show up a few times. What does he know about us?" asked Reuben.

"Rob? He knows that you have occult interests and that's why I consult you sometimes. But he's quiet and discrete, and I trust him."

"He's beyond quiet!" El exclaimed. "He's utterly silent. I've never heard him speak at all."

Newton grunted as he forked some more chicken biryani onto his plate. "He speaks when he needs to. He likes you lot, actually."

Avery was surprised. Most of the time, it seemed as if he barely noticed them. It looked like no one else expected to hear that either, as they all looked puzzled.

Alex brought them back to the subject. "You said, 'strange occurrences.' We need more than that, and I presume it needs to be more than that to trigger a police investigation."

"True," he admitted, "which is why this is nothing as formal as an investigation. There are no grounds for one quite yet. There have been a few disappearances—but there are always disappearances, you know that. However, a body was found on the outskirts of the last town they visited, just outside Torquay in Devon. There was no obvious cause of death, the person was young, and there were no signs of drug or alcohol use, and no visible injuries." Newton sighed and ran his hands through his hair. "But the post-mortem report showed his organs were old, too old for his body. Atrophied and withered."

A trickle of fear ran through Avery. *Atrophied organs?*

Alex said, "That is weird. But why connect that to the circus?"

"Because some bright spark decided to look at where the circus had been and see if anything else had shown up. And something did." He paused for a moment and took a slug of beer. "That's when we found out that at intermittent points on their tour, the same thing has happened. Not every stop—they have been working their way down the country since September—but at least one in three. All found with atrophied organs, all young men, and all with no reason to be dead."

Briar's hand flew to her mouth. "That's horrible. What could do such a thing?"

Newton shrugged. "We have no idea."

"But there's nothing to link the deaths to the circus at this stage?" Reuben asked.

"No. There is nothing to link the deaths to anyone or anything!" He looked frustrated, and he rubbed his stubble before leaning back in his chair and pushing his plate away.

Avery shook her head, incredulous. "But surely you're too busy to look into this? You're still following up the vampire deaths."

"Well, technically there's no investigation to complete. Yes, we're trying to match bodies to victims and find existing family members, but I'm not looking for the perpetrator, am I? He's dead. While the press have been all over this, we've essentially said the killer is a man with a vampire fixation, and he was found dead at the scene, burnt in some freak accident. They've run with it. We're going to have to release a name soon, so we'll probably use one of the victims."

Avery had followed the early news reports before it had depressed her, and had been relieved to know that they were reporting it was a freak and not an actual vampire. The whole thing was turning into a sort of Jack the Ripper-type affair. No one knew who the offender was, but the press kept speculating.

"What about the two girls that we found?" Avery asked. "Have they remembered details?"

"No, and that's a good thing," Newton said, obviously relieved. "As you know, one of them, Alice, was barely alive at the time. She's made a good recovery since then, physically, but mentally—" He shook his head. "She remembers darkness, shadows, pain, cold, thirst, and starvation. The second one, Daisy, who Lupescu had just taken, she remembers someone attacking her from behind, and that's it. She spoke to the press, briefly, and that's all she told them. She just wants to be left alone now, to get on with her life, poor kid."

"Let's hope they both make a good recovery," Avery said, her mind a jumble of thoughts. "Are you saying that the police, your colleagues, now believe in vampires?"

"A small group of us do. The rest believe what the press are saying. I'm now the head of a small paranormal division. There's me, Moore, a detective called Walker, and my boss. It's very under the radar."

Reuben snorted. "Like black ops? That's seriously cool!"

Newton just stared at him. "Not so cool if you ask me, I'd rather they give the job to someone else."

Avery started to feel very uncomfortable. "I know we've talked about this, but just to come back to it again—how honest are you being?"

Newton's grey eyes met hers. "I'm going to be reasonably honest about everything except you five, and the Cornwall Coven, obviously. As for the rest, I have no choice. These things that have been cropping up cannot be ignored."

"By things," El asked, "you mean the strange behaviour of the men down on the beach with the mermaids, in the storm? And the events at Old Haven Church at Samhain?"

Newton nodded. "Yes, but not the deaths at All Souls and the other churches when the Nephilim arrived. There's still no solution to those, and that's how it will remain. I can keep them out of the paranormal bracket. They were violent deaths, easy enough to explain. But the latest stuff, impossible! My boss on this is perceptive and open-minded. A dangerous combination."

"Where are you based?" Reuben asked.

"At the station in Truro. Our main office, where the Major Crime Investigation sits, is in Newquay, but I've always been based in Truro. We've been given our own office there. I think they like us out of the way of the main team. I'll still investigate *normal* murders—if you'll forgive the word—but I'll get the weird stuff, too."

Reuben looked suspicious. "And what's the new guy seem like? I mean, does he have paranormal experience?"

"Woman, actually," Newton corrected him. "I've only just met her. She's come from Major Crimes, too. She seems a bit intense, but open-minded. Let's face it, you have to be to investigate this stuff."

El stood and started to clear the plates, and Alex helped her, but Avery remained seated, thinking. "So, this circus mystery, this is something your paranormal team are investigating? No one else?"

"No one else," he parroted. "And, as I said, it's not even a proper investigation, it's just something that's on our radar. With luck, the circus will leave and nothing will happen."

"Where do they go after us?" Reuben asked.

"Further south—Penzance. Final show before they take a break." He rubbed his jaw absently again. "If there *is* something going on and they're connected to these deaths, and we don't find out who's responsible, they'll disappear for months, or even go abroad, and we might not have the chance to investigate anytime soon."

"And potentially, people will start dying again, elsewhere," Briar pointed out. "So, we have to find out if they're responsible, quickly."

"Happy to help?" Newton asked them.

"Of course," Avery said, answering for all of them, wondering what on earth they were getting themselves into. "Have you got some background on any of the people there?"

"Just coming to it," he said, pulling his notebook from his pocket. "I'll start with the owner, or rather the main owner. His name is Corbin Roberts. He took the circus over from his father. It's been in the family for years, travelling a lot in Europe. It was just a regular circus then. However in the last few years they've been struggling financially, and Corbin has had to find new backers. He's 55 and seems a straight-up guy who runs an honest business.

"For years, Corbin co-owned the circus with a man called Alec Jensen, but he bailed out last year, and within months Corbin teamed up with a younger married couple, Rafe and Mairi Stewart, who are Scottish, originally from Inverness. They were with another circus for a while, but not as co-owners, just managers."

"So this couple invested money?" Reuben asked.

"Yep, and must be responsible for the new direction the circus has taken, because in the summer last year the entire circus headed to the shores of Loch Ness, outside Inverness. I've checked the dates. They didn't have any performances for about three months, and when they re-emerged, they were called the Crossroads Circus."

Briar picked at her naan bread while she listened. "Interesting name. It has all sorts of connotations, especially with boundary magic."

Avery nodded. "Just what we were talking about in my shop. Perfect for their theme."

Alex called over from the kitchen, "Anything suspicious about Rafe and Mairi?"

"Nothing," Newton answered. "Mairi has family in Inverness, Rafe doesn't. But again, there's nothing suspicious about them. I've done background checks on the performers, but to be honest, there are a lot of them. It's a big circus. Again, some of the performers have been with Corbin for years, others are new, and joined them in the summer." He shook his head, puzzled. "They must have been confident of the new show to take on more performers when they were struggling. They are from the UK and all over Europe, with diverse backgrounds. A few convictions for fighting for some of them, speeding tickets, but again nothing too dramatic."

"So no one we should focus on in particular," Briar observed. "That makes it tricky."

Reuben cracked open another beer. "I take it that there were no deaths associated with the circus before, though? Not in Europe?"

Newton loosened his collar. "That's trickier. Not that we know of, but to track all over Europe would be a nightmare, especially based on so little information. We don't think so."

El joined them again after finishing the tidying up. "So, in theory, whoever is responsible is new."

"In theory," Newton agreed. He reached into his pocket and fished some papers out, covered in a list of names. "I wish I could tell you more, but I've got the list of employees here. If you find someone suspicious you think we should focus on, let me know."

"Let's just hope you're wrong," Avery said to him. "I was looking forward to some peace, but I guess we need to start investigating them soon."

"The sooner the better."

"Let's go tomorrow night," Reuben suggested. "We'll wear full Ninja-witch gear. I like feeling like I'm in special ops. We'll meet down the lane, out of sight." He rubbed his hands together in happy anticipation. "I can't wait!"

Three

Halfway through the next morning, Avery left Happenstance Books to buy coffees and pastries from their favourite place just down the road, when she heard shouts, drumming, and the sound of wild piping coming from the centre of town.

Curious, she walked to the high street that snaked down to the sea, and paused to watch the spectacle. Some of the performers from the Crossroads Circus had arrived to promote their show, and they capered down the pavement in their bright costumes. They reminded Avery of their own Yule Solstice parade.

There were about a dozen people, led by a man in a green costume covered in leaves, with a big nest of leaves and twigs on his head. His face was painted green, he carried a staff crowned with leaves, and his boots were made of sturdy brown leather. Avery presumed he was the mythical Green Man, the pagan symbol of fertility and rebirth. He was grinning and waving at the pedestrians, shouting about the opening of the circus. He caught Avery watching and waved, and she laughed, his enthusiasm infectious.

Behind him were a couple of drummers, dressed in shades of green and brown, their hair wild and uncombed, and a piper followed them, skipping, in a jester's costume. A couple of slender acrobats dressed in the skimpiest of Lycra costumes tumbled down the street, doing hand stands, flips, and cartwheels.

A woman trailed behind the acrobats, wearing a long, shimmering blue dress, medieval in design, and she carried a huge sword in her hand. She shouted, "Come meet the true king! Arthur has returned." It could only be the Lady of the Lake.

By her side was a woman dressed completely in straw and corn, a braid of corn around her face. *Was she a corn doll, to celebrate Imbolc?* Avery wasn't sure. And finally two men followed breathing fire, and wearing costumes covered in scales, in bright yellow and reds. *Dragons, perhaps.* One thing was certain—they were all causing a stir. They handed out leaflets, running in and out of shops, and shouting in cackling voices as they entertained the onlookers.

Avery was ready to return to the coffee shop when another woman caught her eye. She looked to be in her mid-thirties, with long, wavy auburn hair, and she wore a mixture of loose clothing in earth colours. The woman paused on the pavement, transfixed as she looked at Avery, and as their eyes locked, Avery felt the strangest sensation, as if she'd been seen completely, inside and out, before the woman broke their connection and continued down the street without a backward glance.

Avery shuddered. *What was that?* As she turned away, slightly flustered, she stumbled into the broad chest of man dressed in dark grey and black. He righted her, his hands on her arms, and she was acutely aware of his steely grip. He glanced at her, his eyes narrowing, before he looked over her shoulder to the woman with the auburn hair. He nodded, and muttered a brief, "Excuse me," before hurrying on down the road. Avery watched as his long stride carried him out of sight.

When she returned to the shop, Dan and Sally were behind the till, talking quietly. Dan was distracted, and he leaned on the counter, looking through a book as they chatted. A Blues album was playing in the background, and the shop felt mellow and welcoming. He looked up. "Finally! I thought you'd forgotten us." His appetite was almost as legendary as Reuben's.

Sally rolled her eyes. "You weren't gone that long, Avery, don't worry."

Avery set the coffees down and pulled an almond croissant out of the bag for herself, before passing it to Dan. "Sorry, I was distracted by the mini-parade. The circus is drumming up trade on the high street."

"Really? Does it look good?" Dan asked.

"The costumes were great. I saw the Green Man and the Lady of the Lake, and there were some fire-breathing men dressed as dragons. I think the acrobats were dryads—they were very energetic. It's a good thing it's warmed up a bit, they weren't wearing much." She paused for a bite of croissant, spilling crumbs over the counter.

Sally watched her over the rim of her coffee cup. "What aren't you saying? You look odd." Sally was surprisingly perceptive.

"There was a woman behind the procession, and she sort of made eye contact with me, and it was the strangest sensation. I felt like she saw right through me and knew everything about me. It was spooky."

"Are you sure she didn't fancy you?" Dan asked, smirking.

"No, you pillock. Our eyes did not meet across a crowded room!"

"Is she a witch?" Sally asked. "Newton's worried about that circus, isn't he?"

Avery had filled them in on Newton's concerns. "He is, but she's not a witch. I don't get that feeling from any other witch. This was different." Avery gazed into the middle distance, shuffling through the possibilities, before she shrugged in frustration. "I don't know, it's weird. And then I bumped into a man who seemed to be watching her, but I must have imagined that. He was probably watching the circus folk. I think he was American."

"Why? Dan asked. "Was he wearing stars and stripes?"

"Oh, you're very funny today! He said 'excuse me' in an American accent."

Dan finished his pastry and wiped his hands on his jeans. "Could it all be related to the deaths, or could she be?"

"It's too soon to say. I'm seeing the other witches later, though." Avery looked behind her and lowered her voice, even though no customers were too close. "We're going to go to the circus tonight, hidden by my shadow spell. We're hoping to see or hear something that might give us a clue."

Before she could say anything else, the bells chimed over the door announcing a new arrival, and Avery glanced behind to see Stan, their pseudo-Druid and town councillor, enter with a couple in their thirties.

Stan beamed when he saw them. He marched across the shop, his tie askew and his hair wind-blown, with the couple close behind. "Excellent, I've got all of you! I'd like to introduce you to Rafe and Mairi from the Crossroads Circus. They are part owners, and I've been telling them what a special place White Haven is! This is Avery, our Mistress of the Occult, Sally and Dan, her occult assistants!"

Avery tried to keep her expression polite as she shook their hands, and forced herself to remember what Newton had told them. "I think you'll find that Stan is exaggerating a bit. I'm not nearly so interesting as to be a Mistress of the Occult, but welcome to my shop."

"And to White Haven," Sally added, and they all shook hands. "Your circus sounds fascinating. I'm going to take my kids."

"I'm sure they'll enjoy it," Rafe said, smiling. "We're certainly enjoying your beautiful town." Rafe was of average height with short, reddish hair, and ruddy skin. Avery could hear his Scottish accent, but it wasn't strong, probably because he'd travelled around. "We debated setting up near Truro, but your town has such a wonderful reputation for ghosts and witches, it seemed like the best place to stay."

Stan rubbed his hands together and looked gleeful—if a fifty-plus man could be said to be gleeful. "I couldn't believe it when you approached us," he said. "The castle will be an amazing backdrop for your show!"

"It certainly will be," Mairi agreed. She was shorter than Rafe, with shoulder-length, wavy hair, and again, a soft Scottish accent. "Hopefully our tales and your history will make a good fit."

"Your circus has been very popular! It makes me wonder why no one has thought of your theme before," observed Dan.

Rafe laughed. "Sometimes, you just need inspiration to strike."

Avery listened and nodded politely as they chatted, but she was watching Mairi, who was the quieter of the two. Her eyes were darting everywhere around the shop, her gaze speculative and unsettling. "Do you like books, Mairi?"

Mairi looked startled, not realising she was being watched. "Yes, of course, but I don't get a lot of time to read. Managing a circus keeps us very busy."

"I'm sure it does. It looks big. You must have a lot of performers. I saw some of them today in the town—very impressive."

She nodded, seeming slightly distracted. "Thank you. Yes, it takes a lot to organise setting up, moving on, booking where to go. It takes months of planning."

"Well, while you're here, feel free to look around."

Before Mairi could answer, the doorbell rang again, and Avery looked up to see Rupert striding in. *Crap.* "Ah! There you are, Stan! I heard you were taking a tour of the town with our guests." He nodded at Avery, a vicious gleam in his eye. "Should have known he'd have been in our favourite witch's shop."

Mairi whipped around to gape at her, and Rafe stilled slightly as he too looked at her, his eyes wide.

Avery's heart thumped in her chest, but she replied calmly, "I think you mean my witch ancestor, Helena, who was so cruelly burned at the stake."

Stan leapt in with a melodramatic shudder. "Terrible business! Terrible! Fortunately, we embrace magic, witches, and the paranormal now, not like back then. I love our pagan celebrations. It's what makes us so special, and Happenstance Books is a part of that. And Avery is so good at dressing her shop for those occasions."

"Sally is, actually," Avery corrected him. She pointed at the table close to the entrance that Sally had filled with a selection of circus and myth-themed books. "She's responsible for our Crossroads theme, as well."

Stan winked at Sally. "Of course. Forgive me, Sally! Did you want me for something, Rupert?" Remembering he hadn't introduced them, he explained to Rafe and Mairi, "Rupert owns the mysterious House of Sprits in West Haven, and he's planning on running some ghost tours of the area. Excellent idea!"

Rafe and Mairi nodded encouragingly, but Avery was aware of Mairi's glances at her.

"Yes, I wanted to discuss my plans with you," Rupert said, smoothly. "However, you're busy, and I'll catch up with you another time. I'd like to add Happenstance Books to the tour actually, Avery. Any objections?"

She had plenty, but she wasn't about to say so. "Absolutely not. It would be great for business. Just as long as you remain outside the shop, of course. Readers like a quiet bookshop to browse and read in. I'm sure you understand. But I guess it depends if you're running them in the day or at night."

Sally backed her up. "Very true, Avery, but so kind to include us in the tour, Rupert. Thank you."

Stan again leapt in before Rupert could answer. "Excellent news! This tour will be a great success, Rupert."

While Stan and Rupert continued their discussion, Rafe smiling politely and nodding, Mairi's phone buzzed, and she pulled it from her bag. She answered it immediately, heading to the far side of the shop to talk, and when she returned, her eyes gleamed.

Stan noticed her return and immediately changed the conversation. "You two must be eager to get on, and we should leave these good people in peace." He started to usher them from the shop, but Mairi pulled a handful of tickets from her bag, thrusting them at Avery.

"You must come to our opening night. I think you would love it! Do you think you can?" She stared at Avery, and then as if she realised she was being intense, glanced at Dan and Sally, too. "All of you, of course!"

Avery stuttered as she took the tickets. "Er, that's very generous of you, and yes, I'm sure we'd love to come!"

Sally rushed in, too. "Absolutely. I can't wait!"

Stan beamed again and winked. "How very generous! Let's hope there are a few more in that bag of yours!"

He escorted Rupert, Rafe, and Mairi out of the shop as they called their goodbyes, and Avery couldn't resist throwing a hex at Rupert. She watched with pleasure as he tripped outside on the pavement, but was careful to turn away when he looked up furiously, brushing himself off.

She waited until they had moved out of sight, then asked, "Why do I loathe that man so much?"

"Rupert? Because he's an arrogant prick," Dan said. "I don't think he likes you, either. I think he's jealous of your ancestry. He's a wannabe."

Sally nodded. "I agree. I'm not sure I like that Mairi woman, either. There was something about her that rankled—despite the free tickets. And she couldn't take her eyes off of you when she heard the word *witch*."

"I noticed," Avery said, feeling unsettled. "Let's just hope it was idle curiosity."

$$+ \quad + \quad +$$

At lunchtime, Avery settled herself into her usual spot at the end of the bar in The Wayward Son, and Zee, one of the seven Nephilim, slid a glass of red wine in front of her.

"All alone?" he asked her.

She nodded. "Just a quick lunch. I needed a break from the shop, and I wanted to see Alex about tonight. We're going to investigate the circus."

He frowned. "Is something wrong with it?"

"Maybe, that's what we're trying to find out. How's Shadow? I gather she's been busy."

Zee looked amused. "Busy keeping Gabe on his toes. She sets off on her horse most mornings, heading across the downs to shoot rabbits and investigate *the wild places*. When she's not working security at Caspian's warehouses, anyway."

"She's settling in then?" Avery asked, in between sips of wine.

"She's settled in just fine. Got a few of us roped into her research."

"Does that include you?"

"When I have time, and the inclination." His face creased with amusement, rippling the faint scar down his cheek. "At least I'm still able to put a few hours in here."

"I remember you saying you might not have time after Christmas," Avery said, thoughtfully. "Caspian's not keeping you too busy, then?"

"Not yet. It's just standard security at the docks." He broke off suddenly, and looked towards the door, grinning. "Speak of the devil—as you say. Look who's here."

For a second, Avery thought he meant Caspian, and then she turned and saw Shadow just inside the door. She looked around the pub, drawing a few double-takes from the customers, not surprisingly. She was still an arresting sight. Today her long hair was a tumble of soft caramel tones, and her high cheekbones and violet eyes added to her unusual beauty. She glanced towards the bar, and seeing Avery, advanced with a speculative gleam in her eye.

"Ha! You've been spotted." Zee waited for her to reach them, and while Shadow pulled up a stool, he asked, "And what trouble do you bring today?"

She gave him a snide look. "No trouble, thank you, Zee. Now, fetch me a pint of Heligan Honey, please."

"Yes, ma'am," Zee said sarcastically, and turned away to grab a bottle of the local beer from the fridge behind him. He plonked it on the bar with a glass, and said, "I'll let you to pour it yourself. No doubt I'll pour it incorrectly."

She arched an eyebrow. "Someone's sensitive."

"Someone is sick of being criticised." He nodded to Avery. "I'll leave you to it. Shout if you want another."

Avery placed a hand on his arm, "Before you go, where's Alex?"

"In the kitchen, chatting with the chef. He'll be out in a minute." And then he headed to the other end of the bar to check on another local.

Avery watched Shadow pour her beer. "Are you upsetting your house-mates?"

Shadow pursed her lips. "Not intentionally. I have high standards. I am fey."

Avery inwardly sighed. *That was wearing thin really quickly.* "Poor you. You're just going to have to get used to us, now that you're stuck here." She sipped her wine, as they assessed each other.

"Yes, you may be right. I'm sure I'll get used to all of you."

"And us, you," Avery pointed out. "So, why are you here? You haven't visited the pub before."

"I thought I should investigate where you spend a lot of your time. And besides, I wanted a drink."

"Is that all?"

Shadow looked away briefly, a guilty look flashing across her features. "Maybe not all. As you know, I've been spending some time with Dan, and he has suggested places that may offer gateways to my world."

"You know that's highly unlikely, though? I'd hate for you to get your hopes up."

Shadow looked into her drink, despondent, and suddenly all of Avery's compassion came rushing back, and she realised Shadow had come to the pub out of more than idle curiosity.

"I know," Shadow admitted. "But I have to try. The longer I am away, the harder it gets. I'm lonely without my kind. I feel..." She stumbled for words, showing a vulnerability Avery hadn't seen before. "Untethered. I still don't know what to do with myself."

"I understand that. But you have to give yourself time. Working with

Gabe and the others will help. Don't antagonise them. They offered you a place to live and work. I wouldn't take that offer lightly. I'm surprised by Gabe's actions. I think he's surprised himself, too."

"The thing is," Shadow said, "those sites that Dan has suggested, most of them probably only have power at certain times of the year, like solstices and equinoxes, sunrises and sunsets. It's hopeless."

"Perhaps you can help us, then, when you're not on security duties?" Avery suggested in a rush, before she could think through the consequences. She filled her in on the Crossroad Circus and the deaths possibly associated with it. "We're going tonight, but that's probably a bit too short notice."

Shadow's face lit up. "Sounds great to me. I know you don't completely trust me, but I will help. I have unique skills, after all. And frankly, if we need to use weapons, I can handle most things."

"All right. But don't go off and do anything on your own. We have no idea what we're dealing with."

Alex exited the door leading to the kitchen and walked over to join them. He leaned over the bar to kiss Avery lightly on the cheek and nodded at Shadow. "To what do I owe this pleasure?"

"I thought I should investigate this pub, I hear it's where you all hang out. I like it. I'll bring Gabe here." She frowned. "I don't know why he doesn't come anyway. He works too hard. It makes him a dull boy."

Avery intervened. "Shadow is going to help us investigate the Crossroads Circus. She's coming tonight."

Alex looked at her, trying to hide his appalled expression. "Really? Great."

"She needs something to do, Alex, and she'll be a great help." Avery wasn't sure who she was trying to persuade more.

"Of course," he said begrudgingly. "The more the merrier."

Shadow's enthusiasm returned in a rush. "Excellent. Do you need to disguise yourselves?"

Avery nodded. "There's a spell we use."

"Good. We need to eavesdrop. That's my favourite form of reconnaissance."

"Of course it is," Alex said, groaning.

Shadow grinned and then stared at the mute TV screen on the wall. "Look. They're talking about the circus."

Avery turned to look at the screen, and Alex flicked the sound on low, just in time to hear Sarah Rutherford, the reporter who had covered White Haven events a few times, talk about the arrival of the circus. Behind her was the castle and the Big Top.

Alex frowned. "The tent is covered in Green Man images!"

"Fits the theme," Avery said. "He was one of the figures in the town today. The costumes are really good! I saw a strange woman, though. She gave me the shivers." Avery told them about her intense stare and that she thought a man was following her.

"This place never gets any quieter, does it?" Alex reflected. "Let's hope it knocks the caves under West Haven off the top spot on the news."

Four

That evening, five witches and Shadow met at The Wayward Son, and then split into two cars, agreeing to meet in a lay-by, just down from the castle's car park.

It was just after 8pm by the time they arrived on the edge of the castle grounds, and a low mist was already rising from the ground. The lights that lit the castle walls were veiled by more coiling streams of mist, and it pooled in corners and swirled around their ankles. The Big Top squatted in the field to the right of the castle, and beyond that, in a large grassy area edged by hedgerows, were the rows of caravans and camper vans that the performers lived in. Wood smoke hung on the air, and the blinking motes of cinders curled on the faint breeze.

"What's the plan?" Reuben asked, dressed like the rest of them in black clothing, what he called their Ninja-witch gear.

Alex adjusted his gloves. "We mingle, listen to conversations, and see if we can hear them discuss anything odd. We should try and find Rafe and Mairi, and Corbin, too." It seemed Stan had introduced Rafe and Mairi to most of the shop owners, so they all knew what they looked like, but Corbin was still unknown. He looked at Shadow. "This is reconnaissance, nothing more. No heroics or grand gestures."

Shadow blinked once, dripping with disdain. "I am quite capable of following the brief, thank you."

"It's what I always expected of one of Herne's hunters," he replied, dryly.

Before Shadow could respond, Briar asked her, "Do you want us to include you in our spell?"

Shadow's face softened. "No, I'll be fine. I am fey and can conceal myself."

Alex continued with his plan. "Let's split into three groups. I'll be with Avery in the field with their caravans. Briar, you go with Shadow into the set-up in the castle, and then Reuben and El can cover the Big Top. Let's meet back here in an hour. Sound good?"

They nodded, but El asked, "What if we hit a problem and need support?"

"Phone us, or scream." Alex smiled slowly. "Phone would be better."

"No shit, Sherlock," El said sarcastically.

Alex flipped her the bird and El laughed, and then Avery said the spell that draped them in darkness. With a blink, the others disappeared, their appearances turning wraith-like and insubstantial. Had Avery not known where they were, she wouldn't have seen them.

Avery and Alex were able to see the details of the tent as they drew closer. A large archway with the words *Welcome to the Crossroads Circus* framed the path to the tent's entrance, flanked by two enormous imitation standing stones. A large raven was perched on one, and his black eyes stared down at them. For a second, Avery thought it was fake, until it cawed loudly, and she jumped. The sound of voices drifted towards them, and music, low and tinny, filled the air.

"Is that coming from the tent?" Avery asked.

Alex nodded. "I think so. Maybe they're practising."

Figures strode to and fro, some quickly, others slowly, usually in groups. The door of the tent was lifted and light poured out, giving Avery a glimpse of seats, ladders, and performers swinging on a trapeze. However, they didn't loiter, instead skirting around it to the field housing the performers' living quarters. They reached a gate in the hedge, jumped over it, and sticking to the dark shadows, walked into the campground.

The smell of cooking and wood smoke was stronger here, and the voices were louder. They edged their way through the mobile homes, noting some had lights within them, and others were dark. The hum of generators filled the air, and with it the smell of diesel, quickly overpowering the scent of food.

Little had caught their interest so far. The occasional figure drifted past in scruffy jeans or combat trousers, boots, trainers, t-shirts, and jackets. The passed a lone juggler, a middle-aged man with long, wild hair, throwing half a dozen balls into the air and catching them with grace and dexterity. He was mesmerising, and Avery dragged her gaze away as Alex pulled her towards the inner caravans. The light was brighter here, and as they peered around the corner of a van, they saw a small, central area with a blazing fire in the middle, and a muddle of seats around the edge in which a few people were sitting, chatting, and eating. They seemed comfortable and familiar with each other, which wasn't surprising, and so far there was nothing untoward happening, just the usual hustle and bustle of a crowd of people who knew each other well.

They walked on, heading to the outskirts, passing more vans grouped together around other fires, and it reminded Avery of music festivals, as every group sounded different; different music, different languages, and different types of performers. Eventually they reached the vans tucked beneath the furthermost hedge. An old gypsy caravan was set apart from the others. It was beautifully decorated, the door open to reveal a colourful interior lit with lamplight. It had its own small wood burner in there, and smoke poured from a tiny chimney, but there was a small fire burning outside, too. As she watched, the woman who she'd seen earlier that day in the town dressed in earthy colours walked down the steps in the same clothes, but with a large jumper and an old parka, too. She was rolling a cigarette between her fingers, but she paused and looked up towards Avery, and Avery quickly slipped back into the dark shadows next to a van, pulling Alex with her.

Alex looked puzzled, but she said nothing, watching the woman and wondering what she would do. For a moment she stood, looking perplexed, and then glanced around quickly as if unsure of her surroundings, but after another brief moment, she carried on down the steps and settled into an old wooden deck chair, propping her feet on a log as she smoked her cigarette and watched the flames.

Avery was rattled. For a moment, it felt as if she'd been seen. She raised herself up on tip-toes and whispered in Alex's ear. "Sorry. She's the woman I saw in town earlier, the one I thought looked into me."

Alex watched the woman. "Are you feeling anything from her now?"

"No, but for a second there, I thought she'd seen me through my spell, but I must be wrong."

"Interesting," he murmured. "I wonder who she is. I also wonder if I'd have had the same feeling if she'd seen me today, too."

"Like maybe she's some kind of witch detector?"

"Maybe."

They watched for a short while, but she remained alone, unmoving and remote.

"I wonder why she's set apart from the others?" Avery mused. "I'm too worried to get any closer to her. I feel as if she has an Avery-radar."

"I'm sure she doesn't, but let's not take any chances and check out the vans further along the hedge. Some of these look bigger than the others—maybe they belong to the managers."

They kept to the shadows, moving between the cars, vans and caravans, hearing snatches of conversation, usually about what crowds to expect, complaints about rehearsals, and relief the weather was warming up. And then they saw a tall, gaunt, middle-aged man exit a large camper van that had been converted from an old army vehicle. He bristled with authority and strode through the vans with purpose, but rather than follow him, they tiptoed up the steps to look into the interior.

It was dimly lit with one small lamp, and it illuminated a sitting area, a small kitchen, and large bed at the rear behind the driver's compartment, and it was a mess. Dirty glasses and plates crowded the surfaces, the bed was unmade, and clothes were strewn everywhere, but what was more interesting was the costume that draped over a chair. It was a cloak of black feathers, and a mask hung next to it—a feather hood and large beak.

"This must belong to the owner, Corbin, aka the Raven King," Alex suggested. "Isn't he the Ring Master?"

Avery nodded. "That's what Dan said. It's an amazing costume, but so were the ones the performers wore in town today. It's going to be quite the show."

"It doesn't tell us anything about who could be responsible for these deaths though, does it?" Alex headed for the exit, but before they could leave, they heard voices, and the man returned with another man behind him. It was Rafe. They walked up the shallow steps, shutting the door behind them.

Avery quickly reinforced their spell and they retreated to the back where it was dark, squashing next to the bed behind a row of clothes. If necessary and they were spotted, they could glamour them so they could escape, but Avery hoped it wouldn't come to that.

Corbin rounded on Rafe. "How is she? Is she keeping it at bay?"

He nodded. "For now. But it grows stronger, and I have a feeling that soon she won't be able to control it for much longer, despite the sacrifice not being complete. It will hunt, regardless."

Corbin punched the wall and swore. "Damn it, Rafe! I thought we'd get away with one more show."

Rafe drew himself up and looked him squarely in the eye. "And I told you we couldn't. It will feed before the first show, it's inevitable, but we'll make sure it happens away from here, as usual. Just stick to your end of the bargain. Caitlin's arrangement feeds this place—and you, don't forget that. Your costume wouldn't be half so impressive without it."

"You didn't fully explain the consequences of this," Corbin said, almost snarling.

Rafe laughed grimly. "Don't give me that crap. We did, but you just heard what you wanted to hear—money and success. You just let Caitlin do what she needs to, and we'll be fine. Hold your nerve, Corbin."

With that, Rafe pushed the door open and left, and Corbin watched him go, his hands clenched and his expression furious. He stood for a moment, breathing deeply, no doubt in an effort to calm himself down, and then he strode to a small fridge, grabbed a beer, and headed out again, slamming the door.

Avery let out a breath she hadn't even realised she'd been holding. "Wow. What did *that* mean?"

Alex was already untangling himself from the clothes. "I don't know, but we need to follow Rafe. He clearly knows more about this than anyone."

Unfortunately, by the time they stumbled down the steps into the night, Corbin and Rafe had both disappeared. For the next half an hour, they hunted between the cars, caravans, and camper vans, desperate to find Rafe, but he'd gone.

Avery scanned the crowd looking for Mairi, but couldn't see her, either. "If Rafe knows about this, Mairi must, too. They're married, so they must all be in this together. But who's Caitlin?"

"Good question," Alex said, as they left the field, frustrated that they had more questions than they'd had before.

They met the others back by the cars. Reuben leant against El's Land Rover, his arms crossed, and his hands tucked under his armpits. His long legs were stretched out on the road, and his head was tipped back, looking up at the stars. El sat inside, the engine running, trying to keep warm. Briar and Shadow were nowhere in sight.

"Any joy?" Reuben asked, straightening up as El joined them.

"You could say that," Alex replied. "Although, what we heard raises more questions than answers. You?"

"We sat on the seats in the dark at the back of the tent, watching the performers. They've already set up the high wires and trapeze, and a couple of acrobats were in there warming up. They're still decorating the inside, though."

El said, "It looks so cool. They're decorating the inside like the out. The walls are covered in paintings of leaves and images of the Green Man, but they're hanging thick curtains of leaves and feathers over the walls, too. The whole place felt like it was rustling, like it's alive, and that there are things watching you. Only half the stuff is up at the moment, but it will feel like we're in the middle of a wood when it's done."

"Any sign of magic?" Alex asked.

"None. Not yet, anyway," Reuben said. "At this stage, I just think it's well put together."

El agreed. "It will be interesting to see what it's like on a performance night, though. I certainly didn't pick up on any magic from the performers. And we didn't hear anything strange, either."

Avery placed her hands on the warm bonnet of El's car, which was still running. "We didn't feel any magic either, but after what we heard, something strange is definitely happening there." She looked beyond Reuben's bulk, up the slope to the castle in the distance. "I'm starting to get worried about Briar and Shadow, though."

Alex checked his watch. "They get five minutes, and then we go and find them."

"Tell us what you heard," El urged them.

Avery had only just started to tell them when they heard footsteps, and Shadow and Briar emerged out of the darkness, Briar glancing nervously behind them.

"Is everything okay?" Avery asked, alarmed. They seemed unsettled, even Shadow.

Briar's eyes were bright with excitement. "Ancient magic is happening up there. I felt the Green Man. Did you?"

"No!" Avery said, startled. "What about you, Shadow?"

Shadow also looked excited, and a bit furtive, which was worrying. "He's here, and he's bringing spring with him. Things are going to get very weird."

"Let's head to my place," Avery said immediately. "See you there."

$$+ \quad + \quad +$$

"How come you could detect ancient magic when we couldn't?" Reuben asked Briar. He sat on one of the chairs that were placed around Avery's dining table, but he'd turned it around so that his legs straddled the seat as he leaned forward on the raised back of the chair.

Briar pointed to her bare feet that were currently flexing on Avery's rug. Her back was to the fire, and she faced the rest of the room, her hands cupped around a mug of tea. "These feet are very sensitive when bare and connected to the earth. Although it was freezing, I decided it was worth trying, and I immediately felt the connection, stronger than I've ever felt before. The Green Man is powering the earth up there. The actual Green Man! The strongest nature spirit of all is truly here! And now that I've felt him, I can't un-feel him. He's here—he's everywhere!"

Avery's stomach fluttered with worry. "Please don't say it's like what happened at Samhain in Old Haven Church." The earth in the wood had been saturated with blood magic, and with the aid of a powerful spell had enabled the opening of the portal. The earth had been tainted, and they had needed to cleanse it after they banished the Wild Hunt.

Briar shook her head vigorously. "No, absolutely not. This was very different. No blood magic, just good, strong Earth magic."

Shadow agreed. "I did what Briar did, and dug my feet into the earth, not expecting to feel anything really, beyond what I normally would, anyway." She shrugged. "As a fey I always have a connection with the earth. It sings to me, responds to me, like it recognises me. But," she paused, her violet eyes darkening to a stormy blue, "something else recognised me. He recognised me." She gazed into the fire and whatever visions lay in there, and her hand flew to her heart. "It felt like home."

The witches exchanged worried glances, and Avery said, "Forgive me for saying this, Shadow, but in the short time I've known you, you seem pretty impervious to anything, and yet, you look upset tonight."

Shadow just stared at her, unflinching. "You would be too if something had tugged at your soul."

"It must have been good to feel your home, though," El said to her gently. She turned to Avery and Alex. "What did you find out while you were hanging around their vans?"

"We found Corbin," Avery told them. "It seems he wears the Raven King's costume, which means he's the Ring Master. Well, that's what Dan told me, anyway." Between them, Avery and Alex related what they had seen and heard, and immediately the collective mood dipped even further.

Reuben reached for another beer and repeated what Avery had told them, "'It grows stronger, and I have a feeling that soon she won't be able to control it for much longer, despite the sacrifice not being complete. It will hunt, regardless.' Have I got that right? What the hell does it mean? Sacrifice sounds ominous."

"But who is Caitlin? And what is her arrangement that gives Corbin's costume power?" Alex asked.

"Whatever it is must be responsible for the Green Man's presence, too," Briar mused.

El brightened. "At least we know there's some kind of magic going on up there, enough to attract the Green Man, and maybe the Raven King—if that's what Rafe meant."

Briar was playing with the ends of her hair as she sat, thinking. "Maybe the circus is named after crossroads magic? Maybe that's what Rafe was talking about?"

Reuben's eyes widened. "Ooh! This sounds fun. Enlighten me."

Briar just looked at him. "Don't you read anything?"

To his credit, he was completely un-offended. "No. You know that. I surf, practice magic—which, admittedly involves some reading of grimoires—and work, when I have to. I'm not the research type."

Alex laughed and toasted him with his beer. "I love your honesty, Reu. You'd better educate all of us, Briar."

Briar settled on the rug, cross-legged, and pushed her long, dark hair back over her shoulders. "I know a little bit. Crossroads are liminal places, and offer a bridge between this world and the Otherworld." She noted Shadow's excited face. "But what the Otherworld is, is debatable. It could be the world of fey, or Hell, or where the spirits live. Common myths talk of being able to summon the Devil at the crossroads, or that the Devil will appear unbidden, promising you your heart's desire in exchange for your soul. They're a powerful place to perform magic, too. Offerings of food or wine can help you make decisions at important times of your life—when you're at a metaphorical crossroads."

"Do these myths occur all over the world?" Alex asked.

"I believe so, all with their own legends and interpretations. In Britain they're commonly linked with standing stones."

Avery sat up straighter. "Is that why there are standing stones at the entrance to the circus?"

Briar shrugged. "I guess so. Crossroads mark thresholds, keep the fey from our doors, and maybe show places where mythical creatures are buried. Like many thresholds, they are more potent at dusk, dawn, and midnight. And of course, they're more powerful on Samhain."

El agreed, adding, "One of Hecate's many roles includes that of the crossroads witch, which I guess fits with her guarding the thresholds of the dead."

The room fell silent for a moment as they thought through the implications, and then Reuben spoke up. "So, the fact that the circus is named after crossroads means what?" He waved his half-empty beer bottle. "It's a good fit for British myth and magic, especially as their performances are based on myths, but is there a deeper meaning?"

A smile hovered on Alex's lips. "Of course there is, because..." He trailed off, looking at them expectantly.

"There's no such thing as coincidence," Avery finished for him. A heaviness settled in her bones and the pit of her stomach. The circus was bringing more than performers to White Haven. She turned to Shadow. "Are there crossroad myths in your world?"

Shadow's face broke into a smile. "We have many stories, old legends that stretch back years—well before I was born—but we would call them less myths than just old tales. The creatures that exist only on the periphery of your world walk about in mine, as real as the sun. But crossroads myths, I'm not so sure."

"What sort of creatures?" Briar asked, her face becoming animated.

That was a good question, Avery reflected. Shadow was a fey; she was a treasure of stories they hadn't even started to unpack.

"There are so many. This world feels only half-alive to me. So many things should be here that aren't." Her eyes dulled as she looked into the fire. "The trees and rivers have spirits—dryads, nymphs, water sprites—all of them are visible, with their own special magic. Satyrs, animal spirits, shapeshifters..."

"We have those," Reuben pointed out. "Briar's boyfriend is a wolf-shifter."

Briar rounded on him. "He's not my boyfriend."

Reuben smirked. "Liar."

Shadow smiled. "I would like to meet him. It's nice to be around creatures with blood from the Other."

Briar looked startled. "What?"

"Of a sort, surely? I told you that Gabe and the Nephilim are half-sylph. These Angels you speak of," she shrugged, unimpressed. "Sounds suspicious to me."

Avery rubbed her face. "This is great, Shadow, but we need to get back to the topic and find out if it is crossroads magic in that circus."

"And if it is, how it works," Alex added.

$$+ \quad + \quad +$$

Newton looked at Avery bleakly. A frown creased his face, and he pulled at his tie, loosening it slightly. "Are you sure?"

"Yes, that's what we heard, and that's what Briar and Shadow felt."

They were in the back room of Avery's shop, which was her stock room and meeting place, and it was just past nine the next morning. Avery had forgotten how energetic Newton was at this hour; he sipped his tea with furious concentration, looking alert and calculating. She, however, felt barely alive. Avery hated mornings.

"But you have no idea who this mysterious Caitlin is?"

"None. We tried to find her, but Rafe had disappeared." She'd told him about the woman who was dressed in earth colours, and she referred to her now. "She might be Caitlin, or she could be unrelated."

"But someone, a woman, controls *it*, whatever that is," Newton pointed out. "And *it* needs to feed. That has to be our killer."

Avery mulled over his suggestion. The woman was perceptive, with an uncanny *knowing* about her. "The woman I saw could be her, but I'm not sure. It's just too soon to say."

After another moment of silence, Newton smiled, and his entire demeanour lifted. "Brilliant work, though. Thanks, Avery, and thank everyone else for me. It's unfortunate to know that we were right, but at least we know *something* about what's going on. I'm going to look into this Caitlin woman, and I think we need to get Ben and the guys involved."

He was referring to the three paranormal investigators, and Avery was startled. "Ben! Why?"

"If they can set cameras up, they might be able to read a weird energy signature."

"But where can they do that? That's nuts. The whole place is buzzing with people."

"On the hill somewhere? Dylan's clever, he'll think of something." He put his mug down. "I'm keen to stop a murder. If we can find whatever it is first, we could save a life."

"Yes, of course, but I'm not sure it's possible with a camera."

Buoyed with positive news, Newton headed for the door. "Can you contact them and let me know? I'm heading back to deal with vampire fallout." He grinned. "Thanks, Avery."

The door banged in his wake and Avery groaned. This was the most cheerful she had seen Newton in weeks, and although it was horrible news, it was also good news. They had an edge. She wasn't particularly pleased about being his deputy, though. She sighed and reached for her phone and tried Dylan first, but he didn't pick up, and neither did Ben, so she called Cassie, who answered quickly.

"Hey, Avery! How are you?" Her voice was warm and welcoming, but she also sounded tired.

"I'm fine, how are you?"

She sighed. "Busy with finishing our papers. We graduate this year, hopefully, so we're trying to get back into coursework after all that vampire madness."

Immediately Avery felt guilty at distracting them with another request. "Of course, I forgot you were in your last year. Have you and Dylan fully recovered now?" They had both been injured after Bethany the vampire had attacked them in the tunnels below West Haven.

"We're fine. Dylan's back to being his annoying, bouncy self, and my head injury cleared up really quickly."

"Good. Well, in that case, I'll leave you to it."

Cassie leapt in quickly. "But you must have called for something?"

"It's fine, you're busy, and you need to graduate."

"But what did you want?" she persisted.

"Newton wondered if Dylan could do some filming for him." She went on to explain what was happening at the circus.

"Of course he can," Cassie said, "and we'll do anything else you need."

"No, you're too busy."

"It's a bit of filming. Dylan will do it." Cassie hesitated for a moment, and Avery could hear other people around her. "I'm heading into lectures now, and then I'll find him and we'll call you. Sound good?"

"Great, but only if you're sure—"

The line went dead, and Cassie was gone.

Avery headed into the shop, taking a plate of chocolate biscuits with her.

Happenstance Books was quiet, with just a few customers browsing the shelves, and the place had a calm, reassuring feel to it. That morning she had reinforced her protection spells, and she felt soothed as she strolled through the shelving units to join Dan and Sally at the counter.

However, as soon as Sally saw Avery, she stood and grabbed a biscuit. "Great, have you finished in the back?"

"Yes, why?"

"I'm going to do a stock take of our children's section, and handle some accounts while we're quiet. That okay?"

Avery shrugged. "Of course, you don't need to ask me."

Sally disappeared, leaving Dan and Avery alone. Dan crunched into a biscuit, and speaking through a mouthful of crumbs, he said, "You look like you have the weight of the world on your shoulders."

"Do I?" She peered into the glass at the front window, hoping to catch her reflection. He was right; she did look slightly dishevelled. She rubbed her hair, pulled a lip salve out from her pocket, and ran it around her lips. "Better?"

Dan squinted. "Only if I look at you like this."

Avery looked over her shoulder to check that they weren't being watched, and then flicked her fingers at him, making a little *whoosh* of air ruffle his hair. "Cheeky sod."

He laughed. "I'm kidding. You look great. Apart from the weighed down-thing. What's happened now?"

Avery explained what they had found the night before, and what Newton wanted Dylan to do.

Dan whistled in surprise. "Wow. So the Crossroads Circus really has crossroads magic? There are lots of myths associated with that."

"So I gather. Got any to add to the list?"

He held up a finger and then pulled out his phone, scrolling through Spotify. In seconds, the music that was playing in the shop changed to an old Blues tune, and an achingly smooth voice filled the shop. "This is Robert Johnson," Dan explained. "Heard of him?"

"No."

"He's an American Blues musician who performed in the 1930s. One day his guitar playing became phenomenal, and when asked about it, he said he'd sold his soul to the Devil at the crossroads in exchange for musical talent."

Avery's coffee cup stopped halfway to her lips. "Really?"

"Really. He was very honest about it. And then he died at that spooky age when all great musicians die."

"27?"

Dan nodded. "The Devil came to claim his soul! This track is actually called 'Cross Road Blues.'"

The Blues guitar and Johnson's haunting voice filled the room. Avery shivered. "Well that's just spooky."

"I'll try and find some more stuff for you later. In the meantime, I'll line up his album."

The bell ringing above the door disturbed them, and Avery turned to see Caspian enter the shop. He paused and listened.

"Delta blues. I like it." He joined them at the counter. Caspian looked smart, dressed in a formal suit and three-quarter length woollen jacket.

"To what do we owe this pleasure, Caspian?" Avery asked him, suddenly self-conscious of her appearance.

"Gabe told me we have a new problem."

"News travels fast!"

"Need my help?" he asked, raising a quizzical eyebrow.

"I'm not entirely sure what we need help with right now. We're just starting to investigate."

Dan waved them away. "Off to your meeting, Avery. I've got this."

Avery wasn't really sure she wanted to spend time alone with Caspian, but this certainly wasn't a conversation for the shop floor. "Fair enough. Follow me, Caspian."

Sally was in the back room, on the computer, and she looked up as Avery entered. Her face fell as she saw Caspian. Reformed character or not, he had kidnapped Sally months before, and she hadn't forgiven him. She went to stand. "I'll leave you to it."

"No, you stay here," Avery said, gesturing for her to sit down. "We'll talk upstairs."

She led Caspian up to her flat, and as soon as they were alone, Caspian took his jacket off and draped it across the back of a chair. "Crossroads magic is complicated, Avery."

She perched on the arm of the sofa. "So I gather."

"We should tell Genevieve."

"But nothing's happened yet."

"Even better."

"I'd like to keep this small. The vampire thing became huge!"

"It needed to be. Vampires are deadly."

"Well, hopefully this thing isn't as dangerous. I think we can handle it."

He watched her silently for a moment, and Avery's living room began to feel very small. He finally spoke. "You're very stubborn."

"It's part of my charm," she shot back.

"I know." His eyes drifted to her lips and then back to her eyes, and a smile crossed his lips.

Shit. Wrong thing to say. Caspian did not need any encouragement. "Behave," she warned him. "Have you some gems of wisdom to share?"

"Not yet, but I'd like it if you'd tell me what's happening."

Avery sighed, and for what felt like the hundredth time, explained what had happened at the circus the night before, and the suspicious events around the country that made them suspect the circus in the first place.

He nodded. "A circus is a good place to hide a supernatural creature. Circuses already have a reputation for odd characters, and they travel frequently."

A thought struck Avery. "True, but although this circus is named after crossroads, it's not actually on a crossroad, is it? So why has it got crossroads magic? It's a travelling circus. They're not even on crossroads up at the castle!"

"Interesting point." He smiled again. "It's a good thing we like a puzzle, isn't it? Are you going again?"

"We're going to go to the opening night, on Saturday, and we'll probably go with Dylan if he agrees to set up cameras. That might be tonight."

"Good. Keep me informed. I can help if you need me." He picked his coat up and headed for the door.

"Thanks, hopefully we'll be fine."

"Hopefully." And then he left, smiling at her enigmatically.

As the door clicked shut, Avery's phone rang. It was Dylan, and he didn't waste time with pleasantries. "Hey Ave, of course I'll help. Let's do it tonight. I can go alone."

"No, you can't. We don't know what might happen. Where are you thinking of putting cameras?"

"I don't know yet, but I'll think of something. I'll come around at eight tonight. Laters!" And then he was gone, and once again Avery felt as if her life was spiralling slightly out of her control.

Five

Avery, Alex, Dylan, and Ben stood on the ridge of the hill looking down on the castle, which had become an apparition of itself; the yellow lights that illuminated the walls were webbed by a heavy mist, which had become steadily thicker as night fell, draping the landscape in veils of illusion. They had pulled onto the verge of a road further away from the castle and trekked across the fields, approaching well away from the grounds.

Once again, the circus tent was lit up, and fires burned sporadically across the campsite next to it, but like the castle, they were ghostly. Avery glanced around and shivered. It was eerie here, surrounded by darkness and the sticky fingers of mist. She imagined she could hear things moving beyond her vision and stepped closer to Alex.

"Where are you thinking of putting the cameras?" Alex asked, shuffling on his feet to keep warm.

Dylan pointed to a black shape further down the hill. "That tree will be great. Close enough to get decent images, but far enough away for them not to see it. Besides, I'll put it up high. But I'm not sure about the other two."

"Something will suggest itself," Alex said, setting off down the hill. "Let's get this one in first."

The wet grass was spongy, and Avery was glad she'd worn Wellington boots. The others, however, wore trainers or short leather boots, and their jeans were already wet around their calves when they reached the huge oak in the middle of the field.

Dylan opened his backpack and scrabbled around, pulling out a small, lightweight camera. He checked the batteries and the settings, while Ben pulled a wooden box out of his own pack and a cordless drill.

"This is what we'll house it in," Ben explained. "We've used them before at Old Haven Church and other places, and it means the camera is fixed and protected from the weather, at least for a short time." He looked around, worried. "However, it's cold and damp out here, and I'm worried it will affect the camera's performance. The box is insulated, though."

Dylan grimaced. "It wasn't too bad at Samhain, but I'll have to come in the morning to get it, in the light. I should be far enough away that no one really notices what I'm doing, but I'll leave it to tomorrow night if it looks risky."

He took the box, drill, and screws from Ben, put them in a much smaller pack that he had pulled from the larger one, and started to climb the tree. He was quick and agile, and he swung up through the branches effortlessly. After another few minutes Ben's phone buzzed, its volume muted, and he read the text aloud. "He's ready."

Alex said a small spell designed to muffle sound, which would stop the noise of the drill from echoing across the fields. After another few minutes, Dylan reappeared, exchanged the drill for the camera, and headed back up the tree.

Avery and Alex watched the castle and their surroundings, wary for any intruders. However, everything was silent, other than the rubbing of bare branches overhead, clacking like disapproving old women. Avery could see movement around the campsite, and people going in and out the circus tent, and there were a lot of smaller stalls now erected within the castle walls. A few shouts reached them, but nothing that could be understood. Avery closed her eyes and reached her awareness out, feeling for magic. She didn't take her shoes off; that would be pointless. She couldn't feel Earth magic as strongly as Briar, but the wind could carry things to her.

She reached out, pulling air towards her from the campgrounds, and all of a sudden, the faint noises grew louder. She stepped away from Alex to allow her to concentrate on the snatched conversations: questions about performances, complaints about someone's noise, an argument about costumes.

And then she felt *her*—the mysterious woman.

Avery was momentarily startled, but rather than retreat, she shielded herself and the others with a protective spell, blocking her probing mind. She was pretty sure she'd detected her first, before the woman became aware of her presence. She waited, feeling her mind like the gentle brush of a feather, as it moved past her and the others, moving up the hill and out across the fields. If she had detected them, she would have loitered, pushed harder to try to find out who they were. Fortunately she didn't, and Avery relaxed.

Now that Avery had detected her, she could follow her easily. She was searching for something, but what? And then she vanished. *Damn it.* She'd gone too far, past where Avery could follow her. *How did she do that?* Avery wasn't sure she could send *her* mind so far from her body, not without spirit-walking anyway, and this wasn't spirit-walking; she was sure of that. Unfortunately, there was nothing that would tell her more about who she was, or what her powers were, but Avery was sure she wasn't a witch. After another few moments, Avery turned her concentration back to the circus below.

Alex disturbed her, gently taking her right elbow in his hand. "Are you okay? You're miles away."

"That woman has been here, searching for something."

"Did she detect us?"

"No, I don't think so. I shielded us, and she passed on, across the fields." She nodded in the general direction that she had gone.

"I felt your magic flare, and I wondered what for. I thought you were searching."

"I was. It was good timing."

Dylan landed on the ground behind them with a *thump*. "Done. On to the next." He looked between them. "What's happened?"

"Someone's *essence* is out here, searching for something," Avery told him. "But don't worry, we've got it covered."

"Good, let's get a move on," Ben said decisively. "I want to get to the far outer wall of the castle. There's no one near there. We can mount a camera on that."

He turned and led the way to a large bulk of blackness that was dense against the grey of the sky. There was no moon or stars to guide them, and it was tricky going, especially in the mist. Avery stumbled in rabbit holes and over patches of gorse, until eventually they reached the outer wall, which stood a good distance away from the main part of the castle. It enclosed a smooth, grassed area that ran to the edge of the castle's interior.

"Do you want me to focus on the campsite, or the circus tent?" Dylan asked as he pulled another camera from his pack.

"Campsite," Avery said immediately. "There are all sorts of things going on there."

All the while they had been walking, Avery had kept the protective shield around them, and now she focused on trying to feel the woman's presence again, while Dylan climbed the crumbling wall, and Alex and Ben supported him. The mist was growing thicker, and its cold fingers stroked Avery's cheek and reached down her neck. She felt moisture on her eyelashes and skin but ignored it, as she concentrated on the campsite and the surrounding area.

Then she felt the beat of wings, low overhead. Their span felt unnaturally large, and the wave of air threatened to push her into the earth. She felt Alex jump besides her as he felt it too, and they crouched to avoid being hit. A presence loomed above them, silent and oppressive, and she felt an unknown power smother her, silencing all other night sounds. Then it magnified a hundred times, and the sensation of one single span of wings exploded into hundreds of birds, all flapping above her as they streaked away across the land and over the sea.

They leapt to their feet as the oppressive feeling disappeared, and looked to the horizon.

"What the hell was that?" Alex asked her in urgent, hushed tones.

"I've no idea. What is happening here?" Avery felt breathless with panic.

But before he could answer, she felt a surge of *something*, and the unmistakable feeling of malevolent glee. She grabbed Alex's hand and felt the flutter of wings return overhead, back to the campsite where they vanished to a single point, and normal night sounds returned.

"It must be the Raven King," Avery suggested. "Did you feel wings, too?"

He nodded, looking as bewildered as Avery felt, but Ben's voice disturbed them. "What is going on with you two?"

Ben and Dylan were watching them from the shelter of the wall, both wide-eyed.

"Didn't you feel it?" Alex asked them in a low voice.

"No," Dylan said. "Why were you both crouching?"

"It felt as if there were hundreds of birds flying overhead, and I had this feeling of doom," Avery explained, for want of a better word.

Ben and Dylan exchanged a confused glance, and Dylan said, "*Birds?* We didn't feel a thing."

Now it was Avery and Alex who were exchanging worried glances. "Not surprising, really," Alex finally said. "It's a magic thing. You done here?"

Dylan nodded. "You want me to place the final camera?"

"Part of me wants to say yes. The more we know, the better. But most of me just wants to get out of here," Alex answered.

Avery nodded in agreement, and looked back over her shoulder to the campsite, where everything looked surprisingly normal. "I agree. Forget the last camera. Let's get back to the car. Are you sure they're set up?"

"Absolutely," Dylan said, reassuring them.

They headed back across the fields, but within a few minutes the light from the castle grounds disappeared behind them, and they were in pitch darkness, surrounded by mist that was so thick, they could barely see each other.

Avery faltered, gripping Alex's hand tightly. "Are we going in the right direction?"

He paused, too. "I think so, but I can't see a damn thing. Dylan, Ben? What do you think?"

Ben's voice was tight with worry. "I don't know where we are, but we're heading uphill, so we must be going the right way."

"Let's stay close together," Dylan suggested. "No wandering off!"

They trudged onwards, and the field seemed to go on forever. Alex gripped Avery's hand as they stumbled over uneven ground, and with unspoken agreement they quickened their pace. Suddenly, an unexpected wind rustled the grass beneath their feet, and the scent of loamy earth surrounded them, rich and overwhelming, almost cloying as it filled their nostrils.

They stopped again. "Feel that?" Alex asked Dylan and Ben.

They nodded and Ben said, "I can *smell* that."

"I don't know if that's a good or a bad thing," Alex admitted, perplexed. "Let's keep going."

They pushed on as the rustling sound and the smell of earth became more insistent, until Ben said in a panicked, whispered tone, "Why aren't we coming to a hedge? We should be at the boundary by now. We only crossed one sodding field."

"Things seem further when you can't see where you going," Avery said, trying to be logical in the face of increasing panic. She strengthened the protection spell, and as she did so, felt the unmistakable presence of the woman again. She suddenly started to doubt herself. *Were they as protected as she thought? Was this a game? A ruse?*

Avery's voice was strained. "I think we're being hunted."

"What?" Dylan hissed, whirling around.

"I can feel something stalking us—despite my spell," Avery said, almost stumbling over her words.

Alex squeezed her hand. "I feel something, too. We need to think smarter. I think we're being led astray. This smell of earth is bewildering, and the rustling all around us is misleading."

Avery thought of the spells she could say without needing her grimoire. "What about a finding spell on Ben's van?"

"Try it," Alex urged.

Avery turned to Ben. "Give me some of your hair and the keys."

Without question, Ben yanked a few strands free and placed them and his keys in Avery's hand. Trying to block out everything else, she said the spell, and within seconds a blue light appeared before them, and then set off across the grass, barely visible in the mist.

"It's going the wrong way, I'm sure," Dylan said, watching it go.

"Trust it. Go now!" Avery cried, and ignoring their instincts they virtually ran after it, stumbling and falling occasionally in their haste.

Avery could feel it now. Something was behind them, gaining ground, but just as Avery was prepared to turn and fight, they ran headlong into the break in the hedge, the van appearing in front of them. It beeped as Ben unlocked it, and he slid across the bonnet in his haste to get to the door. Dylan dove for the passenger door, and Alex and Avery threw themselves in the back. The doors were barely shut as Ben sped away, tires squealing.

Avery pressed her face to the glass, watching as another face manifested out of the swirling mist. She fell back in shock, but a wave of magic exploded from Alex's outstretched hand behind her, and he sent a spear of concentrated power at the mysterious entity. It exploded into fragments as Ben put distance between them.

"Anyone want to tell me what happened back there?" Dylan said, turning around in his seat to look at them. He sniffed his jacket. "I think I can still smell that composty stench."

Avery and Alex exchanged a troubled glance, and Avery said, "I think we were pursued by the Green Man, the Raven King, and the unknown woman. One of them was threatening us, and I'm not sure who it was."

"Me neither," Alex agreed.

Ben drove recklessly through the country lanes, glancing back at them to ask, "Just back up a moment. I thought the Raven King was just a costume, and the Green Man was the theme of the circus. How they can now be *real*?"

Alex spread his hands wide, shrugging. "We don't know, but Briar and Shadow are convinced the Green Man is here, courtesy of boundary magic, which must apply to the Raven King, too. And don't ask us how that works when the circus isn't on a crossroad either, we have no idea. I'm very confused right now."

"Essentially, you're saying something is bringing those myths to life?"

Avery nodded as she remembered what Rafe had said in the camper van only the night before. "And we know *something* is inhabiting *someone* and its hunger is growing, and it will hunt."

Alex looked at her, perplexed. "Did you feel that pulse of power, while we were sheltering under the castle wall? That feeling of pleasure that something had?"

"Yes. Why?"

"Maybe *it* already hunted. Maybe someone is already dead."

Ben groaned. "Bloody brilliant. Maybe we were next on the list. We were in the middle of that field, alone, unseen, and being shepherded away from safety, until you did that spell, Avery."

"But I had put a protection spell around us. Does that mean it was useless?"

"Maybe not," Alex said. "We're still here, aren't we?"

"But whatever it was, it was gaining ground on us. We all felt it."

"We need to hit the books again, soon," Alex suggested.

"Yes, that's a good idea. If you guys do pick up those cameras tomorrow," Avery said, "don't go alone."

Dylan laughed dryly. "You don't need to worry about that. We'll go early, as soon as it's light, and change the card and batteries. I'm betting circus folk aren't early risers."

"Don't take any chances!" Avery warned them.

"We won't, and with luck, the mist will cover us," Dylan said, as Ben pulled into the outskirts of White Haven and made his way to The Wayward Son.

"You two coming in for a drink?" Alex asked.

Ben twisted around in his seat as he stopped outside the pub. He still looked damp from the mist, and his hair was tousled. "I'd rather get home. Then I can have a hot shower and several stiff whiskeys."

"I hear that," Dylan agreed.

"All right," Alex nodded. "We'll be in touch. And stay safe."

Six

"Whatever was chasing us somehow got through my protection spell," Avery murmured to Alex as they curled in bed, holding each other.

"Not true," he said, his warm breath tickling her ear. "It's not meant to hide us, not like your shadow spell. It did as it should—it protected us. Whatever was chasing us couldn't get close."

She snuggled against him. "I suppose you're right. But I did shield us earlier, when I felt that woman's presence in the field. She couldn't find us then."

"But then other things happened, and you probably dropped it unconsciously." He rolled on top of her, a forearm on either side of her head supporting his weight as he looked down at her. "I think it's a good thing they know we're watching. It might make them hesitate."

Her hand traced the contours of his face. "They didn't seem too worried to me. They chased us across the field. The Green Man was around us! It had to be him! I just wish I knew what it all meant."

"We'll work it out, we always do," he said before kissing her and leaving her breathless. "Now, I think we have better things to do than talk about that damn circus." And as his hand trailed down her body, Avery blocked out the night and their pursuers, focusing only on Alex, his touch, his lips, and the delicious heat spreading from her stomach.

Unfortunately, Avery didn't sleep easily. She dreamt that she was in the field again, and this time the mysterious pursuer was closer and Avery was alone. The mist was once again wrapped around her, and the rustling of the hedges and grass beneath her feet was vividly real. For a second she stood her ground, and then as she felt the strange presence grow closer, Avery ran as fast as she could, but she had no idea where she was running to. Something was close. She thought she heard breathing behind her, and a whisper of some undecipherable word, and she stumbled as something on the ground wrapped around her ankles. She fell heavily, her breath knocked out of her, and she felt the wet grass against her cheek and beneath her palms. She struggled to rise, but she couldn't get up. Something was smothering her, suffocating her, and she tried to scream, but she couldn't do that, either.

She was going to die, and she couldn't summon her magic. She couldn't do anything. With a monumental effort she pushed her attacker away and her eyes flew open, and suddenly she was back in Alex's bedroom, sitting upright, eyes wide open.

Her heart was pounding in her chest, and she took some deep breaths. Alex was asleep at her side, oblivious to her panic. It was just a bad dream, she told herself. But she couldn't shake the ominous feeling the dream had brought with it, and she shuddered as she tried to go back to sleep.

When Avery woke the next morning, she smelt bacon, and she slipped out of bed and headed to the kitchen, pushing the strange dream of the night before to the back of her mind.

"You're cooking! Thank you."

Alex smiled, his hair tangled around his face and stubble creeping across his cheeks. He pushed a cup towards her across the counter. "My pleasure. Here's your coffee." He watched her for a second as she took a sip and said, "Have you ever considered if we should move in together? We're at each other's place most nights anyway."

She paused as she met his eyes, feeling a flush of pleasure. "I had, actually. But I guess it's tricky with us both living above where we work. And I have my cats, so..."

"You'd rather be at your place than mine." He smiled as he moved closer.

"For the record, your place is bigger, as well as the fact that you have two cats, so it would make sense to me, too."

She grinned. "Are you saying you want to move into my place? Properly?"

"I guess so. Sound okay?"

"Sounds great," she said, a warm, fuzzy feeling filling her. "But your flat is gorgeous. What will you do with it? And all of your lovely furniture?"

"I'll keep it empty for now and we'll see how it goes. You never know," he teased her, "your mess might start to drive me insane."

"My mess!" she said, wanting to throw something at him. "I'm not messy. That much."

He laughed and kissed her. "You know you are. But that's okay. It's part of your charm. Now, let me finish breakfast, because we have somewhere to be."

"Where?"

His face fell and he became serious. "Newton just called. Someone found a body on the beach this morning. He wants us to look at it."

Last night's activities came flooding back to Avery. "Oh, no. It's not a natural death, then?"

"Maybe not. Get dressed, food will be ready in a few minutes."

+ + +

The beach was silent, other than the steady lap of waves on the shore. The sea was oddly calm, but so was the weather. There wasn't a breath of wind, and although the mist had lifted slightly, there were still ribbons of it undulating across the sands and winding up the steep cliff face.

They were at the same beach where Avery had first met Caspian. A set of rickety wooden steps led from the car park on the hill to the beach below, and rock pools edged along the far side, under the cliff. Avery wrinkled her nose as she looked around, wondering what felt so different. And then it clicked.

It felt like early spring. Shadow was right about the Green Man's influence.

Avery and Alex reached the bottom of the steps together, and Newton walked over to join them, a woman next to him. She was in her mid-thirties and had olive skin and very dark hair, and she looked curiously at both of them. Avery felt uncomfortable under her direct gaze. It was something the police did well, and she assumed she had to be the new detective, Walker.

Newton greeted them. "Thanks for coming. This is DS Inez Walker, the detective I was telling you about."

Inez shook their hands. "Good to meet you. Newton has told me how you help his investigations sometimes, although I feel he's not telling me everything." She gave Newton a long, sideways glance.

"This way," Newton said, not rising to the bait, "and wear these." He handed them plastic overshoes, watched while they put them on, and then walked over to the man's body, which was on the dry sand, just above the tide mark.

Officer Moore was a short distance away, watching them silently, and a dog sat next to a policeman who had it on a lead. It whined and pawed the ground, agitated.

Avery eyed it regretfully. "Is that the victim's dog?"

Newton sighed. "I'm afraid so. It seems they went for a late night walk and never came back. Someone jogging on the cliff path," he paused and pointed over their heads, "saw him lying here, and called it in."

Avery looked at the man at her feet. Other than being dead, he looked normal, nothing to indicate how he'd died. "Is there anything you want us to focus on?"

He shook his head. "Just see if you can detect any magic, or anything odd. The coroner will be here soon, and SOCO. I'll tell them that you two were here to consult. I was given clearance for it."

Avery thought she detected Inez flinch when Newton mentioned magic, but she recovered quickly. Alex had already crouched and he held his hands out above the body, so Avery sent her magic across the beach, trying to feel anything further afield. She shook her head. "I can't feel a thing," she said regretfully. "What about you, Alex?"

He looked up. "I sense a powerful type of energy I haven't felt before. You try."

She'd hoped to avoid this, but she crouched next to him, echoing his movements. He was right. "Yes, I feel it. It's like that oppressive power we felt last night."

Inez narrowed her eyes. "A power?"

Avery nodded. "Malevolent. Well, that's how it seemed to me."

Newton intervened. "Alex mentioned something has happened."

Avery rolled her eyes in disbelief. "Lots of weird things. We can tell you later. We might know more, too, if Dylan had success with the camera."

"Good. Can you narrow down this sense of oppression?" Newton asked. "Would you recognise it again?"

Alex and Avery exchanged glances, and Avery shrugged. "Probably."

"Good."

It looked as if Inez wanted to ask more questions, but the noise of cars from the car park above disturbed them.

"That will be the coroner," Newton said. "We'll see you later." And with that, they were dismissed, and Alex and Avery headed up the steps, aware of Inez watching them all the way.

"Well, it's clear Newton hasn't told her that much about us yet," Alex noted as they reached his car.

"No. But that won't last long, and then it will be interesting to see just how open-minded she is. He didn't say if he'd found out who Caitlin was, either."

"I guess this has side-tracked him," Alex said. "I'll ask him later."

+ + +

Sally's hand was already at her mouth as she listened. "You had to do *what*?" She closed her eyes briefly. "Please don't tell me something else is happening here."

"Sorry," Avery said, feeling inexplicably guilty. "It seems someone at the circus is responsible for those deaths after all."

Sally's expression changed as she spat out, "Bollocks. The kids were so excited about that circus. I can't take them now!" She looked at Avery, outraged. "No one should be taking their kids there."

Avery's mouth fell open and she looked at Sally, shocked. "We can't announce this! We have no evidence. And besides, everyone who has attended the circus in other towns has been fine! The performance will be safe enough."

Sally continued to glare. "I don't care. I'm not taking the kids."

"That's fair enough, but it's not my fault, you know."

Sally deflated like a popped balloon. "I know, but I was just hoping life would get back to normal around here, or at least relative safety. I'm fine with magic, just not the deaths."

"No one's fine with the deaths, Sally, you fruit loop."

The shop was quiet, and Sally, Dan, and Avery were chatting around the counter in a lull between customers.

"Someone needs a chocolate biscuit," Dan said, holding out the open packet.

Sally glared at him, too. "It will take more than a digestive biscuit to make me feel better."

"But it will help, right?" he said, wafting it under her nose. "I'm as upset as you, Sally, but we're here to stop this. It's our job now."

Avery looked at him, surprised. "That's very sweet of you, Dan."

He puffed his chest out. "I'm Team Witch all the way, you know that. I'm tackling Raven King and Green Man myths for you later. "

"Thanks," she said, taking a biscuit for herself. "I should call Genevieve."

"Why are you putting it off?"

"I just think it's something we can handle, that's all."

"But she has collective knowledge, and you've got Oswald and all the oldies to ask. Although, you do have me, and I'm awesome."

"True, so awesome," she said, sarcastically. "I'll call her soon, before Caspian beats me to it, and outs me like a grass."

"However," Dan continued, jabbing his half-eaten biscuit, "I have been thinking about the Green Man and his connection with the crossroads, and I would argue that he's another liminal figure. He sits on the boundaries of earth, nature, growth, decay. He's a nature spirit, essentially, and here we are, blind and unknowing in the presence of nature's true face. It's there, just beyond our understanding, a wild force we can't control."

"Holy cow. Have you drank extra strength coffee this morning?" Avery asked, looking at him, amazed.

"Master's in Folklore," he said, poking at his chest. "Almost. By the way, I'll need a few days off to finish up soon."

"Sure," Avery agreed, not fully focusing on what he was saying.

"That's pretty cool, actually," Sally said, her expression softening. "The Crossroads Circus has all sorts of crossroads figures in it. Maybe I will go, after all."

Avery leant on the counter. "I just wish I knew who the other woman is, the one I saw behind the procession, and at the campground. I wasn't sure she was with them at the time, but she has to be. She's camped with them, admittedly a little bit separate from the rest. I wonder what her role is? I felt she looked straight through me, and her mind—her awareness—travelled far beyond where mine can." She thought through the attack in the field. "I'm convinced she was the presence I felt."

"Maybe she's the conduit for the crossroads magic," Sally suggested. "As you said, the circus isn't on an actual crossroads, so if the name refers to the magic from a crossroads, maybe she's it. She carries it within her."

Dan and Avery blinked at her, and Avery said, "That's quite brilliant, Sally."

Sally looked pleased. "Is it? Oh, good."

Dan continued to theorise. "She could be that Caitlin woman."

Avery's voice filled with excitement. "Rafe said 'Caitlin's arrangement feeds this place,' but it didn't make sense at the time. That could be what it means—an arrangement to get crossroads magic. I feel something is just beyond our reach, though."

Dan nodded. "Yeah, we're not quite there yet, but it will all drop into place."

"But when? We're running out of time. They've killed once already. What if once isn't enough this time?"

"Let's hope Dylan's film suggests something," Dan said, before falling silent as the doorbell chimed, announcing a customer.

"I'm hitting the books," Avery announced, aware they'd know exactly what books she was referring to.

They nodded, and Sally called, "Good luck!" as Avery made her way up to her flat

.

✛   ✛   ✛

As Avery walked into her lounge, she looked around, wondering how her home would feel once Alex moved in. She smiled. It would feel great. *As long as he didn't try to make her tidy too much.*

She glanced at the sofa. Hers was a little worn compared to his. Maybe they should bring his sofa here. It was important that he had some of his belongings here, too. She stroked the cats that curled around her legs, and headed to the kitchen to give them snacks, thinking about what Dan and Sally had suggested. It was an intriguing suggestion that someone was carrying crossroads magic, essentially boundary magic.

What would this mean for Shadow? Was that a way for her to get home? She shook her head. Unlikely. As they knew from past experience, the power needed for that was huge, and she couldn't feel that much magic so far.

After feeding the cats Avery headed to the attic, spelling on lamps, candles, and the fire as she went. The day was gloomy, and the mist that had lifted earlier was back, blurring the outside world, and making her rooms dark.

She'd already checked the occult section in her shop for books on boundary magic, but hadn't found anything particularly relevant. However, she knew that all the best books were in her private space, anyway. She pulled a few off the shelves and spread them across her wooden worktable, trying to decide where to start, when she realised she hadn't yet phoned Genevieve. Steeling herself for rebuke, she called her, and Genevieve immediately picked up.

"Hi Genevieve, how are you? It's Avery."

"I'm fine, are you? You don't normally call to chat."

"Damn it. Sprung already," Avery admitted.

Genevieve groaned. "What's happened now?"

She updated her as succinctly as possible and then asked, "Do you know much about crossroads magic?"

Genevieve was silent for moment. "Not really, but there are ways of linking yourself to a crossroads, to carry the power with you. I'll have to do some reading to check exactly how, though."

"No, don't bother, I'll do it. I'm sure you're busy."

"To be honest, I am. Are you sure you don't mind?"

Avery breathed an inward sigh of relief. "No, this call was just to keep you informed. Caspian's offered to help, too."

"Has he now? He's quite the reformed character," she remarked. "Thanks, Avery. Do continue to keep me informed, and if I think of anything, I'll call you."

Happy she'd kept Genevieve up to date and also escaped her ire, Avery turned back to her books, and spent the next half an hour identifying all the ones that had the most relevant articles. Then she turned to her grimoires. She found more crossroads spells in them than she expected, but then again, she'd never looked for such things before. Most talked about the power of boundaries and performing spells on crossroads, and also suggested ways to draw on spirits for their aid. She shuddered. She had no intention of doing that.

As usual, whenever she worked with her original grimoire, she thought of Helena, her ancestor who'd been burned at the stake, and whose ghostly presence inhabited her flat. Naturally, it wasn't long before Helena appeared. She manifested on the opposite side of the table, watching Avery with her cool brown eyes, and she brought the scent of smoke and violets with her. Helena had saved her life when Bethany the vampire had knocked at Avery's window in the middle of the night, trying to tempt her to let her in. As much as Helena unnerved her, and the fact that their past together was complex, Avery liked to see her. She made her feel grounded with her history.

Avery smiled. "Helena, good timing. I'm investigating crossroads magic. Any idea how you link to a crossroads? You know, bring its magic with you?"

Helena was unable to speak, but she did help in other ways, depending on her mood. She frowned, and floated around the table, her long black skirts moving across the floor silently as she arrived next to Avery. She leaned forward over her grimoire and a gentle wind ruffled the pages, finally falling open on a page with a scrawl of writing on it and the images of keys. The spell was written in Middle English, and was difficult to read; no wonder Avery hadn't found it. One word, however, was clear. Hecate, the Goddess of crossroads magic.

Having found the spell, Helena moved away, towards the fireplace. She settled on the small sofa and stared into the flames, a very human activity that was more sorrow-inducing than scary.

Avery called over to her, "Thanks, Helena. By the way, Alex is moving in."

Helena nodded, disinterested, and Avery turned back to the spell. She needed her dictionary if she was to understand this. She settled on a stool and lost herself in the translation.

It was well over an hour later when her phone rang, and she jumped as her silence was disturbed. "Dylan. How did you get on?"

"Pretty well," he said, cautiously. "Do you want to see it?"

"Of course."

"Great. Get the beers in and the witches round, and we'll see you at seven."

After talking to Dylan, Avery decided she should call Shadow, too. It was only fair, and she had proven useful the night they had first surveyed the campgrounds. It was a short conversation. She agreed to join them without hesitation.

Avery had one more call that afternoon from Newton, and his mood was grim. "We prioritised the post-mortem on the young man we found this morning. His death is like the others. His organs are atrophied and old, as if his insides were older than his body."

Avery fell silent for a moment as she took in what he was saying.

"Are you still there?" Newton asked.

"Yes, sorry. I guess that was only to be expected. I think we are making progress, though. Dylan is bringing the footage we've captured around later if you want to see it."

"Of course I bloody do," he said brusquely.

"Did you find any evidence on the body?"

"Nothing. Just like the others. I hope you have something on this, Avery. Otherwise, this will keep happening, and the pressure's on."

"We're moving on this as fast as we can, Newton!"

Now it was his turn to fall silent, before he eventually admitted, "I know. I miss Briar."

Avery's heart sank. "She's still your friend—most of the time."

Newton made a grunting sound. "Is he coming down again?" He meant Hunter.

"Not for a couple of weeks. It's too far to travel very often, so you don't have to force yourself to be polite."

"Good. And I'm always polite."

Avery threw her head back and laughed loudly, disturbing both the cats and Helena, who still reclined on the sofa. "You know that's bullshit, right?"

"Oh, sod off," he said, impatiently. "I'll see you later."

Seven

Briar was the first to appear that evening, and she brought crisps and dips to share.

As Avery welcomed her, she couldn't help but notice how pretty Briar looked, and how content. "Have you been chatting to Hunter?" she asked her.

Briar glanced at Avery as she filled a bowl with crisps. "Yes, why?"

"You have a glow."

She wrinkled her nose. "I do not."

"Yes, you do. Don't deny it. I'm pleased for you. Is he treating you well?"

Briar blushed. "Yes. He says the sweetest things."

"Sweet is not the word I was expecting to hear describing Hunter."

She grinned mischievously. "There are times that he's very naughty."

"How naughty?"

"Too naughty to share with you!"

Avery laughed. "Excellent. You deserve some naughtiness. No regrets about Newton?"

Briar met her eyes. "No. It was the right call. Does he ever say anything?"

"He grumps about Hunter, but he knows he has no right to. He'll get over it. We met his new detective friend, Walker, today. He doesn't seem to be sharing much about us at the moment, which is a relief until we know her."

"Good. It will be interesting to see how she deals with the paranormal world."

"Maybe she's involved because she knows a lot of it already. Looks like she'll keep Newton on his toes, anyway."

They were disturbed by the arrival of some of the others, and before long, everyone was present. After a flurry of snack-grabbing and finding drinks, they crowded onto seats in Avery's living room, wedged either on the sofa, the floor, or on chairs pulled in from the dining table.

Dylan quickly loaded the footage on to Avery's TV. It was taken from the camera that he had wedged into the castle wall, and it was, as usual, shot using thermal imaging. The images were startling.

Reuben leaned forward, watching the screen with his forehead creased. "Is that some kind of spectral mist?"

"It looks like it, doesn't it?" Ben said brightly.

Newton almost growled. "You're not supposed to be excited about this crap!"

Ben looked affronted. "It's not every day you see a spectral mist and get it on camera!"

"I think it's cool!" Reuben declared, still staring intently at the screen.

Briar looked confused. "But where is it coming from? And is it really spectral?"

Dylan narrowed his eyes. "Mist does not normally have a red, pulsing glow. And besides, the whole place was misty! Why is it concentrated around the campsite?"

"And," Ben cut in, wagging his finger at the screen, "you can see it rolling up the hill. This started recording as soon as Dylan put it in the wall, and then these two," he pointed at Avery and Alex, "starting to behave all weird. And then look at this!" He broke off as the image of huge, spectral wings filled the screen, and then dissolved into thousands of birds.

"What the actual f—", Newton started to say. He looked around at the others. "Where did those come from?"

"If you slow the footage down," Dylan said, "you can see the place where the wings seem to come from, but it's quick—a split second. And then, in a few minutes' time, another figure emerges from the mist, walking out of the campsite and up the hill, too. We'd gone by then."

"Can you tell who it is?" Newton asked.

"No, sorry," Dylan said regretfully.

Cassie shook her head in disbelief. "No wonder you were so spooked. Where did the wings come from?"

"The Raven King," Alex answered grimly. "Corbin, the owner, is the Ring Master, and that's his costume. The mythical figures on the site are coming to life."

Newton started to look excited. "So he's the cause?"

"Not necessarily. Remember that conversation we overhead the other night?" Alex pointed out.

Avery nodded in agreement. "We think someone is using crossroads magic."

"Why?" Newton asked. "And why feed on young men?"

"Because they're youthful and vibrant, and their energy will be strong," Shadow said confidently. She had sat on a chair to the side, as if she was unsure of how involved she wanted to be with the group, but she had listened and watched intently, her concentration absolute.

"That makes sense, I suppose," Newton admitted. "That also probably explains why there's a gap between kills. But is this all about powering the circus? It seems extreme." He looked unconvinced.

Alex agreed. "And risky. Why kill to get a few extra customers?"

"There has to be some other reason, then," Shadow suggested. "The circus could be an elaborate cover."

"Or a convenient cover," Avery said.

"Where did the deaths start?" Reuben asked. "If we know that, it may help us work out what the aim is."

Newton pulled his notebook out of his pocket. He was dressed in his jeans and a sweatshirt, rather than his suit, but he still exuded authority. He ruffled through a few pages and then said, "The circus started in Inverness, but the first death didn't happen until they reached Edinburgh. They stay in place for three weeks on average before moving on, and tend to sit a short distance outside of cities, but it varies as it moves down the country."

"You'd think it would be set up outside Truro or Falmouth, rather than here," El said.

Reuben shrugged. "Except for the fact that we are paranormal central right now."

"And how many deaths do you think are associated with it?" Cassie asked.

Newton grimaced. "It's hard to be sure, but we think at least half a dozen."

The collective mood shifted as Briar said, "That many? This is worse than we thought."

Reuben continued to muse on the circus's source. "I wonder if there's a crossroads in Scotland that this circus links to? It would make sense, seeing as how that's where the new concept originated."

Alex reached for a handful of crisps as he said, "I doubt we'll ever know that, but I'd like to know how it's done, if it is."

Avery decided that now was a good time to share the spell she'd found. "I was doing some research this afternoon," she explained, "when Helena appeared and showed me a spell in her grimoire."

Cassie shuddered and looked around as if Helena might appear at any moment. "I don't know how you cope with that! I would freak out if a ghost kept manifesting in my home!"

"You're a ghost hunter," Reuben said, incredulous. "Shouldn't you be excited?"

Cassie looked equally incredulous. "Not if one was in my own home!"

Avery laughed. "I've got used to it, and she's very helpful most of the time. And don't worry—it's mainly upstairs where she appears."

Cassie looked slightly relieved as Avery continued. "The spell suggests that the witch links two keys together using a red ribbon or cord, measured from your heart to the wrist of your left hand, and then you carry them around for one full cycle of the moon. You have to handle the keys every day, developing a personal connection to them. Then when the cycle is complete, you bury one key in the centre of the crossroads, cutting the cord between them. You then keep the other key on you, allowing you to access the boundaries of the crossroads."

"Wow, so there is a way!" El exclaimed, her curiosity piqued.

"There's probably more, and I'm sure that spell could be adapted, but it's the only one I've found so far."

Shadow was even more excited. "It allows the user to cross boundaries between worlds? This could be my chance to go home!"

"I don't think it's that straightforward. I think it's more to draw on the power of the boundary," Avery warned her, but it was clear Shadow wasn't listening.

"But again, something to work on," Newton said, relieved.

Dylan changed the footage. "Here's what the camera picked up from the oak tree. The mist looks similar, but you can see a better shot of the wings, and the figure—whoever it is—moving up the hill. And you can see us, retreating from the wall."

"No wonder we got lost," Alex said, watching the screen. "We veered off in the wrong direction partway up the hill."

"Yeah, but," Ben said, pointing, "we were being herded by the mist, just as we thought. And then unfortunately we move out of view and you can't see us anymore, so we can't tell what may or may not have been stalking us. It might be that figure, but—" he shrugged, his meaning clear.

"But we've made progress," Newton said encouragingly. "We know it's the circus that's behind this, and we know there are at least three key figures involved in some way. But I need more. There's nothing I can act on, not legally, anyway."

"Did you find out if there's a Caitlin employed at the circus?" Alex asked.

Newton grimaced. "No, unfortunately. We're re-examining the list again, just to make sure we're not missing anything. I'll let you know. Is anyone going to the first show on Saturday?"

"A few of us were planning to go," Avery said. "I was thinking we should split up again. Some of us could watch the show, others could patrol the grounds, especially since the campsite should be deserted."

"Great idea," Newton agreed. "There are the stalls in the castle walls, too. We'll need to investigate those. Who wants to do what?"

There was a brief argument about who should go where. Most people wanted to investigate the campsite, but Newton stood firm. "Avery and Alex need to be at the campsite. They already know the layout and where Corbin's van is, but someone there to help them would be good."

"Me," Shadow said forcefully.

Briar, as ever, was diplomatic. "I'm happy to watch the show. I want to see if they use any magic in the performance."

Cassie groaned. "I'd love to join, but I'm just too busy right now. Coming here tonight was tricky."

"Same for us," Ben said, speaking for him and Dylan. "Uni work is stacking up."

"That's fine," Newton told them. "Just keep an eye on the cameras in case anything else appears."

Dylan shook his head. "I'm afraid that's not possible. I checked them today and it's too damp out there. Sorry, guys. I've had to retrieve the cameras. There'll be no more footage."

"Then we'll manage without it." Newton turned to El and Reuben. "That leaves you two to check out the stalls within the castle grounds."

"Excellent," Reuben said sarcastically. "I can gorge myself on candyfloss and try to win a teddy bear."

"What about you, Newton?" Briar asked.

"I can't be too obvious about investigating anything, so I'll come and watch the show with you, Briar, if that's okay?" He looked as innocent as

Newton could be, which wasn't very.

Briar merely nodded. "That's fine." She looked perplexed. "Has anyone else noticed how unseasonably warm it is? February is usually miserable. Green shoots are appearing on plants that shouldn't even start to grow until late spring."

"I have," El admitted. "The courtyard plants outside my workshop have sprung to life."

Reuben agreed. "Our nursery is blooming, too. I just thought we were having an unseasonable bit of warmth."

"I told you, it's the Green Man," Shadow said. "He's affecting everything."

"But why hasn't it happened in other places?" El asked. "Surely someone would have said something?"

Shadow shrugged. "Maybe no one noticed. Not enough to comment, anyway."

"For all we know they did, but it didn't make the papers or the Internet," Alex suggested.

"We're supernatural central," Reuben pointed out. "And we have a lot more magic in White Haven than most places. I think it's feeding him. Let's hope it doesn't become too obvious. Anyway, where shall we all meet before the show?"

"Castle car park," Alex said immediately. "But what's our plan? Surely we don't want to engage in some kind of magical battle?"

"Reconnaissance, that's all," Newton said. "Observe, fact find, but nothing else! I'm presuming you don't want to out your magical abilities to the watching crowds?"

"No need for sarcasm, Newton," Reuben said. "But if we're attacked, we may have no choice. Anyway, it must be time for another beer. And can we please order some food before I die of starvation?"

Eight

After a quiet, uneventful Friday, during which Avery tried to forget all about crossroads magic and suspicious deaths, Saturday was busy. White Haven was again inundated with circus performers as they paraded through the town, drumming up business for the afternoon and evening performances.

Acrobats and jugglers in bright costumes handed out flyers during the morning, and there was a palpable air of anticipation in the town. Two performers on stilts were dressed as giants with huge heads on their shoulders, and although it wasn't clear which giants they were supposed to be, everyone was excited, because Cornwall was well-known for its giants. Everyone who came into the shop was talking about them, and it sounded like the first performances would be sold out. However, by lunchtime the street performers had gone. The afternoon show started at two, and the evening show at seven. Avery hoped they'd avoid most of the crowds of screaming children for the night performance, although that wasn't really an issue for her.

"I thought you wanted to see the show?" Sally asked Avery at lunch.

"I do, but it's more important to investigate the campsite again. I can see it another time," she pointed out. "It's here for over another week before it moves on. I didn't think you were going at all!"

Sally shrugged. "I reconsidered, and the kids were driving me mad. And you're right. Nothing will happen at the show in the middle of the afternoon. I managed to swap the tickets Mairi gave us for the afternoon performance, so it's free too!"

"Just stay away from the ravens," Dan warned. "It's like Hitchcock's The Birds out there."

"What?" Avery asked, thinking he'd gone mad.

"Haven't you noticed? There are a lot of ravens around the town." He walked to the shop window and pointed upwards, and Avery craned her neck to see the roofs above.

Dan was right. Ravens were gathering on gutters, chimneys, and electricity poles up and down the street.

"Oh, wow. I didn't notice," Avery confessed.

"Well, if the Green Man is here, it makes sense that the Raven King is, too. The magic is rising, Avery," Dan said ominously.

Sally laughed and checked her watch. "I'm not scared of birds, and I'd better go, if that's okay."

"Sure," Avery said, waving her off. "Have fun, and see you Monday. But let me know if you notice anything odd."

"Are you going?" she asked Dan, after Sally had left.

"Probably. I'll give it a few days in the hope that the rush dies down—I gave Sally my tickets. Although, it's been all over the news. Have you seen it?"

"No, I've been preoccupied with research. Which reminds me, have you found out anything else?"

"Not much at this stage. Nothing significant, anyway. I'll let you know as soon as I do. And Avery, be careful tonight. This thing worries me because of all we don't know. It's so odd!"

Avery held her hands up and jiggled them. "Competent witch here! Don't worry."

Dan looked over her shoulder and out the window, a frown creasing his face. "That guy's back."

"What guy?" Avery said, turning quickly.

The street was crowded with pedestrians, and cars crawled down the road, stuck in Saturday traffic.

He inclined his head. "That man wearing dark clothes, with grey hair. He's in the entryway between the second-hand store and the butchers, and he seems to be watching our shop. That's the second time I've seen him there."

Avery stared, waiting for a gap in the crowd, and then caught a glimpse of him leaning against the wall. She took a sharp intake of breath. "I know him! Well, not know, but I bumped into him a couple of days ago—literally walked directly into him. He was right behind me, and he seemed to be watching that strange woman."

"Really? And now he seems to be watching us—or rather, you."

"Why me?" Avery asked, startled.

"Well there's nothing interesting about me," Dan said. His eyes narrowed again. "Looks like he's leaving."

Avery made a quick decision. "I'm going to follow him."

"Avery! I'm not sure that's wise."

"I don't care. I want to know who he is. Don't worry, I'll be fine."

And with those brief reassurances, she ran out to the street. The man was striding down the pavement, back towards the high street, and Avery hurried after him, wishing she'd thought to grab her jacket. It might be mild for February, but it still wasn't warm.

The man was tall, and she could just see his head above the crowds as she struggled to keep up. She hadn't decided what she wanted to do. Should she try to speak to him, or just try to see where he went? She struggled through the shoppers, edging between them as quickly as she could, but it was hard going, especially as she didn't want to appear too obvious.

He paused at the bottom of the road, looking left and right as if he couldn't make up his mind where to go, and she slowed as she got closer. Then he turned right swiftly, and headed towards the harbour. For a second, she lost him. The main street was much busier, and she hesitated, uncertain, but then she saw him again just as he turned into an alleyway.

She quickened her pace, and when she reached the entrance, she paused and peered around the corner, feeling like a spy. What was she thinking?

He was nowhere in sight, so reassured, but annoyed at the same time, she started up the street, and then cursed herself as she saw him sitting on a large black and silver motorbike. The engine was already running and his helmet was in his hand, but before he rode away, he turned back to look directly at her, and raised his hand to his eyebrow in salute, a slow smile spreading across his lips. And then he pulled his helmet on and roared away.

$$+ \quad + \quad +$$

El stood with her hands on her hips as she surveyed the circus tent and the sprawling castle grounds. "Wow. This is pretty impressive. No wonder it's had such rave reviews."

"And we haven't even seen the performance yet," Reuben pointed out. His arm was slung across El's shoulders as they paused at the edge of the site.

El was right. It was spectacular. The castle was always eye-catching, especially when lit up from below by the lights that illuminated the castle walls, but there were now strings of coloured lights as well that added to the party atmosphere. Small vans and stalls created a village to stroll through via narrow walkways, all displaying typical carnival fare, albeit with a twist. Everything was Green Man-themed, with the occasional glimpse of the Raven King's image, and there were huge painted ravens on the sides of some stalls. Dominating everything was the Big Top, camouflaged by paintings of leaves and trees with multiple images of the Green Man peeking through. The arch leading into the main area beckoned the crowd, and instead of just two huge imitation standing stones next to the archway, more now lined the path to the tent. The flaps were drawn back, offering a tantalising glimpse inside, but the lighting was low and mysterious, and

Avery felt everyone's excitement rise.

The queue to get into the circus was long, but Briar and Newton had arrived early with Avery's free tickets, and Briar texted to confirm they had got seats.

A dark figure emerged from the Big Top, throwing his hands wide in welcome. As he stepped into the light, Avery caught her breath. It was Corbin, dressed as the Raven King. He looked magnificent. The cloak and mask they had glimpsed the other night were only part of his costume. His calves were covered in shiny, slick black Lycra, but the rest of him was clad in feathers, his chest puffed out. His mask incorporated a long black beak, and the only thing visible of his face was the glint of his eyes. He threw his arms open and the cloak lifted like wings. He must have had something in the sleeves, because as he extended his arms, the wings grew longer. It was quite dramatic. He shouted, "Welcome to the Crossroads Circus! Beware all who enter. The boundaries between worlds are thin tonight! Who knows what may come through?"

With that statement, it seemed as if hundreds of ravens were suddenly overhead again, their wings beating noiselessly, but their caws deafening. Several people flinched and ducked, but they were high-quality visual and sound effects, and as the Raven King dropped his wings and re-entered the tent, the illusion vanished.

"Clever," Reuben observed. "Are you sure that's not what you felt the other night?"

Alex just looked at him, deadpan. "No. I know the difference between an illusion and magic."

Reuben winked. "Just checking."

It was already dark, but fortunately the mist had lifted, leaving a damp, cloudy evening that threatened rain. They had parked in the car park like everyone else, and Avery, Alex, and Shadow joined El and Reuben as they strolled to the stalls.

"We'll separate when the show begins," Alex told them. "The campsite should be at its quietest then."

They entered the mini-village together, and Avery's senses were quickly overloaded with smells of food—candyfloss, doughnuts, burgers, hot dogs, and chips—and also the shouts of teenagers, the hum of generators, and garish lights. She fell into step beside Shadow. "I forgot these places were so loud. Do you have anything like this where you're from?"

Shadow was looking around with curiosity, but she nodded. "Always, but without these— what do you call them? Generators?" Avery nodded and Shadow continued. "We don't have electricity. But the themes are the same, just with a lot more magic and fey, of course."

Avery raised her voice to be heard, "You don't have electricity?"

Shadow looked at her, amused. "No. But we have magic that provides lights beyond candles and oil lamps. It's complicated to explain, but I guess it would be something like your witch lights." She lifted her gaze and frowned. "What's Reuben doing?"

Avery looked across to where Reuben was picking up a pellet gun and talking to a stall owner, and she laughed. "We have to watch this. Reuben is going to try and shoot the targets. The sights are always out, so people can't win."

They watched Reuben square up to shoot the little tin targets that were set up at the back of the stall. He called across to El. "What do you want if I win?"

There was a range of cuddly toys hanging up around the stall, as well as key rings, mugs, and t-shirts. In the middle of the display was a large raven soft toy. "The bird, please," she said, pointing it out.

The stall owner, a florid man dressed all in green, laughed. "You'll need to hit a dozen targets for that."

"No problem," Reuben said. He took the first shot, which missed, and he grinned. "Okay. Now I've got it." And then he reeled off the next several shots like a firecracker, and the tin targets fell one after another.

The stall owner looked flustered and confused. "That was impressive."

"I know. Raven, please."

The stall owner handed it over, and Reuben passed it on to El with a flourish. "For you, my lady."

She laughed as they strolled away, tucking it under her arm. "And what am I supposed to do with this?"

"I don't know. I just wanted to win it. You can give it away, I suppose." He looked insufferably pleased with himself.

"Good," she answered. "I'll give it to the next deserving child I see."

They continued to stroll through the stalls, some of the performers still entertaining the crowds, and when they spotted a hot dog stand, they came to a halt while Alex and Reuben queued for food. Shadow and Avery walked on for a short while, Avery curious to see if they could exit through the back of the stalls to the campsite.

"What do you think we're going to find tonight?" Shadow asked her as they stopped in a corner where they could watch the comings and goings of the crowd.

"I don't know, probably not much if I'm honest. I'm wondering if we gave ourselves away the other night, and now they'll hide everything."

"Maybe, but whoever is behind this has been doing it for some time. They might not worry."

"But anyone who recognises magic—as we do—would know what we are and what we do, even though I thought I'd blocked us the other night." Avery was still annoyed with herself, and frustrated. She must have dropped her guard, which allowed them to be chased across the field. But something was niggling her. She was usually so careful, and she was sure she hadn't acted carelessly.

"No point worrying about it now," Shadow told her. "They're here for a while yet. If we don't find anything tonight, we can come back."

"The other night, you felt the Green Man. Can you feel him now?"

A wicked glint entered Shadow's eyes. "Yes, I can. He's stronger than before. There's a real energy here now. You must feel it, too!"

"I can feel something, I'm just not sure what it is." She considered Shadow's excited expression. "Is he good in your world, or a figure of fear?"

"Generally good, but like all Gods and spirits, they have their own agenda. It's hard to know what he wants here."

And that was the trouble, Avery thought, but while they were speaking, she heard a swell of music come from the big tent. The show must be starting.

Within seconds, Alex joined them, taking final bites of his hot dog. "Are we ready, then?" he asked them.

Avery pointed further along where there was a break in the stalls that led to some portable toilet blocks on the edge of the section. "We can get through that gap."

They wound their way through the still considerable crowds, and finally emerged behind some generators. The campsite was ahead. Avery cloaked them all, and Alex threw in a protective shield, as well.

They threaded through the vans, generators, and general camp detritus, trying to sense anything unusual. Unfortunately, the campsite wasn't as quiet as they'd hoped. There were still plenty of people milling about, some seeming to act as security, and others were performers, now dressed in their outrageous costumes and elaborate makeup as they made their way to the discrete doorway at the rear of the tent where they could enter unseen. Avery saw a dozen acrobats all dressed in green again, but made to look like trees.

"Dryads," Shadow whispered, before she disappeared in her bewildering way, leaving Alex and Avery alone.

"We should try to find Corbin's van," Alex said, striding determinedly ahead, barely visible with the spell that protected him. "We know that will be empty."

Before she could follow, Avery sensed the strange woman's presence again and she whirled around, trying to see her.

She stared into the pools of blackness cast by the vans. Nothing moved, but she could sense the woman just ahead, out of sight. She followed almost blindly. It was tantalising, a wisp of magic she couldn't explain. And then Avery reached the edge of the camp, slipped through a gap in the hedge, and the world fell away.

Nine

A very was standing alone on a road made of beaten earth, and ahead she saw a crossroads with four huge standing stones, like sentinels, marking the four corners.

Where was she? More importantly, how was she here?

The sounds of the circus had disappeared, and instead the ragged caw of a bird broke the silence. There was no moon that night in White Haven, it had been covered by thick clouds. But here—wherever here was—the sky was clear and the full moon's ghostly light showed a large raven perched on the furthest standing stone, watching her.

Avery's heart beat wildly in her chest, and she glanced around trying to orientate herself. Nothing looked familiar, and all she could see were four roads stretching into the distance. She glanced behind her. The hedge was gone. Avery started to panic, and she took a deep breath. *I'm a witch. I've got this. This has to be an illusion.* But creeping dread filled her. This didn't feel like an illusion. It felt very real.

She froze, uncertain of what to do. *Breathe, and take notes. This could be important,* she reminded herself. She looked around again, trying to find landmarks. There was a gentle rolling hill ahead, and trees covered some of the landscape, but other than the standing stones and crossroads, her surroundings were uneventful. It was as if she was in the middle of the moors somewhere. And why was the road of beaten earth? Why wasn't it made of tarmac?

In the middle of the crossroads a swirl of mist appeared, and within seconds a figure stepped from it. It was the woman from the procession. She stared at Avery, grim amusement in her eyes, and fear struck Avery as she'd never experienced it before, not even when facing the vampires. Avery heard drumming, a faint beat at first, and then it grew louder, wilder, and suddenly she wasn't afraid anymore. She was furious.

"Who are you and what do you want?" she yelled. "I know this isn't real!"

"Isn't it?" the woman said softly, her voice almost husky. "Look around, Avery. Do you know your way home from here?"

"How do you know my name?"

"I know many things. "

"So it seems. Would you like to share?"

"All in good time. You're interfering in things you shouldn't."

"Don't bring your business to my doorstep, then."

The woman laughed. "You're feisty."

"Yes I am, and I don't know what you're doing, but I'll stop you."

"Will you?" the woman asked, walking towards Avery. "You won't have time. I have other plans for you."

Instinctively, Avery gathered air around her, and then hurled it at the approaching woman. The woman staggered as her hair streamed behind her, but she recovered quickly and kept advancing as Avery retreated. What the hell did she want?

Avery shouted, "Stop! Don't come any closer."

The woman ignored her. "Or what?"

As she drew closer, Avery whispered a spell that should have stopped the woman from walking, freezing her steps and sinking her into the earth, and for a moment, it did. But then she pulled her feet free, shaking the earth from them, and advanced again. Avery balled pure energy into her palm and threw it, but again the woman deflected it easily, sending it crashing into a standing stone. She kept coming, and Avery saw that she was older than she had first thought, fine lines marking her face and around her eyes.

Avery had no idea what would happen if she reached her, but sensed it couldn't be good. In fact, she had the distinct impression the woman was absorbing the power from her spells.

A single idea filled her mind. Witch-flight. She didn't know where she was, but she knew where she wanted to be. She envisaged the space in the back of her van that was currently parked in the castle's car park, and summoning all of her power, she disappeared, pleased to see the woman's frustrated look before she vanished from sight.

However, for what felt like several long minutes, Avery felt suspended in time and space, and she was briefly aware that the flight was taking far longer than it should. She focused on her van and only her van, until with a thump, she landed sprawling on the plywood floor behind the front seats. She gasped for breath she didn't even know she needed, and then realised she felt nauseous. She stumbled upright and threw the rear door open, half falling onto the tarmac below where she retched, a cold sweat covering her brow. She took a moment to appreciate that everything was as it should be: the car park, the circus, and night sky above, heavy with clouds. She was safe.

Then she had another thought. Alex.

Avery dragged herself to her feet, and raced up the path towards the circus and then, bypassing it and the stalls completely, she ran around the back to the campsite, pulling her phone from her pocket as she went, and flicking to Alex's number. And then she hesitated. If he was hidden and she alerted someone to his presence, that could endanger him.

Damn it!

She slowed as she entered the campground, knowing she needed to be stealthy and not having a clue as to who may be a threat, or if the mysterious woman was here again. She edged in and out of the vans, once again draped in the shadow spell, although now fearing it was useless to protect herself from her attacker.

In the camp it seemed as if nothing had changed, although the place seemed emptier. Maybe more of the performers were now in the tent? But, she couldn't see Alex or Shadow.

What if they had also been spelled away into in another place? She tried to calm herself down. For some reason, the woman was targeting her, not the others. Logically, this meant the others must be okay.

The sound of the crowd in the Big Top erupted behind her as a huge cheer went up, and the sound of clapping and stamping of feet resounded through the night. The clapping kept going and Avery paused. It sounded like it was the end of the performance, but it couldn't be, surely. It had only just started.

She stopped and checked the time on her phone, and nearly stumbled with shock. It was just after half-past nine, and the performance was end-ing. She had lost two hours of time. Two hours? How?

Avery leant against the side of the closest camper van, checking and re-checking the time. This wasn't possible. She had been gone for minutes only. Before she could think or do anything else, Shadow appeared next to her looking furious. "Where the hell have you been, Avery? Alex is panic-stricken." She stopped long enough to let out a piercing whistle, and then she frowned. "You're as white as a corpse. What happened?"

Avery's mouth felt dry. "I don't know. I ended up on a crossroads, somewhere."

Before Shadow could respond, Alex, Reuben, and El emerged out of the darkness, all of them looking worried. Alex ran forward and hugged her. "Thank the Gods! Where have you been? Are you all right?"

Shadow answered for her. "She's been somewhere else. Let's get out of here, now, and ask questions later."

And with that, Avery was hustled back to the van.

+ + +

"Will everyone stop looking at me as if I've gone mad?" Avery said, frustrated. "I'm fine, honestly."

They were all in Alex's flat, and Reuben had just pressed a large glass of mulled red wine into her hand that he'd fetched from the pub below. "I'm sure you are, but let's face it, alcohol always helps."

She couldn't disagree with that, and she took a healthy sip, enjoying the spicy warmth as it flowed down her throat, heating her whole body. She hadn't even known she felt cold, and she shivered. "Thanks, Reuben. That is good."

Briar sat next to Avery, looking at her anxiously and running her hands over her, several inches from her body. "I have never seen you so pale, and your aura has been depleted." She looked up at Reuben. "Grab my bag, please."

Briar had arrived a few minutes after everyone else, having gone home first for her herbal healing kit, and it was this she asked for now. Reuben placed it at her feet, and Briar reached inside, rummaging about, while Avery tried to focus on the room, which was increasingly hazy. She looked at the wine, confused. She hadn't had that much.

"What's the matter?" Alex asked. He sat on the other side of her, watching her every move.

"I feel slightly weak, as if something is missing," Avery told him, trying to explain the weird sensation.

Shadow weighed in now. "Your magic has been weakened, that's why, not just your aura. I can feel it."

El was sitting on the floor, in front of the fire. "What happened, Avery?"

"It doesn't make sense," she said, struggling to articulate her words.

"That doesn't matter. Just tell us as you remember it."

Avery told them about her mysterious journey to the crossroads, her encounter with the strange, still unknown woman, and the loss of time. "I tried several spells on her, but nothing worked. She seemed to be absorbing my magic."

Briar pressed a large, black gemstone into her hand. "Hold this. It's black onyx and very grounding. I'm going to make you a potion." She leapt to her feet, grabbed her small case, and headed to the kitchen.

"Are you still connected to her in some way?" Alex asked.

Avery tentatively explored her magic and sent her awareness further afield. "No, I don't think so, but I don't feel right. I feel disconnected somehow. Like I'm here, but not here." Avery closed her eyes, feeling ridiculous, but as soon as she did, the crossroads appeared in front of her, wreathed in mist, timeless and draped in power. Her eyes flew open again. "The crossroads, I can see it..."

Shadow stepped closer, extending her own strange fey powers. "You *are* connected, Avery. That's why you're not feeling better."

Everyone turned to her in shock. "What?" Alex asked, his eyes haunted with worry. "How?"

"Boundary magic," Shadow said. "She's connected to you. It's faint, but it's there. I think she's feeding off your power."

Avery put her drink down. "Shit. I think you're right. It's the only thing that explains how I feel. How do we stop her?"

"Protective circle, salt, our magic, the works," Alex said, leaping to his feet. "We break it, now."

Shadow shook her head. "You'll need more than that."

Avery started to feel frightened. Some unknown woman with unknown magic had connected to her like a leech. "Why?"

"Because I think she's connected to your spirit body."

"We can spirit-walk," Alex said immediately. "I can do that easily, and find a way to break it."

Shadow nodded, though slightly apprehensive. "Maybe. But if you cut the link in the wrong way—" She broke off, shrugging.

"It could do more damage," Reuben finished for her.

She turned her violet gaze to him. "Possibly. I don't know much about this—please don't think I do—but that woman's magic is more closely aligned to mine than yours. I can sense the difference, and her odd connection."

Alex sat down again, deflated. "So, what do we do?"

Briar answered from the kitchen, where she was furiously crushing herbs. "We enhance Avery's strength; keep her topped up with magic. It's not ideal, because it means the woman will continue to draw from her, but at least Avery will continue to function. I'm making a potion right now that will help."

"It's a waiting game, then," El said.

Briar nodded. "I'm afraid so."

Avery felt her head spin again. This was all so weird. She felt tricked—manipulated. "I feel like an idiot."

Newton was leaning against the wall, his eyes narrowed. "Of course you're not. But this is our chance to learn more about her and what she wants. The questions we have will eventually give us valuable answers. For example, how could she just take you away without your knowledge?"

"I don't know," she answered, looking up at him, baffled. "It was like nothing I have ever experienced before. Her magic is unlike ours—as Shadow says. I'm sure she's not a witch."

"And you had no idea about the time?" Reuben persisted. He was sitting on the rug next to El, a beer in hand.

"None. It felt like minutes only."

"It's because of the crossroads," Shadow explained. "We know it straddles worlds, and time is different in Otherworlds."

Reuben looked impressed. "Wow. So, you were in some sort of time-flux. That's very *Star Trek*."

"Lucky me," Avery said, feeling not very lucky at all.

Alex sighed heavily. "But why you? We're all witches, with varying strengths, why choose you?"

"Maybe it's to do with your elemental Air powers?" El suggested.

"But what can you do with elemental Air that you can't do with other elements?" Newton asked.

Avery shrugged. "Witch-flight, obviously. But everyone here can use elemental Air to some degree."

"But not as well as you," El reminded her.

Avery flopped against the back of the sofa. "I don't know. I'll need to do some reading about crossroads magic, try to work out why she needs me, and for what."

"*We* need to do some reading," El told her, gently. "You're not alone in this. We'll all help, like you got me out of that curse. I guess the big question is whether this is also linked to the Green Man and the Raven King."

"Bollocks!" Newton said forcefully. He pushed away from the wall and started pacing. "Just when I thought we were getting somewhere, we have more questions!"

"Why don't you tell me what you found while I was elsewhere?" Avery suggested to everyone.

"Very little," Shadow said. "Other than the fact that I could sense the Green Man and his Earth magic again. He's getting stronger."

"I found Corbin's van again," Alex added, "and searched it, but there was nothing in there to tell us what's happening, and I couldn't find Rafe or Mairi."

"There was nothing odd happening around the stalls," Reuben told them. "Just people spending money and eating lots of food. I sensed nothing magical or Otherworldly. No wild magic, nothing like we experienced on Samhain."

"What about inside the tent?" Avery asked Newton and Briar.

Briar continued to prepare ingredients in the kitchen. "I did sense magic in the tent, it was subtle, but there. The performance was amazing."

Newton stopped pacing. "It was very clever. The Raven King commanded the whole thing. It felt like the tent had come alive. The walls were covered in fake greenery, and when you were close enough, you could see it rustling, like it was alive. That was down to wind machines, but it was effective. The light tricks were clever. It felt like ravens flew overhead at one point, and all the performances were folklore themed. The stilt walkers were there, playing Cornish giants, the acrobats were dryads, there was even Beowulf fighting Grendel the monster in some crazy aerial acrobatics, and loads more. "

Briar agreed. "It wasn't quite Cirque De Soleil, but it was close. The subtle use of magic definitely gave everything an extra fizz, but no one without magic would ever know it."

Newton rubbed his face, and suddenly looked incredibly tired. "You can't tell me that the deaths and the crossroads magic is just about putting on a good show? That's nuts."

"No," Alex agreed, "there is definitely something else happening. We just have to figure out what."

"And you," Shadow said to Avery, her eyes bright with intrigue, "are in the perfect position to find out more about our mysterious woman. You're linked to her now. The connection goes both ways."

Avery looked up at her, trying to feel positive. "That's true. I just need to work out where that crossroads is. It's the key to everything."

Once the others had left, Avery turned to Alex. "I don't even know if I can sleep. Every time I close my eyes, I see the crossroads. I'm scared that she'll take me back there in my sleep."

Alex pulled her close, kissing the top of her head, and they sat next to each on the sofa, staring into the bright flames of the fire. "I don't think that will happen. Besides, Briar's potion will help you sleep, deep enough hopefully to dull your connection."

She ran her fingers across his face. "I hope you're right. But if not, promise you'll come and find me? That place felt so eerie."

"I'll find you anywhere," he vowed, taking her hand in his and kissing her fingers one by one. "And if she hurts you in any way, I'll kill her. I'll raze the whole circus to the ground if I have to."

Ten

For the first few hours of the night Avery slept heavily, drugged by the herbs that Briar had put in the potion, but at some point that all changed, and once again she stood on one of the four roads leading to the crossroads, drenched in the shadow of a standing stone.

It was night, and the full moon was still high above her, giving a silvery sheen to the landscape. Ground mist snaked around her ankles, and undulating moors spread around her to the horizon, except for the low roll of hills ahead of her. A second moon closer to the ground confused her for a moment, before she realised it must be reflected in water. The woman was nowhere in sight.

Avery looked around, desperate to see something that may indicate where she was, but the landscape was almost featureless. The standing stones were the only things of significance. The one closest to her was twice her height, and several feet thick. Up close she could see shapes carved into it, and she frowned, frustrated. She didn't recognise them at all, but she tried to memorise them, hoping to find them later. If there was a later.

Tentatively, she placed her hand on the stone. It was cold, but Avery felt it humming with energy, and with her touch the carvings began to glow with a golden light, as if they were illuminated from within. Avery's first instinct was to step back, but she felt that wouldn't help. Whatever was happening, she needed to understand. She pressed her hand on the surface firmly, watching as the signs continued to light up until they almost burned, and suddenly realising that she could be summoning something, she tried to pull her hand away, but couldn't. It started to pull her closer, and Avery had the terrifying thought that it was trying to absorb her, to pull her in and swallow her whole. She screamed as she struggled to break free, sweat pouring from her. The sound of drums once again filled the air, primeval and tribal, and her blood pounded in her ears.

Alex's voice broke through her panic. "Avery! Avery, wake up!"

Her body was shaking violently, and all of a sudden the crossroads had gone, and she felt Alex's hands on her shoulders. Her body felt like lead, and as if her eyes were welded shut, but she forced them open, her breath short. "I'm here. I'm okay!"

"Thank fuck for that!" He pulled her close, his warmth thawing her immobility. "You scared the shit out of me."

He must have spelled the lamp on, because soft, warm light flooded his bedroom, and reality rushed in. Avery pressed herself against him, soaking up his warmth. "How did you know I was in trouble?"

"Because you were screaming the place down," he said, pulling away and staring down at her. "What happened?"

"I was at the crossroads again, in my dream. It was a dream, right? I was still here?"

"You were still here," he said, reassuring her.

She pushed him away and sat up. "What the hell is happening to me?"

"I don't know, but we'll work it out, I promise." He caught her hand, and went to kiss her palm, but frowned. "What's this?"

"What?"

"This mark?"

A strange, silvery shape glowed within her palm, and she groaned. "It's from the standing stone." She explained what had happened and what caused her to scream.

Alex was annoyed. "I can't believe you touched it! What were you thinking?"

"I don't know, it seemed a good idea!"

"Avery, that place is messing with your mind! She's screwing with you! She needs your power for some reason, and now you're truly linked. You can't trust anything you see or think there."

Avery felt tears well up. "Don't shout. I didn't know. I've never had to doubt my instincts before, never!"

He pulled her close again. "I'm sorry. I didn't mean to yell, but I'm terrified I'm going to lose you. You're strong, Avery, but you can't do this alone. Promise me you won't try."

"I promise," she said, feeling exhausted. "I think I need to sleep again, although I'm terrified of what will happen."

"I'll be right here. Just don't touch anything again."

✝ ✝ ✝

The next time Avery woke, it was morning, and grey light seeped into the room. She smelt coffee and bacon, and she stretched out, noticing how heavy her body felt.

She had managed to sleep well for a few hours, with no dreams. She examined her right palm again, hoping the mark would have disappeared, but it was still there, glowing just beneath her skin.

Alex appeared at the door, and he smiled. He had just come out of the shower and he was half naked, his towel wrapped around his hips, showing off his flat, muscled abs and tattoos. "You're awake. Feeling okay?"

She nodded. "I think so. I actually managed some decent sleep."

"I could tell—your breathing was heavy and slow. Hungry?"

"Starving."

"Want breakfast in bed?"

"No, I'll get up. Thank the Gods it's Sunday and the shop is closed."

She padded into the kitchen, wrapped in his heavy robe, and sat at the counter watching him finish making breakfast. He pushed a coffee in front of her. "This will perk you up." He watched her take a few sips. "I've been thinking about what we should do today, and the first thing should be to decipher that." He pointed at her palm.

"You're right. The more we know, the better. I also want to look up crossroads, famous or otherwise, see if I can find some images that will help find out where it really is." She sighed. "I'm wondering if I could use witch-flight to try and get back there, physically, but I'm not sure that's a good idea."

"It's a very bad idea. Don't you dare try that. But researching it sounds fine." He finished preparing bacon and egg sandwiches for them both, and she tucked in. "Briar has already phoned. She's coming around in about half an hour with another potion. It sounds like she woke up early to make one, and apparently El and Reuben are coming, too. She has some jewellery for you."

"Full house, then."

"For a while." He pointed to the table in the corner where a pile of books was already waiting, including his grimoires. "And then we have some reading to do."

$$+ \quad + \quad +$$

When the other three witches arrived, Avery was the centre of attention for the next hour, and she didn't like it one bit. "Please, stop fussing! I'm okay."

Briar placed her hands on her hips and stared Avery down, although she was looking up at her. She was petite and shorter than Avery. "No, you're not. You're going to have to put up with fuss until we work out what's going on and sever the connection to this bitch." Briar hardly ever swore, and everyone looked at her, wide-eyed. "What? She *is* one! And she has really pissed me off. I have made half a dozen potions for you, enough to last a couple of days. One with breakfast, one with lunch, and the red ones are to have before bed."

She handed Avery four small turquoise glass vials filled with a thick liquid, and two red ones. Avery pulled the lid off one and sniffed. "What's in them?"

"Many things. The turquoise ones will enhance your energy. The red ones are to help you sleep. I'm working on some more, too. Take one now."

Avery braced herself and downed it in one go. She knew from experience that potions sometimes tasted horrible. She winced. This one was no exception. "Yuck."

"It will work, that's all that matters."

Reuben laughed. "Briar, I had no idea you could be so bossy."

Briar turned to him and frowned. "Don't you start."

Reuben smelt of the sea again, and his hair was still damp. It was obvious that despite the grey, cold weather and freezing water, he had been for an early surf. He held up his hands in mock surrender. "No chance."

El leaned forward, passing Avery a silver necklace with an oval black stone in a simple setting. "This is from my Crossroads Collection. Jet protects you from evil, violence, and psychic attacks, and will hopefully slow down the pull of your magic that woman is using." Avery slipped it over her head, feeling the weight of the stone rest just below her throat; its steady, thrumming energy soothed her.

"Thanks, I feel it already."

El nodded, pleased. "Now, show me your hand. Alex told us you're marked."

Avery held her hand out and the others crowded around.

"It's not a rune," El said confidently. "Unless it's of a type I have never seen before."

"I agree," Reuben said, taking Avery's hand in his rough one and tracing his finger over it. "Is it a sigil of some sort?" He looked at her with piercing blue eyes. "Was this on that standing stone you touched?"

Avery nodded. "Yes. It was covered in them, of different designs, all carved by hand, and I didn't recognise any of them. They started to glow when I put my hand on the stone. It hummed with power, and then started to suck me in... Sorry, it sounds mad, but that's exactly how it felt." She shuddered at the memory.

"What about the other three stones?" Reuben asked. "Did they glow?"

Avery paused for a moment, thinking back to her dream. "No, I don't think so, but I was so focused on the stone I was attached to that I didn't really look."

"That's a good question," Briar said, looking bleak. "It would indicate if they're all connected. And you have no idea where that crossroads is?"

"No. The landscape was completely unrecognisable. Surely a crossroads with four standing stones marking each corner is weird, though?"

Alex frowned, "Maybe, maybe not. Standing stones are littered across the UK, and in Europe. They might not be obviously on crossroads now, but maybe some were in the past. There are hundreds of standing stones and strange cairns in Cornwall, and there's the Castlerigg Stone Circle close to Hunter, but I don't recall any crossroads."

Avery closed her eyes for a few seconds, but already the crossroads was fainter in her mind, harder to recall. "I think this is good news—it's not as close to me now."

"That's the potion and the necklace working," Briar told her. "Was the woman there? I presume not."

"No, fortunately, but I felt her guiding hand on all of it. But," Avery continued, "something I do remember is how old the place felt. I mean, truly ancient."

Alex headed to his coffee machine and started another brew. "What if this isn't just a distance location, but a time one as well?"

"Surely I couldn't have travelled to my van on the car park last night so easily?" Avery reasoned, feeling a chill sweep through her. "I mean, if I had moved through time in any significant way, that would have affected everything."

Alex stared at her for a moment, nodding. "Probably. It was just a thought."

"You know, there is something I forgot to tell you," Avery confessed. "There's a strange American man in town who seems to be watching our mysterious woman, and my shop."

"What!" Alex exclaimed. "Why didn't you say?"

"I forgot, sorry."

"Tell us everything," Reuben instructed.

Avery related her two encounters with the man, and how he'd disappeared on a motorbike.

"Bollocks!" Alex said. "What the hell has he got to do with all this?"

"If it's any reassurance, I didn't feel threatened by him," Avery told them.

"I'll keep an eye out for him, and let Newton know," Reuben said. "You concentrate on feeling better."

Briar picked up her bag, and slung it over her shoulder. "Right, we'll leave you to it. I'm heading back to do some spell research for you. I'll let Eli know about this man tomorrow, just in case he's seen him in town."

El and Reuben made to leave, too. "We'll see what we can find," El said, pulling Avery into a hug. "In the meantime, Avery, stay safe, and don't rush off on your own. This woman will be around for a while. We have time to deal with this. We only have a few pieces of the puzzle so far, but we'll work it out."

For the next few hours, Avery and Alex worked quietly side by side, looking through signs and sigils, before moving on to standing stones and crossroads, but by lunch, Avery was ready to tear her hair out.

"I am utterly stumped," she confessed. "And I'm hungry."

Alex slapped his book shut with a resounding *thud*. "I think we should go and see Shadow."

"You do? Why?"

He looked at her for a second, and Avery could see the worry in his eyes.

"I don't want you to freak out, but I've been thinking about that mark and why we can't find out what it is. Last night you were at a boundary, an active boundary. What if the marks aren't from our world?"

Avery looked down at her hand, and then back up at him. "You might be right."

He leapt up, and grabbed his keys. "Come on, I'll drive."

"Can we swing by my flat on the way and feed the cats? I'm afraid they'll think I've abandoned them."

"Ah, the children," he said, laughing. "Of course."

By the time they got to the old farmhouse on the hill, a fine drizzle had set in, and the surrounding fields were a murky grey and green. Alex complained all the way up the bumpy lane, as they jolted along. "I'm sure Gabe makes this road even worse, just to deter visitors."

He pulled into the courtyard surrounded by outbuildings, and they ran to Shadow's place, the converted stable. There was no answer there, so they headed for the main house instead, Avery running with her coat over her head to keep from getting wet.

For a few moments their knocking went unanswered again, and then they heard heavy footfalls. Gabe answered the door, dressed in black fatigues and a black t-shirt, but his feet were bare, and his short dark hair, which was slightly longer than usual, looked damp. He frowned. "Alex and Avery! Didn't expect to see you two. Come on in."

He led them up the hall into the big rustic kitchen at the rear of the house, and Avery noticed that although the place looked as bare as usual, at least it was warm. To her surprise, Shadow was in the kitchen, stirring something in a pot, from which an aromatic smell drifted. A fire was burning in the fireplace, and plates, bowls, and cooking paraphernalia covered most surfaces.

Shadow looked around and smiled. "Hi, guys. I'm cooking. I've found it's a great way to de-stress." She wore an overlarge set of striped pyjamas, which draped her slender frame, and Avery found her mouth dropping open in surprise before she clamped it shut.

Gabe rolled his eyes as he headed to the kettle. "What de-stresses Shadow, distresses me. Look at the mess. Tea, coffee, or beer?"

As one, Avery and Alex said, "Beer, please."

"Good call," Gabe said, heading to the fridge and grabbing four beers. "I've just got back from work, and this is what I find." He popped the caps, handed them out and took a drink. "Grab a seat," he told them gesturing towards the table and taking a seat himself.

"Were you working for Caspian?" Alex asked, as they joined him.

Gabe nodded. "Yeah. He had a big shipment last night, at his Falmouth warehouse, so I was supervising that."

Alex looked puzzled. "I thought you did security?"

"It involves a few things. Turns out that Caspian likes having us Nephilim around."

Intriguing, Avery thought watching him. It made her wonder quite what Caspian's business was sometimes. *Perhaps best she didn't know.* "Are all of you helping him?"

He jerked his head back, indicating Shadow. "She helps sometimes, just enough to earn her keep, and the other guys roster through, although Barak, Nahum, and Niel do most of it."

Shadow snorted. "Enough to earn my keep, indeed! You great-winged idiot. I pull my weight." Avery sniggered. *Great-winged idiot?* She continued, unabashed. "I'm making a hot pot for you! Do you want to try some?"

"Is it safe?" Gabe asked, his eyebrows rising.

"Of course. I'm fey."

"Always with the fey thing," he said, sighing. "Dish it up then, and I'll try not to throw up."

"You know you won't," she retorted, as she grabbed some bowls and started to spoon it out.

Avery and Alex exchanged an amused glance. *What was this weird, domestic set-up?*

"What about you two?" Shadow asked.

"Saves us a pub lunch," Avery found herself saying. "And to be honest, it smells great."

"It's rabbit. I shot them yesterday, using my bow, obviously. I need to keep my skills up."

"Great," Avery said, hating the thought of hunting, but the dish that appeared in front of her looked delicious, and she tucked in regardless.

Shadow sat next to them, placing some slices of fresh bread on a plate in the middle, and then looked at Avery knowingly. "What happened to you last night?"

"You know what happened. I ended up at some weird crossroads."

"I know that. I mean afterwards. In the night. You look terrible," she said bluntly.

"Thanks so much for your honesty. I visited the crossroads again, in my dream, sort of." Avery shook her head, confused. "I don't know if I can call it a dream, because I was there. It was so real!"

Alex interrupted. "She screamed the place down. I had to shake her out of it."

Shadow looked nonplussed. "I told you that you were connected, psychically. I'm not surprised."

Avery put her spoon down. "Well, go you! This isn't that easy for me to accept. It was bloody scary! I almost got sucked into a standing stone, and now I'm marked!" She thrust her palm in front of Shadow.

Shadow blanched. "By Herne's curly horns. That's fey script! How did this happen?"

"Fey script?" Avery looked at her hand. "No wonder we couldn't decipher it."

"I did think it was a possibility," Alex said, "but I honestly hoped I was wrong. It seemed too surreal."

Shadow's nonchalant attitude disappeared and she became very excited. "If you have fey script on your hand, it must mean the boundaries are weakened. This could be my chance!" She narrowed her eyes at them. "I told you there was more than one way!"

"Do you think we can forget about your way home for one second?" Avery asked, annoyed. "I've been marked. What the hell does it mean?"

"You have been claimed."

"I've been sodding *what*?"

"Claimed. By the Goddess of the Crossroads."

The room fell silent as they all stopped eating and looked at Shadow.

Alex found his voice first. "Do you mean Hecate?"

"The three-headed Goddess who sees past, present, and future? Yes."

"The maiden, the mother, and the crone," he said, elaborating.

Shadow looked confused. "If you say so. We have many Gods and Goddesses in our world. She is one of them. We keep out of their business and they keep out of ours, most of the time. Apart from, you know, a few months ago."

Alex was struggling to remain calm. "What do you mean, *claimed*?"

To be fair to Shadow, she looked a bit flustered, too. "Avery has been marked as a sacrifice. That's what that writing says. It's ancient."

Avery closed her eyes, willing herself to be calm. She opened her eyes again, staring into Shadow's violet ones, which were beguiling and cunning all at the same time. "The writing on the standing stones must have all been in fey script."

A calculating look swept across Shadow's face. "Probably. Tell me more."

Avery resumed eating, and in between mouthfuls told Shadow exactly what had happened in her dream.

"We need to find this crossroads," Shadow said, and looked to Gabe for support. "I need to go there!"

"Just slow down a second," Alex said. "Of course we need to go there, but we need to find out more about it! Why is Avery being targeted? There are four other witches that woman could have picked on. *And who the hell is she?"*

But it wasn't Shadow who answered—it was Gabe. "The Gods always like their sacrifices."

"Well, Avery won't be one," Alex said, jabbing his fork forcefully at him and Shadow. "We need to break this, but to do that we need to know what she is to be sacrificed for."

"Not will be, will *try* to be," Avery pointed out, annoyed.

"Well, that's the big question, isn't it?" Shadow said, absently playing with the food in her bowl. "The obvious answer would be to increase Hecate's power. But of course, it could be to strengthen the woman's power. She could be drawing on power from Hecate for a spell. Or it could be that something needs to manifest from the crossroads, and they need Hecate's power for that to happen."

"But surely they're already drawing on that power," Avery said. "That's how the Raven King and the Green Man are becoming real! And what about the deaths? And the strange conversation we heard: 'Its power feeds this place, don't forget that.' Who or what is *it*?"

"I wonder if there's a way for me to travel to the crossroads with you," Shadow mused. "It would allow me to decipher the script on the standing stones."

"That would be useful," Alex conceded. "What if we psychically linked with you, Avery? Like we did with Gabe once. Remember, we were able to see the cave where you were?" he said to Gabe.

Gabe grunted. "I remember that. You were surprisingly strong."

Alex flashed him a surprised grin. "Thanks. We could use the same technique. Then hopefully, wherever it is that you go, Avery, we could go with you."

Avery started to feel the tiniest bit hopeful. "Maybe, but that could be dangerous. You had to drag me back last night. If you're there with me, who brings us back?"

"Our coven. I'll need them, too."

"Where do we do this?" Shadow asked.

"My place," Alex volunteered. "I've been thinking about the other night, when you and Briar felt Earth magic, and you said you could feel something drawing on you. Do you think that's because of the boundary magic, that it knew you were fey?"

Shadow nodded. "I've been thinking on that too, and I think you're right. In the end, though, whatever it was wanted you more, Avery."

"Lucky me."

Alex rose to his feet. "Thanks for the food, Shadow, but we better go. I want to prepare for tonight." He held his hand out for Avery. "Come on. Let's get you home."

She stood, feeling lethargic and heavy. *Damn it.* Whatever was happening was not stopping. It was a strange sensation knowing that something was draining her power. A chill swept through her as she realised she could lose her magic, if not her life. That could not happen. A life without magic was no life at all.

Eleven

Avery and Alex spent a quiet afternoon at Alex's flat, and while Alex prepared for the ritual ahead, Avery continued her research.

Halfway through the afternoon, he declared, "I'm going to need Caspian."

"Why?"

"You'll be in the circle centre with me, linked over the crystal ball, and so will Shadow. We need someone to represent elemental Air, and he's strong."

"Do we have to involve him?" she asked, groaning.

"Yes. You know I wouldn't suggest him if we didn't need to, and he did offer to help. Besides, we need as much power as we can to do this, and he's powerful."

She sighed dramatically. "All right, then."

While Alex made the arrangements, Avery continued to research crossroads and stone circles and found out one fact that was particularly unpleasant. "Do you know that standing stones are supposed to represent witches in some places? They were frozen in place, transformed!"

Alex was in the kitchen grinding herbs in his pestle and mortar. He stopped and looked up at her. "No, but you said you felt you were being sucked in."

"This gets worse. I'm going to be immortalised in stone."

"No, you're not. Go on, tell me more."

She glanced down at the page again. "Standing stones in many places are supposed to represent witches, or other figures frozen in time. One of the most well known is Long Meg and her Daughters. It's a stone circle, not far from where Hunter is from. Apparently, they were turned to stone for dancing on the Sabbath. The circle is supposed to be magical, and many say you can't count the same number of stones twice. To do so will break the spell. Some legends also suggest that witches were buried at crossroads under standing stones, as a way of neutralising their power."

Alex resumed grinding his herbs. "That's good to know. It's a link. You can't identify four standing stones on a crossroads, though?"

"No, annoyingly."

"That's okay. We'll find a way."

"What if this is exactly what that woman wants us to do? We could be walking into a trap!"

"And that's why we have back-up."

+ + +

As the afternoon progressed, Avery felt more and more lethargic, so that by the time everyone else arrived, buzzing with energy and intent, she was drowsy.

Alex had prepared the salt circle in front of the fire again, and the room was filled with candles and was bathed in firelight.

Briar took one look at Avery and ran over to hug her. "You look worse."

"Thanks Briar, I thought Reuben was the one who was going to tell me that."

"You do look terrible," Reuben agreed.

Briar ignored him. "I've been working on spells to break this connection, and I'm struggling."

"We all have," Caspian told her, as he arrived partway through their conversation. "But to break a psychic connection with force is very dangerous."

118

His dark eyes fell on Avery. "That alone could kill you."

"Is there any positive news?" Avery asked, trying to subdue her panic.

"Yes, your link to her is her weakness," Shadow said confidently. She had dressed for battle, wearing black fatigues, and Avery could see the glint of her knives in the sheaths on her thighs.

"Exactly," Reuben said. He pointed at the salt circle on the floor. "Shall we sit?"

Alex nodded. "Yes please. The elemental places are marked by candles and compass points. The usual. Avery, Shadow, let's take our place in the circle, too. Caspian, are you ready?"

He nodded and sat between Briar and El, opposite Reuben, a purple candle in front of each of them. Alex, Shadow, and Avery sat virtually knee-to-knee around one solitary candle in the centre.

"We're going to raise a protective circle before we begin," Alex instruct-ed, "and then we three need to drink this potion. It will help relax us to enter the necessary mind state."

"We're not connected, then?" El asked. "We were last time."

"I'm not going to link to you. You four are our magical protection and support," Alex told them. "It may also take longer than we think, considering Avery thought she'd been gone for minutes and it turned out to be a couple of hours. Are we all clear?"

They nodded, and the four witches in their elemental positions started the ritual to raise protection, while Alex drank some of the potion from the silver goblet and handed it to Shadow and Avery.

Avery could feel the heat and low lighting begin to work on her already weakened state, and the potion quickly exacerbated it. Within seconds she felt the protective circle around her activate, and all noises of the outside world disappeared.

Alex held his hands out. "We need to join hands, and then say the spell after me. This will link us, so that where you go, we follow."

Shadow looked wary. "I have never done magic like this before."

"Trust me, it's safe. Do you want to see this place?"

She nodded.

"Come on, then."

She linked hands with Alex and Avery, and as they repeated the spell after Alex, Avery felt their energies connect; Shadow's sharp, wild energy was distinctly different to Alex's. They all took a moment to adjust, and then Alex guided them again. "Avery, just focus on the crossroads. Don't resist it."

She nodded and closed her eyes. It didn't take long. The crossroads was lurking just beneath her waking mind, a constant presence that she had battled to ignore all day long. But in this state, it rushed in, and so did her fear.

She stood next to the standing stone she had connected to before. A full moon was again overhead, illuminating everything with its silver light. She stepped away from the stone, already feeling its hum of energy, and it took every part of her to resist its pull. The markings on it were already starting to glow with the strange light that looked like molten gold. Once again, no one was here, and the landscape stretched around her, devoid of life.

Avery immediately heard Alex's voice in her head. *You're blocking us, Avery.*

I'm not, I promise.

It's your fear, he replied. *I can feel it. Relax, let us in.*

Avery took a deep breath and then another, willing herself to calm down. She hated it here, alone. She needed them.

For another few seconds nothing happened, and then suddenly they were there, standing on either side of her.

"Wow," Shadow said, turning slowly. The crossroads enhanced her otherness in ways that were indefinable, but obvious at the same time. "This is amazing. I feel the fey magic rising." She trembled slightly. "It's so odd to feel my home when I haven't in weeks."

Alex squeezed Avery's hand gently. "I knew it would work. I can see why you were freaking out. This place definitely has Otherworldly vibes." He looked at Shadow and his voice was sharp. "Focus on the stone. What does it say?"

Shadow ran her hands gently across the surface, and the writing became more visible. She was silent for a few moments as she read the script. "It's ancient and I don't recognise some phrases, but essentially this stone calls to the energy of the wind. It demands that someone who commands it be made sacrifice so as to give honour to Hecate, Goddess of the Crossroads. Those who are sacrificed will receive her eternal blessing."

Avery felt a cold fear wash over her. "She chose me because I wield elemental Air. Which means—" She broke off, looking at the other three stones, and Alex followed her gaze.

Shadow had already anticipated them, and she reached the next closest one. She didn't need to touch it; the writing was already glowing with golden light. "The language is identical. I presume they were all placed here at the same time, but the script calls to the Fire element instead. They must represent the four elements," she said, confirming their suspicions.

While she made her way to the two remaining stones, Alex asked Avery, "But why only you? Why aren't the other witches being called here?"

"I don't know, but the other stones remain lit from within, unlike this one. I have a bad feeling about this. We need to get out of here."

Alex turned around, taking in their surroundings. "Not yet. Is there something that will help us find this place again, in the real world?"

Avery threw her arms wide. "Look at it! It's virtually featureless! And the moon never changes. It should be waning by now—I've been here three times. It's still full and overhead. I feel as if we're in a bubble."

Shadow re-joined them, and it was clear she'd overheard the conversation. "We are in some sort of stasis, like a spell that has frozen this place in time. That's how it feels to me, anyway. The fey magic that surrounds here is," she frowned, as she tried to find the right word. "It's less wild...harnessed, like a horse."

"And why isn't that woman here?" Avery asked. "I keep expecting her to appear at any time!"

"Because she doesn't need to appear," Shadow explained. "Her job is done. She brought you here, and now you're linked to that." She pointed at the stone dedicated to elemental Air. "It's draining your power, even now. I don't know about you, but I can feel its energy growing. And I think I know why the other stones are lit, and it's not good news. And I think you know why, too."

Avery swallowed, fearing she also knew the answer, but she'd been trying to ignore her suspicions. "I think these have already been activated—if that's the right word."

Shadow nodded. "Yes. Their power is already complete, which means—"

"Other witches have already been sacrificed to them," Alex finished for her. He raked his hands through his hair, his eyes wild with worry. "So how do we break the connection before Avery dies?"

Avery felt sick. Three witches with strong elemental magic had already been sacrificed to these stones, and she could be next. "Where did that woman get the other witches from?"

"It might not be where, but *when*," Shadow suggested. "This stasis could have existed for a very long time."

"Which suggests that this woman has also been doing this for a long time," Alex said. "Who the hell is she?"

Before she could answer, Avery staggered as her energy dipped and her vision dimmed, and Alex quickly stepped forward, supporting her before she could fall. "Time to get you out of here."

Alex extended his left hand to Shadow, still holding Avery with his right arm. "Grab my hand and don't resist."

For endless seconds, nothing seemed to happen, and then with a rush, Avery was back in the centre of the circle, and the room dissolved into blackness.

Twelve

Avery heard the murmur of voices all around her, and then slowly a warm, orange light began to seep into the blackness that surrounded her like a shroud.

As the voices grew louder, Avery began to make out words. It sounded like a spell. *Why could she hear a spell?*

A male voice shouted, "Her eyes are fluttering, she's coming around!"

And then she heard Alex's voice and felt his hand slide into her own. "Avery, can you hear me? Are you all right?"

She tried to speak, but it felt like her mouth was full of dust and grit. With the greatest effort, she opened her eyes and then quickly closed them. The light seemed blinding. "I'm fine," she finally muttered, realising as she said it that she was not fine at all. "Water."

"Here," Briar said, and she felt arms slide under shoulders and lift her so she was sitting up.

"Let me," she heard Reuben say from somewhere behind her, and suddenly she felt a warm, solid mass behind her, and she leaned into it with relief.

Alex said, "Have some water, Avery, just a sip."

A glass was pressed to her lips and she took a few sips of cold water, thinking she'd never tasted anything so delicious in her life. It was only when she finished drinking that she opened her eyes again, squinting against the light for a few moments until her vision adjusted. The fire still burned, candles still illuminated the room, and Alex's worried face swam in front of her.

"Hello, gorgeous. Glad to have you back."

"Glad to be back," she croaked. "What happened?"

"Crossroads bloody magic, that's what," Reuben said from above and behind her. Avery realised a pair of legs were stretched out on either side of her, and she twisted to look up into Reuben's anxious face. She must be leaning against Reuben's chest. "You had us worried then, Ave."

"Sorry. It wasn't exactly what I planned."

Now that she was awake, she could see Alex next to her, and beside him was Caspian. On her right was Briar, and at her feet was El, all of them white-faced with worry. Shadow was watching from beyond the circle.

"By the Goddess," Briar said, "you had me worried. You're very weak."

"I feel as weak as a kitten. What happened?"

Alex explained, "I think that stone drained your magic while at the crossroads, far quicker than it would by just your psychic link. We shouldn't risk you going there again."

"How can I not go?" she asked. "It's there, all the time, in my head! I see it every time I close my eyes!" She could hear her own panic rising, and she tried to subdue it.

"I have made a suggestion," Caspian said, his voice low. "It should help, but not everyone agrees."

Alex shot him a look of annoyance. "I'm just not sure that another magical link will be a good move."

Briar's calm tones interjected. "But it could buy us valuable time—at Caspian's expense."

"I've told you that I'm happy to do it. I'm the only one who can." He looked around at the other witches. "And you know I'm right."

Avery held a hand to her head. "I'm not thinking particularly clearly right now. Can you be more specific?"

Briar took Avery's hand in her small, soft one. "Since Caspian also commands elemental Air, his power will supplement your own, and hopefully feed that standing stone that continues to drain your power, until we can sever the link completely."

Avery looked at Caspian and knew he was completely serious. "I think that's too dangerous, Caspian."

"But it's too dangerous for you not to have support. How long do you think you've been out for, Avery?"

She looked around at the others' faces and noted how tired they looked. "An hour or two?"

"Try five or six."

"What!" She tried to sit upright, but her limbs still felt heavy, and she sagged back against Reuben again. "How is that possible? How long were we at the crossroads?"

"For us, a matter of minutes," Alex said. "But in reality, over an hour."

"We were starting to panic," El told her. She still sat cross-legged at Avery's feet, her blonde hair loose around her shoulders. "You three were motionless. It was freaky. And when you finally came out of your weird psychic trance, you just collapsed. For the last few hours, Briar has been trying a variety of healing spells on you."

"With very limited success," Briar said, grudgingly.

Caspian was impatient. "You haven't got time to wait, Avery, and you have very few options. Do you want to link with me? It will help slow the drain of your power."

Avery glanced at Alex, not sure what to do. Caspian was probably right, but she wasn't certain it would be a good thing, and she wasn't sure Alex would like it, either.

Before she could respond, Briar said, "For the record, I think it's a good idea, Avery. Tell us honestly how you feel."

She met her calm, quiet gaze. "I'm shattered. My limbs feel heavy, and my thoughts are clouded. I can't feel my magic as much, either. It actually feels pretty scary."

"Well, I think you have your answer then," she said softly. Briar looked at Alex. "You know Caspian is right, and I know you want to do this, but Caspian is the only one to truly wield elemental Air like Avery. And his magic is strong. Your powers are different, and we're going to need you to help Avery break this link. That is *your* strength, Alex."

Alex looked stricken for a moment, and then nodded. "Agreed. Avery?" She nodded. "Agreed."

Alex turned to Caspian. "Thank you. What do you suggest?"

Caspian could swagger when he wanted to, but he must have realised how difficult this was for Alex, because he said, "You're the expert on this. What do you think?"

Alex thought for a moment, looking at their arrangement within the broken circle of salt. "I don't think what we three have just done is the way to go. That was for a short-term connection only. A type of binding might be more effective."

Caspian nodded thoughtfully. "But it has to link me to the crossroads too, or it's pointless."

"I think whoever links to Avery now will be bound to the crossroads, re-gardless," Briar said. She held her hands a few inches above Avery, sweeping over her body. "I can feel it. You're sort of vibrating with it. It has changed your energy."

"I agree," Shadow said. "As soon as we connected, it was obvious."

Alex nodded as he started to look excited. "Yes, you're right. We needed to connect mentally and psychically because we needed to visit the cross-roads with you, but Caspian doesn't. He just needs to lend his power to yours. The connection you have to that place will automatically feed from Caspian, too."

"I think you're right," Avery agreed. "But Caspian, I think you'll get flashes of the crossroads anyway."

"Good. There are positive aspects to this link. It links us to *her*, too—whoever she is."

"Exactly," Reuben said from behind her.

Alex rose to his feet. "I'm just going to get my grimoire. I have a binding that should work, but happy to take any suggestions."

"We trust you," Briar said, still gauging Avery's energy levels. "I've brought more potions with me. You have to drink them every two hours. I've upped the dose."

"Whatever, I'll drink anything at this stage. I might have to increase my alcohol consumption, too."

"I've already beat you to that," Reuben said. He shifted slightly, and Avery tried to sit up on her own, but failed. "Stay put," he commanded, his hands resting on her shoulders. "I can cope with a numb ass."

Avery reached up and rested her hands on his for a moment. "Thank you."

Alex returned to the circle, and sat cross-legged with his grimoire on his lap. "You two need to sit in the middle, knee to knee, hands linked," he instructed Avery and Caspian.

Avery reluctantly pulled herself away from Reuben, summoning all of her remaining reserves of energy to sit upright, and sat opposite Caspian.

She watched his expression, wondering if this was really a good idea. He liked her, he'd made that clear, and she hoped this link between them wouldn't make his feelings stronger. But he gave nothing away; he just looked his normal, collected self. He held his hands out and she took them in hers, uncomfortably aware of his strong, sure grip, and the light touch of his knees resting against hers.

Alex pulled a white cord from his pocket. "I'll say the spell, and you repeat it after me. As we continue, I'll wrap this cord around your wrists. The cord will then be kept safe in a cedar wood box until we break the binding." Alex then spoke to El, Reuben, and Briar. "You all can join in, too. Our magic will reinforce the binding and act as a sort of secondary defence."

They murmured their agreement, and moved back into their positions, and then Alex began to chant.

The spell was short and succinct, and they all repeated it over and over again, as Alex wound the cord around Avery and Caspian's linked hands. Avery felt the power of the spell rise quickly, and a tingle ran up her arms and across her body as the binding took hold.

Her link to the standing stone and the crossroads reverberated through her, as if it recognised a second power enter her body. Avery watched Caspian carefully. He shuddered, and Avery guessed he could feel the crossroads magic now, too.

Caspian's magic felt cool in her veins, and she started to sense it beyond her arms, as it travelled across her body, along her trunk, and down her legs. His magic was strong. She'd always known that, but feeling it flow through her now, she realised how much she had underestimated him. He met her eyes as the binding took hold, and she thought she detected a hint of triumph in his face, which he quickly masked. She knew her magic was flowing around him too, as weak as it was right now.

The chanting continued, and with relief Avery felt her magic and energy lift, and her muddled thoughts became clearer. For the first time in hours, she began to feel they could defeat this woman, and that she would not become stone fodder in some time-frozen place.

Alex ended the spell, and the cord that bound her and Caspian's hands burned with a bright white light for a few seconds before extinguishing. She was now bound to Caspian until this thing was over, and he looked a damn sight happier about it than she was.

Alex gently untied the cord. "Feeling better, Avery?"

She smiled at him. "Much better. It happened quicker than I thought. It's very odd to feel someone else's magic in your body." She kept it light as she looked at Caspian. "Thank you. How are you?"

He rolled his shoulders. "Fine so far, but I can feel the pull of the crossroads. Blunted though, probably because I'm not directly linked. Unfortunately, I can't feel that woman. I'd like to pick up her power signature. It might help us work out who she is."

Briar wriggled closer to Avery and extended her hand again, her face impassive as she concentrated furiously for a moment. Then she relaxed and sighed with pleasure. "Excellent. I can feel your magic rising. Great job, everyone."

Reuben scooted around, looked at her, and then nodded wisely. "Yes, I agree, you do look less like shit than you did earlier."

"Thanks Reuben, you always say the nicest things," Avery replied.

"Always here to please, you know that, Ave. So, what now?"

"Now we find out who that woman is and what she wants."

"She must have some other role in the circus," Caspian suggested.

El shrugged. "Maybe her role is to give the circus magic? Odd though, that she should parade around the town with the other performers."

Avery eased away from Caspian and stretched out her cramped limbs, and the others started to move too, breaking up the circle. "The more I think about it, the more I think she has no circus role, not as a performer anyway. She has to be our number one priority. She's the key to everything."

Shadow warned, "That will be hard. She protects herself well, and can obviously defend herself against magic."

"So there are two things going on, really," El surmised. "The creature that is hunting people, and the woman who controls the crossroads—who could be Caitlin, if Newton can find out who she is. And yes, they have to be linked, but essentially there are two problems. We need to keep searching for that crossroads."

"Two teams," Shadow said. "We divide and conquer."

"But," Alex said, looking at Avery. "You can't come to the campgrounds."

"Why not?" she asked, annoyed.

"You know why not. She knows you. A trip to that site could trigger another trip to the stones. We can't risk that."

"No, you can't," Caspian said, unexpectedly agreeing with Alex. "You had just enough energy to fly out of there last time—which, by the way, suggests it's located here in this world somewhere, but is a long way from here. You might not be able to do that again. We need to know where it is and how that woman links to it. We should concentrate on that."

"As in, *we*," Avery said, gesturing between them.

"Yes. If we find the crossroads, we're halfway to breaking the link. She is anchored to something there."

Briar groaned. "So many questions. It hurts my head."

"That's tiredness," Reuben said, as he rose to his feet and extended his hand, pulling Briar to her feet, too. "We all need sleep. It's nearly three in the morning."

El grabbed her jacket and headed to the door with Reuben next to her. "And it's Monday. So no lie-in either. Do we meet tonight, then?"

Alex put his grimoire away in the large wooden chest he kept a lot of his magic paraphernalia in. "After the show. It has to be then. We want them in the campground, not in the tent, if we're to spy effectively."

"Midnight then," Reuben said. "I'll call you to confirm. You in, Shadow?"

"Of course."

Briar confirmed that she would be there too, and left with Shadow, Reuben, and El, leaving Caspian the only one remaining. He pulled on his coat as he spoke. "I'm going to chat to Estelle. She has a knack for 'finding' spells. There must be something we can adapt to help us find the crossroads. I'll call you later, Avery. Perhaps while the others are searching the campgrounds, we could try this. Midnight would be a good time for us, too. Liminal boundaries are stronger at those times. You should come to my place."

"Are you sure Estelle will want to help?" she asked. Estelle, Caspian's sister, had never liked them, and despite Caspian's acceptance of the White Haven witches, she had never softened her stance. And Avery didn't like Estelle, either. She was abrupt and rude, with a solid superiority complex.

"She has no choice. I'm the head of the family now, and the head of our coven."

Alex shook Caspian's hand. "Thanks, that sounds a good plan. And thanks for tonight."

"Anything to help Avery," Caspian murmured, and with a final glance at her, he left.

Alex shut the door and turned to look at her. "I hate that you're bound to him." His dark eyes burned with a fierce intensity she didn't often see. Behind it she could sense his worry, and maybe some fear.

"I hate it, too," she reassured him, "but I really do feel better. And I love you even more for doing this. You have nothing to fear, you know."

He reached forward and pulled her close, kissing her passionately. When he released her, she was breathless. "I don't want to lose you, to anything or anyone."

"You won't. Now come to bed." She grabbed his hand and pulled him after her.

Thirteen

Avery's eyes felt gritty the next morning, and she stumbled into her flat with a heavy head from too few hours of sleep. But at least she *had* slept, which must have been a result of extreme tiredness, Briar's potions, and Caspian's magic.

She felt horribly guilty. She'd hardly been home at all the previous day, and she gave Medea and Circe a big fuss when she arrived. They meowed loudly, and wound around her legs until she'd fed them, and then she headed down to the shop.

Sally and Dan were already in the kitchen, and the smell of coffee filled the space. Avery inhaled greedily. "One for me please," she said as she stepped through the door.

"No problem," Sally called, reaching for cups, and then she turned to look at Avery and frowned. "What have you been up to?"

Avery just groaned. "Too many things. Mainly getting myself into trouble with some crazy circus lady."

"Again?" Dan said, as Sally poured the coffee, sugared it, and then handed Avery her cup. "Tell us everything. No, wait. Let me guess. It must be the mysterious woman."

"Spot on, and our connection just got a lot weirder." She filled them in on everything that had happened over the weekend.

Sally gaped at her. "You're linked to Caspian now?"

"Temporarily! His magic is shoring up mine. It's weird. I didn't think such a thing was possible, not like this anyway. I mean, you connect to another witch's magic when you do spells together, but this is something else entirely."

"Does that mean he's in your head?"

"No! That would not be okay. This is a magical link, not psychic. But I'm really annoyed—they've banned me from going to the circus with them tonight."

"Sounds sensible," Dan said, leading the way into the shop, ready to open the doors for the day. "You're clearly very vulnerable right now. Do you want to do your thing?" He gestured around vaguely.

"Do you mean enhance my protection spells? Yes, that's probably a good idea."

Sally and Dan gave her space as she walked around, lighting incense and reinforcing her spells—one for protection, and one that helped her customers find that special something they didn't know they needed. Her rituals calmed her, so that by the time the doors opened, she almost felt her usual self.

Avery joined Sally and Dan at the counter, where they were finishing their coffee. Dan had found Robert Johnson's blues music, and its moody sounds already filled the shop. "Did you go to the circus in the end, Sally?" Avery asked.

She nodded. "I did. It was amazing. The kids loved it. But I did feel the slightest bit of magic, although I doubt anyone else could."

That made Avery pause. "You can sense magic?"

"Only slightly, and only because of you. I think I've been overexposed to it. Anyway, I felt it at the circus, but it didn't detract from the performers. They were still brilliant."

Avery shifted her weight as she leaned against the counter. "What do you think the magic did?"

Sally thought for a moment. "I think it gave the atmosphere a buzz, and the tent walls seemed to rustle as if something was alive in that fake greenery. But, the whole performance was magical, really."

"Interesting. Briar said the same thing."

"What will you do while the others are at the circus?" Dan asked.

"Try to find the crossroads with Caspian and his sister."

"That bitch, Estelle?" Sally looked appalled.

"I don't have much choice. We need to find the crossroads to break my link to it—and the mysterious woman's. Estelle is good at 'finding' spells, apparently."

"What happens if you can't break the link?"

"The standing stone will eventually sap all my power and I'll die."

Dan and Sally fell silent, looking at her wide-eyed and open-mouthed. Dan recovered first. "You'll solve it, Avery. You always do."

Avery's usual positivity was failing her, and she confessed, "Yes, but I'm not normally the one at risk. I'm already not functioning as well as usual. You should have seen me before Caspian helped."

"I did try and find out more about the Green Man and the Raven King," Dan said. "But, to be honest, I've found nothing ground-breaking."

"Tell me what you have found. I need something to cheer me up."

"Well, the Green Man is a nature spirit, and has been around for centuries. Images show him surrounded by green leaves and vines, and he's associated with death, rebirth, and fertility, and particularly with Beltane and May Day celebrations."

Avery nodded. "I remember. Isn't he the consort to the May Queen?"

"Usually. His title is quite recent. It's attributed to a woman called Lady Raglan, back in the 1930s, if I remember the date correctly. Before then he was called Jack in the Green. People mostly associate him with nature, forests, and woods. He's always been depicted in pagan beliefs, but his image is commonly found carved into stone and wood in churches. Depending on where you are in the country, he has been mixed up with Robin Hood, and even Herne the Hunter."

"Really?" Sally asked, surprised. "Why would churches have pagan images carved on them?"

"It's believed that many churches were built on pagan places of worship. And many people who were involved in building churches would have still clung to the old beliefs. He's likely carved into All Souls and Old Haven Church."

"I love how the old beliefs sneak into Christianity. I might have to go and have a look at All Souls," Avery said, thinking it would be good to speak to James anyway.

Dan continued, "He's also been associated with the Green Knight, you know, from the Arthurian Legend, Sir Gawain and the Green Knight. He was interesting! Gawain chopped his head off, and the knight picked it up and challenged him to the same thing the next year."

"You think he's here now because he's linked to the Otherworld, and has been summoned by crossroads magic?" Avery asked.

"I reckon," Dan said. "The circus is all about boundaries and English folklore, and how figures from our ancient past shape our present." He smiled. "I always like to think he's around when I'm walking across the fields and down country lanes, especially in the woods, and particularly at twilight, when the light is fading and the animals are busy. I can almost sense something else there, just beyond my vision."

"That's exactly what I think, too," Sally agreed. "I like to think the old ways lurk behind the everyday."

"You two never cease to surprise me," Avery said, laughing.

"And that's why we like working here," Sally said. "Go on, Dan. What about the Raven King?"

"He's based on Welsh mythology. Have you heard of Brân the Blessed, or *Brân ap Llyr*?"

Avery frowned, thinking that something about the name sounded familiar. "Vaguely."

"He's the legendary Welsh King of Britain. Brân is the God of music, poetry, and prophecy, and *brân* means 'raven' in Welsh. Ravens are associated with prophecy, too, and seen as messengers between the Otherworld and our world." He shrugged. "They have their place in lots of other cultures, and were associated with Apollo in Greek myths. Anyway, here in Britain, the raven is identified with Brân. He's the son of Llyr, which is why you might remember him, Avery."

"Llyr, as in the father of the crazy mermaids we fought in the summer last year?"

"The very same. The God who represents the powers of darkness. But Brân wasn't a dark figure—he was revered and honoured as being wise and brave. Ravens have always been associated with him."

"And hence he's a liminal figure, because ravens carry messages between our world and the Otherworld," Avery said, grasping the connections. "And he was a God of prophecy."

"And as a God, he stepped between worlds anyway," Dan agreed. "Did you know he's the source of the myths of the ravens and the Tower of London?"

Avery shook her head. "No."

"Brân was injured in a fight with the Irish, shot by a poisoned spear. He commanded that his head be chopped off and buried on the White Mount, in London, with him facing France. The White Mount is where the Tower of London now stands. It is believed his head is a talisman, protecting Britain from foreign invasion. And it was a talking head, too! He continued to advise and entertain on his journey to London."

Sally gasped. "That's so cool! I did not know that. And that's why ravens are associated with the Tower?"

He nodded. "Yes. The ravens gather to respect their fallen king, and it is rumoured that should ravens leave the Tower, Britain will fall. Therefore the Tower has a raven master to ensure that the Tower always has ravens."

"So the Raven King is another figure who crosses between worlds," Avery said thoughtfully. "The circus master's costume certainly did it justice the other night. I just wonder how much Corbin has to do with what's going on there. He certainly didn't sound very happy when we overheard him the other night."

Dan finished his coffee and thumped his cup on the counter. "Maybe he's the weak link—someone to work on to help you."

Avery looked at the shelves stacked with books, seeing nothing but the Raven King in her mind. "Maybe he is, Dan." Her hand itched, and she looked at her palm as the mark glowed again.

Sally had followed her gaze, and she frowned. "What's that on your hand?"

Avery looked guilty. "I neglected to mention that. The stone I mentioned marked me. It's fey script."

Sally edged around the counter, grabbed Avery's hand, and pulled her closer to the front window to examine it carefully. "Wow. That's scary."

Dan took her hand too. "That's some dream that can do this."

"I know. The power of the crossroads is real. No wonder they used to bury their dead there. Maybe they thought it helped their souls cross to a better place."

Dan dropped her hand and rubbed his chin thoughtfully. "You know, you talk of the crossroads as an evil place, and Hecate can be a dark mistress, but she isn't always. She's a chthonic Goddess, a Goddess of the Underworld, but she's not inherently evil."

"I know. What are you suggesting?" Avery asked.

"Well, neither are the Raven King and the Green Man. They're liminal figures, after all. Their presence is not evil, even though it probably felt scary the other night when they were in the field with you. But surely the presence of a God and a nature spirit is bound to feel scary. You're in the presence of powerful beings. More importantly, Brân was a power for good. He protected the weak, and if you believe the myths, he protects England right now."

For a moment, Avery was speechless as she processed Dan's words, and a bright spark of hope started to fill her. "You're absolutely right! If anything, they should be on our side!" She started to pace the front of the shop as her head filled with possibilities. "We need to use them, or at least trust in them."

Sally sat on the sofa beneath the window of the shop, watching her pace. "I don't know. They haven't helped so far—those young men have still died. That doesn't sound positive to me."

"But it's like what Shadow says, and what you have said before too, Avery," Dan reminded them. "Gods don't interfere in the affairs of men, and neither do pagan spirits. They are separated from the affairs of mortals—in general—unless you appeal to them. Whoever this woman is, she appealed to Hecate for help, and there was clearly a price to pay. You could appeal for help too, and enlist the Raven King to Team Witch."

Avery stopped pacing and looked at them both. "But what if there is another price to pay?"

Dan folded his arms across his chest. "You're already paying the ultimate price. I don't think you've got much to lose."

$$\dagger \quad \dagger \quad \dagger$$

Avery looked up at All Souls Church and squinted at the stone work. It was a gloomy day, and the sky was filled with heavy clouds. She felt it had been days since she'd seen the sun, but that wasn't unusual in February. What was unusual was the warmth to the air, and the ever increasing number of ravens in the town and up at the castle.

The image of the Green Man with his mischievous, grinning face stared down at her from the archway above the church entrance. It was tucked to the side, but it was unmistakable. Other faces were also there, strange gargoyles with their wild, ugly expressions. She felt they watched her as she set off around the church, trying to spot more carvings. She was so lost in her thoughts that she didn't hear James, the vicar, until he spoke from behind her.

"What are you up to, Avery?"

She looked around, jumping with surprise. "You were quiet! I was looking for the Green Man. He's in quite a few places." She pointed up at him, high up the wall on a buttress.

James laughed. "Oh, yes. He's a cheeky thing, isn't he?"

"Do you mind that he's carved here? He's a pagan symbol, not Christian."

"Of course not. He's an ancient symbol of fertility and rebirth. I quite like it that he connects us to our past. Besides," James said, grinning, "he was probably put there to encourage the pagans to come in. You know, make the Church a place for everyone, and then convert them to the true faith."

He said this with a glint of humour, and Avery laughed. "Of course! That makes perfect sense. What about those, though?" she asked, pointing to the gargoyles that projected from the corners of the building.

"Oh, now they have two purposes. They funnel water from the roof to prevent erosion, and also remind people that the devil exists. That's why they're so grotesque—to encourage people to pray."

Avery was surprised. "They funnel water?"

James pointed. "See, its mouth is open. I believe the word is French originally, it means throat or gullet."

"That's so cool. I'm learning so much today."

"What else are you learning about?"

"The Green Man and the Raven King."

"Is that because of the circus?"

"Sort of," she confessed. She hadn't seen James for a while, and he looked good; happy, and free from worry. He also seemed pleased to see her, which was nice, as they'd had their ups and downs in the past. Fortunately, when she'd last seen him before Christmas, he'd been happy to bless some water for them to help in their fight with the vampires.

James became serious again. "Is something happening again?"

"Yes, but you don't need to be involved."

"I think I owe you a coffee or two, and maybe some biscuits. And if I'm honest, you look a little pale. Come on in." He turned and led the way to the vicarage, clearly not accepting no for an answer, and Avery fell into step beside him.

"I'm sure you're busy, James."

"Never too busy for one of my flock."

"I'm pretty sure I'm not one of those."

"You are to me," he said softly, in a way that had Avery pausing in surprise.

He headed inside and she followed him through the toy-strewn living room, into the kitchen, and watched him as he filled the kettle and prepared cups.

"Where's your wife?" she asked him.

"Volunteering at the children's nursery. She does a few things to help the community." She remained silent, and he looked at her. "Did I surprise you?"

"Yes, actually. You know I'm not a believer in your faith."

"That's okay, Avery. I've decided that I don't need you to believe. And besides, you look after our community, too. I imagine the vampires were pretty scary to deal with?"

"Terrifying. I hope I never have to face them again."

He switched the kettle on, grabbed a packet of shortbread, and then sat at the kitchen table, gesturing her to join him. He offered her a biscuit as he asked, "Were you the ones to tell the police about the bodies in the caves beneath West Haven?"

"Yes. That's where we found Lupescu, the chief vampire."

"And you found those two girls?"

"Me and my coven, yes."

"In the middle of the worst snowstorm that we have seen for years?"

She smiled ruefully. "It was pretty bad, wasn't it? But yes. We tracked it and found its lair, and then waited for it to return. Lupescu killed Grace, the girl who worked at The Wayward Son."

His eyes closed briefly. "I thought it must be so. Poor girl. But you saved two more."

She took a bite of her biscuit, enjoying the sugar hit. "I wish we could have saved even more. The vampire had been hunting for years."

"Were there others?"

"I'm afraid so, but we think we killed them all."

"Only think?"

"We can't be sure, but we're pretty confident."

"And what do the police really think?"

"They know vampires were behind it all."

The kettle boiled and he stood to make their drinks, and then brought them to the table, placing one in front of Avery. "Do they know about you?"

"One of them does."

"And the press?"

"I hope not!" She sipped her drink, watching him over the rim of the cup. "We try to keep a low profile."

He nodded. "And you do. What about that house they found the passages under? The medium's house?"

She tried not to roll her eyes. "That was the root of the problem, actually. But hopefully that will never get out, even though the owners are going to run tours."

"They want to run tours of White Haven, not just their house. That's what Stan was telling me, anyway."

Avery felt a stir of worry deep in the pit of her stomach. "I know. He wants to put my shop on his tour."

"He strikes me as an opportunist."

"Oh, he's definitely one of those."

James looked at her thoughtfully for a moment. "I feel I should tell you that I've heard rumblings of concern from my parishioners."

"Concern about what?"

"Black magic. They think that's what the deaths and all those bones were caused by."

For understandable reasons, angry hordes and Helena flashed into Avery's head, and she had a vision of Helena's final moments as she was burned at the stake. "What did you say to them?"

"I've told them it's ridiculous, of course. Have you had any problems in your shop?"

"None!" Avery's customers were always book and occult lovers in general anyway, and she certainly hadn't detected any animosity.

He nodded, relieved. "Good. The last thing we want is a modern day witch-hunt."

She shook her head, perplexed. "No. I hadn't even considered it."

"Just to reassure you, there were only a few concerned people. Many who live in White Haven appreciate it for what it is, and love its mysticism and magic, but I just wanted to warn you. I hope that man doesn't stir things up. What's his name again?"

"Rupert." She remembered his resentment once he'd learned she was a descendant of Helena, and wondered if he would create trouble for her. There was something about him that none of the witches liked.

"That's it. Are you sure I can't help you with anything? I mean, this current issue with the circus. There was a death the other day, on one of the beaches."

Avery nodded. "Yes, there was, and someone in the circus is responsible, but we're working on it. You can stay out of this one, but thanks for asking anyway." She didn't see any point in sharing her current predicament. There was nothing he could do.

He smiled, but it didn't mask his worry. "Fair enough. Have another biscuit."

Fourteen

Alex nearly spat his pint out as Avery repeated what she'd discussed with Dan and Sally.

"Will you please stop talking about dying!"

"It's a possibility, you know that. Facing my own mortality is weird. But I have to trust this will work tonight. I haven't got a death wish! And as much as you don't want me linked to Caspian, I don't want to trust Estelle. But we have to find the crossroads!"

"But do we? I've been thinking on this all day. Is there another way?"

Alex and Avery were sitting in a secluded corner of Penny Lane Bistro, the former home of Helena, waiting for their starters to arrive. Avery had brought him up to date with all the latest developments, theories, and suggestions, before they went their separate ways later that night. She was drinking a hearty red wine, and Alex was drinking a pint of Skullduggery Ale, his latest favourite tipple.

Avery lowered her voice and leaned closer to Alex. "I could not affect that woman in any way with my magic. And I have great magic, as you know. I can only presume that Hecate's magic protects her, and wow, I wish I had that protection. She was virtually immune! If her link to the crossroads is protecting her, we have to sever it. Only then will she be vulnerable. Only then can we stop me from turning into a standing stone, and stop whatever is killing those young men."

Alex scowled. "I hate it when you're so logical."

She smirked. "Like you, I've also been thinking this through all day, and

I believe it's our only option. I haven't seen the woman again since the other night. Some of the circus performers have been all through the town this morning, and she wasn't with them—well, not that I saw anyway. Or the American."

Alex sipped his pint thoughtfully. "Dan might be right about Corbin. If we can see he's still doubtful, I'm happy to talk to him. We have to know who the other woman is. I can't believe how many performers there are. It's like looking for a needle in a haystack."

He was right, Avery reflected. The circus was much bigger than she had anticipated, and a very slick affair. "I think he's right about the Raven King and the Green Man too, but how do we recruit them to our side?"

Alex was silent for a moment as their starters were delivered, but as soon as they were alone, he suggested, "What about an invocation?"

"Like summoning a demon or a spirit?"

"They are spirits of a sort, so why not?"

"Wow. I hadn't considered that as an option, but I guess you're right. But, because they're already present at the circus at certain times, wouldn't that mean they are under someone's control?"

Alex groaned with exasperation. "Maybe? We still don't know enough about how this works. But I really don't think you can control them like that. I think they've just been released, you know what I mean, like they have found a way to cross to our world and are tethered to the circus, but are otherwise free to do what they like. Maybe Hecate summoned them." He shrugged and paused to take a few mouthfuls of food and then said, "Rationally, when I think back to that night in the field when we were pursued, it didn't feel threatening, initially. It was disorientating and confusing, but it wasn't until the end when it changed and we felt something else pursuing us. It's a bit jumbled in my mind, but I think that's right."

"I agree, but I think we need to shelve that idea for another time." Avery chinked her glass with Alex's. "Good luck, and be careful."

✝ ✝ ✝

Caspian's manor house was dark except for a few windows on the ground floor through which a subdued yellow light peeked, and subtle garden lights illuminated the drive, shrubs, and specimen trees.

Avery knocked on his front door, feeling nervous for what the night may bring, and her mood wasn't helped when Estelle answered. Her long, dark hair was loose around her shoulders, and her face was pinched with annoyance. She looked disapproving at Avery. "Avery, you'd better come in."

"I better had, unless we want to do this on your lawn."

Estelle just ignored her, leading the way wordlessly into the large reception hall. She turned left down a long corridor and headed to Caspian's study, which Avery knew from her previous visit was at the rear of the house, overlooking a knot garden, which had been there for years but was recently renovated.

Caspian was standing in the middle of the room wearing a black t-shirt and loose black cotton trousers. The room was painted dark moss green, the parts of the wall Avery could see, anyway. The rest was lined with oak bookshelves, and a large desk sat to the side of the room, covered in old leather books. On the opposite wall was a stone fireplace, and a fire blazed within it. The whole place was masculine and expensively furnished.

However, it was the arrangement on the floor that caught Avery's eye. A large map was spread out on a Persian rug, and a salt circle had been drawn around the whole area, leaving plenty of space for people to sit within it.

Caspian was staring at it, and he looked up as they entered, a trace of a smile on his face. "How are you today, Avery?"

"Better, thank you. I've been taking Briar's tonic all day, and with your magic, I feel stronger. How are you?"

"Pretty good, but I can feel the pull of the crossroads, very faintly."

Estelle was dismissive, watching her brother with her arms crossed over her chest. "You're an idiot. It could have affected you, too. It still could."

Caspian didn't even look at her, looking back at the map. "We've been through this. I wasn't about to let Avery die for the sake of father's old grudges. I've moved on, and so should you." He looked up suddenly, flashing her a hard look, before turning to Avery. "I've put this map together from several maps I had. We needed something detailed and big, and this is it. It's the best I could do in the short term. However, I have a feeling we need only concentrate on Scotland."

Avery took her coat off and placed it over the back of a chair, and put her bag next to it, before she joined Caspian. "That makes sense. It seems it's where all this started."

"There was an article on the circus in one of the Sunday papers. Did you see it?"

"No, I don't read them, and besides, I was busy feeling terrible."

"I didn't read it until today. It expands on what Newton told you, and talks about how the circus became so successful."

Avery was intrigued. "Did it give details?"

He shook his head. "Not really. It was a piece about how long the circus has been going, and how they were struggling until Corbin had the brilliant idea to reinvent it after a summer break. He said the history and the wildness of his surroundings inspired him. It mentions Inverness and Loch Ness, but nothing more specific."

Avery stared at the map. "It's a shame we can't narrow it down further. I didn't notice any recognisable landmarks, other than water. It could be the loch or the sea. Inverness is close to both. The only reason I could tell there was water close by was because the moon was reflected in it."

"Excellent. Knowing it's near a body of water will help."

Estelle interrupted. "You don't need to know anymore if you'd both have a little more faith in my spell," she said acerbically. "We can pinpoint the area—if you two can get your part right."

"I think you know better than to doubt my magic, thank you, Estelle," Caspian said dryly.

Avery winced inwardly. There was certainly no sibling affection between them, but maybe that was because she was there, and she knew Estelle didn't like her. That was confirmed when Estelle said, "It's not yours I doubt."

"You should know better than to doubt mine, too," Avery pointed out, resisting the urge to smack Estelle's arrogant face. "But I think it's best we don't look back, don't you?" She was referring to a couple of their previous battles, where she had beaten Estelle, and saved her from attack by the Nephilim when they were still in spirit form.

Estelle chose to ignore her. "We should start to prepare, then. You two sit on the rug, next to the map. I'll get my grimoire."

While Caspian and Avery sat at the base of the map on the soft rug, Estelle collected her grimoire from the table, and sat at right angles to them. "This is a reasonably simple spell," she told them. "We don't need potions or herbs, it's just an incantation. However, we are following your magic, Avery, which means we need a thread of it to follow. And I guess yours too, Caspian, although your connection will be weaker."

Avery frowned. "A thread? How do you mean?"

"The magic you release when you throw energy balls or command air, but rather than releasing it in bulk, we need a tiny part of it."

"It's like when we use witch-flight," Caspian explained. "When I showed you how, we slowed it down. That's what we do now."

Avery nodded. "I know what you mean. What then?"

Estelle huffed, impatient. "You're tethered to a place. That thread will lead us there—in theory. I haven't tried to do anything such as this before. However, I have used a version of this to find lost objects that are closely associated with someone."

Caspian added, "Because my magic is linked to yours, we should have double the magic to find it."

"All you need to do," Estelle said, "is clear your mind, and let the spell do its work. Don't resist it. I'll seal the circle first. You two need to link hands."

Avery shuffled closer to Caspian, until they were both in the same position they had been the previous night, cross-legged and knee to knee, but as Avery reached her hand out, Caspian took her right hand and turned it palm upward. "The mark is still there."

"Unfortunately, yes. It itches sometimes."

Gently, his index finger traced the lines, almost intimately, and Avery was suddenly grateful that Estelle was there, as she subdued a shiver at his touch. She felt the power of his magic again, boosting hers. It was a strange feeling, and one she'd be glad to see the back of. "The mark is unfortunate," he said, softly, "but it will help us tonight."

"Done," Estelle said, satisfied, as Avery felt the circle close. "Now, bring forth your magic."

Caspian cupped his left hand beneath her right one, and Avery cupped his right hand in her left. Within seconds a thin stream of what appeared to be smoke left the centre of Caspian's palm and floated upwards, and it reminded Avery of the cord that linked her to her spirit body. She did the same with her magic, focusing on releasing some into her right palm. Her magic had a similar appearance, but it was golden rather than smoky. It curled in the air as it rose, stopping in her eye line.

Estelle then started the finding spell, her voice low but clear, and Avery's magic started to swirl lazily, drifting across to the map, followed by Caspian's. Avery watched, fascinated as the spool of magical thread uncoiled, still linked to her hand. And then she felt a pull in her stomach, and an image of the crossroads flashed before her eyes. She blinked, suddenly dizzy, and took a deep breath to steady herself.

Caspian murmured, "Don't resist it, Avery. We must follow it."

She nodded, and opened up her mind to the crossroads again, desperately trying to keep anchored in Caspian's study, rather than lose herself at the standing stones. Her magic drifted over the map of Cornwall, and then it was joined by Caspian's, both swirling over White Haven, and then they started to snake their way up the country.

Their threads of magic passed over Bodmin Moor and into Devon, then through Salisbury, across to London, and then northwards, moving back and forth across the country.

"Why is it moving so haphazardly?" Avery asked.

"It's not. It's following the path the circus took," Caspian told her. "See how it's lingering over certain spots where they performed? Places where the boundary magic surged for a brief time."

Avery was impressed with the strength of Estelle's spell. While they watched, Estelle continued to chant, and unbidden the image of the crossroads became stronger in Avery's mind, and she shivered. Caspian's hands gripped hers tighter, sending a pulse of magic her way, and she embraced it hungrily. The farther north they moved, the stronger the image became.

Avery closed her eyes, almost unwillingly, and suddenly she was there, standing at the edge of the crossroads again. She heard Caspian, his voice almost muffled. "I can see it too, Avery, open your eyes."

But Avery's eyelids felt as if they were welded shut, and once again the standing stone glowed, its script pulsing with golden light, and the itch in Avery's palm began to burn.

Then a searing white light flashed into her mind, and Caspian's voice boomed in her head as he commanded, "Avery, open your eyes! Now!" Magic raced through her, and her eyes flew open. She found Caspian staring at her, panic-stricken, and her hands ached through the fierceness of his grip.

"I'm here. It's okay."

"You almost weren't," he said, his voice rough.

Estelle spoke calmly. "It worked. Look." The threads of their magic whirled lazily above a spot in the far north of Scotland. "Don't move." She jumped to her feet, headed to the top of the map, and then crouched, her face close to the surface. "It's by Inverness, a place called Lochend, which is at the end of Loch Ness." She looked smug. "See, I told you it would work."

"How the hell do we get there?" Avery asked, bewildered. "It's so far!"

Caspian looked at her, a smile playing gently across his lips. "You forget I've seen it now, too."

"But how? I don't understand. We're not psychically linked."

"We didn't need to be. The further north you went, the stronger the pull, the stronger the image. And because my magic is linked to yours, and I *am* an elemental Air witch, I saw it too, clearly. Fortunately, I am not anchored there as you are, and could pull back. However," he smiled triumphantly, "I can take us there."

"I'm not sure that's a good idea," Estelle said. "You may be good at witch-flight, Caspian, but it works best when going to a place you know well."

"To a place I've *seen*," he reminded her, finally dropping Avery's hands. "I saw it well enough to take us there, especially now that I know where it is."

Avery hated to agree with Estelle, but... "I think Estelle's right," she said. "Taking me could be a disaster. I only have to creep towards it on a map and I can't think straight. And that's probably where I flew back from the other night. That's why it seemed to take longer than usual, *and* I was nauseous when I arrived. It was pretty scary."

Estelle's superior expression changed. "Wait a minute. How did she get you there?"

"She called me, sort of, in my head. I passed through a gap in the hedge, and I was just there!"

"No sensation of flight?"

"None! I can't explain it."

Estelle frowned, looking interested for the first time all evening. "Fascinating. How did she manage that?" She clearly didn't expect an answer. Instead, she narrowed her eyes at Caspian. "You don't know what links the woman to that place yet. Whatever it is, it's strong, abnormally strong. To break her link, you have to know what it is. If you go there, you need to be fully informed with a clear plan."

Avery eased away from Caspian. "Let's do some more investigating. If Alex and the others have managed to find Corbin tonight, we may be able to discover more. Or they may even have seen the woman again. She must have something that links her to the boundary magic. They might know what that is. In fact," she said, becoming excited, "we may be able to break her link from here, if we can get close enough. We might not need to go there at all!"

"All right," he said crossly, "you win. For now. But I have a feeling we will have to go there regardless. Hecate's magic makes her too strong—you know that better than anyone."

Avery's phone started to ring, and she headed to her bag and grabbed it. It was Alex, and she answered quickly, asking, "Any luck?"

"Yes, we managed to get Corbin alone, and he's willing to talk, tomorrow morning. No, this morning now, at ten. Neutral ground."

"That's fantastic," she said, breathing a sigh of relief. "Where's neutral ground?"

"Old Haven Church."

"Excellent, that's nice and quiet. Any reason he's decided to help?"

"Haven't you heard?" Alex asked, his voice dropping. "There's been another death tonight. They found the body before midnight on the edge of town."

Avery sank into the closest chair, turning to Caspian to find him watching her. She said, "Are all of you okay?"

Alex laughed dryly, "Sort of, but I'm knackered. I'll head to yours, meet you there?"

"Sure, I'll be leaving soon."

She rang off and looked at Caspian. "There's been another death, outside White Haven. But the good news is Corbin has agreed to help. We're meeting him tomorrow at Old Haven Church."

"Good. I'll come, too."

"No, that's a bad idea," Avery told him. "You haven't been to the circus, and no one—as far as we know—knows you. We should keep it that way. You're our secret weapon."

He laughed. "I've never been called that before."

"You may never be called it again, either," Avery said, teasing him.

"All right," he said, softly. "You're welcome to stay here tonight."

Estelle frowned at Caspian, but Avery shook her head, "No, I'll head home, but thank you, both of you, for tonight. We're one step closer to stopping this. Hopefully I won't end up sacrificed to Hecate after all."

Fifteen

A fine drizzle was falling by the time Alex and Avery reached Old Haven Church the next morning, and they ran up the gravel path to the large porch that covered the entrance and sheltered beneath it, waiting for the others to arrive.

After an argument on the phone that morning about who should go and meet Corbin, mainly from Reuben who wanted to meet 'the mad bastard' who had agreed to use crossroads magic, they had finally agreed that for all to show up would be equally mad. The less Corbin knew about them the better, and he had only met Alex the night before. Alex had told Avery how they had waited until the camp had finally fallen silent, and Alex had snuck into his van, using glamour to momentarily silence Corbin while he spoke to him. It seemed Corbin was so shocked about the second death in White Haven that he agreed to help. They had, however, agreed that Shadow should join them. Her knowledge of fey magic might be useful.

Alex leaned against the thick wooden door of the church, looking out at the increasingly heavy rain. "What if he changes his mind?"

"Then we got back to plan B, and try to break whatever links the woman to the crossroads."

"I don't like that option. She seems to have disappeared."

Avery watched the rain spatter off the bare branches and headstones of the dead, and felt the gloomy day lower her spirits. "Well, she can't have gone far. If the second death is caused by whoever is responsible at the circus, and I guess we're waiting to have Newton confirm that, she must be close by, pulling strings."

"At least *you* achieved something last night," he said, watching her. "Even if we never see her again, we know where the crossroads is."

She nodded. "It was a great spell. I was surprised by how accurate it was, and Estelle was a pain, but she helped. But it was also a bit too real, *again*. I don't like how close it is to my reality, and I told you how it affected Caspian, too."

"He'll like that. It makes him feel closer to you."

Alex's voice had an edge to it, and Avery tried not to feel annoyed. If he was linked magically to someone she knew fancied Alex, and didn't particularly hide it, she'd hate it, too. She would be scared she'd lose him. "I don't like it any more than you do, but right now, we couldn't do this without him. In fact, I think I'd be dead. I imagine that woman is feeling pretty damn angry I'm still alive."

"Yes, she is," a deep voice said, making her jump. Avery and Alex raised their hands, and a ball of fire appeared in Alex's palms as Avery summoned what little magic she had available. They hadn't heard Corbin arrive, and he raised his hands as if surrendering. "Sorry. I didn't mean to startle you."

It was the first time that Avery had seen him properly, in daylight, without his costume. He was tall and gaunt, his face long like his limbs, with a thick shock of black hair, greying at the temples, and his eyes were dark, almost black as well. He stared at both of them, taking in their appearance, too.

Alex relaxed his stance, the fire disappearing. "You came. I wasn't sure you would."

Corbin glanced at Alex's hands uneasily as he stepped into the shelter of the porch. "How did you do that?"

"I'm a superhero," Alex answered dryly.

"I mean it. If I'm to trust you, I want to know."

"I need to trust you, too," Alex said. "But I guess you're here. I'm a witch, a good one. And so is Avery, when some bitch isn't messing with her powers."

Corbin swallowed nervously, and despite his height, almost seemed to cower in the corner. "Caitlin is stronger and more dangerous than I realised. I hadn't expected the death toll to be so high."

"Caitlin is the woman who controls the crossroads. The woman with auburn hair?" Alex asked.

Corbin nodded.

"We suspected as much," he said.

Avery subdued a snort. "But you did expect a death toll?"

Corbin glanced at her nervously, and then away, looking out to the graveyard. "Not exactly, but I thought there may be. I guess I willingly misunderstood."

"But you didn't try to stop this sooner!" Avery said, incredulous. "It clearly didn't bother you that much."

Corbin glared at her. "And just who should I ask to stop this madness? Should I have told the police? I would have sounded insane. I had no idea what to do—until now!"

Alex shot her a glance and Avery fell silent, knowing now wasn't the time to antagonise him. Before anyone could say anything else, Shadow appeared at the porch entrance, staring intently at Corbin. "Sorry I'm late to the party."

Alex said, "No, you're just in time. Let's head inside."

Alex unlocked the church door with a spell, and they headed inside, walking to the rear pews to take a seat. Avery shivered. It was colder in here than outside. Corbin folded himself into the narrow pew, looking around nervously. It seemed that even here he was scared.

Alex sat next to Corbin. "We didn't have time to talk last night, not properly. Why don't you tell us how this all started?"

"Last summer, the circus was in trouble. We had returned from Europe with poor sales and little money, despite our performers being excellent. We'd actually cut our tour short because we couldn't afford to keep going.

Unfortunately, we looked tired, and weren't competing, and some people were threatening to leave." He smiled briefly. "Fortunately we've been running for years, and most people are loyal. I'm lucky that they wanted to keep trying. We all agreed that we needed to do something new. And then, Rafe and Mairi, my two newest managers, suggested we go to Scotland. They're originally from there, just outside Inverness. They said the place would inspire us, allow us to rebuild and re-think, so that's what we did."

Alex frowned. "Sounds pretty innocuous."

"It was, and they were right. We stayed outside Inverness. It's beautiful there, close to Loch Ness. It gave us time to think. And then Rafe suggested something else." Corbin shuffled in his seat. "Rafe and Mairi as well as being managers are also investors, and have sank a lot of their money into the circus. They had been with us for only a year, but they were hard working and ambitious, and everyone seemed to like them, but I guess now I can say they were always odd. Anyway, they said they knew of a wise woman who could help the circus. They reassured me, joking almost, about how old magic would make us rich. I admit, I was desperate. We were running out of money, and I was intrigued, so I agreed to meet her." He fell silent for a moment, staring at the back of the pew in front of him. "I could tell Caitlin was unusual from the start. She had a strange intensity—eyes that saw too much, if you know what I mean."

"What did she propose?" Shadow asked.

"She said I should embrace the old ways, the myths and the magic of the wild, and the stories would bring their own reward. We talked about the Raven King and the Green Man, King Arthur, Beowulf, giants, pixies, goblins, elves, so many things, and how a circus based on these would be unique and exciting. I loved it!" He became animated, his voice rising as he looked at them. "I could see it all, and I became excited about our future for the first time in a long time. And then she said that she had ways of allowing the magic of the Otherworld to fuel our performance." He shook his head. "I laughed, initially, not realising she was being literal. She said she could ask at the crossroads for the spirits to join us, and asked if I would give my permission. I thought she was mad, but essentially harmless, so I said yes. Caitlin then explained that she would perform the ritual on the night of the next full moon, and I thought that was that."

Avery looked at Alex and Shadow. "That explains the full moon over the crossroads, then."

Corbin looked confused. "You've been there?"

"Unfortunately, yes." Avery looked at his confused face and sensed he was genuinely shocked. "Don't you know what has happened to me?"

"No, I don't think I do."

"I have been marked for sacrifice to Hecate. I should be dead right now—if it wasn't for my friends."

Corbin blanched. "Hecate? How?"

"I've been linked to one of the standing stones there. It's draining me of my magic."

Corbin looked really uncomfortable now. "I've never been. I stayed away from all that. Only Rafe and Mairi went with her."

"Go on," Alex prompted. "What happened next?"

"I focused on developing the new programme, with other key performers. No one else knew about Caitlin's involvement, just the three of us. Nothing more was said about the full moon ritual, and I forgot about it, almost, and when I did think about it, I thought it was probably some crazy something she did in her back garden. Anyway, two weeks or so later, I felt a change in the camp, the stirrings of something happening, something I couldn't quite place."

"Like what?" Shadow asked. "Or are you in denial again?"

Corbin frowned at her. "I worked out, eventually, that what I felt was the presence of a wild spirit, something bigger than all of us. I called Rafe and Mairi into my office, and asked them what was going on, and they laughed, said the ritual had worked, and wasn't that fantastic? At that point, I knew I'd entered into something I couldn't control, but even then

I had no idea of the extent of it."

"When did you?" Avery asked.

"Not until weeks later. We were ready to start performing by the end of the summer, and our first performances were for the local crowd. From the start we were a huge success, and that first night I experienced the power of the Raven King for the first time. I felt him, actually *felt* him!" Corbin looked at them, wide-eyed with surprise. "I felt him fill me up, take over me, animate my costume...it was subtle, but it was there. And the Green Man was on the grounds, everywhere, every night. I admit, for a while I loved it."

Shadow watched him, her hands in her pockets as she leaned against the pew. "But not anymore?"

"They exhaust me, and I know it sounds odd, but I sense their frustration. They are as tied to us as we are to them."

"Has anyone else noticed?" Avery asked.

He shook his head. "That's the weird thing—no one else seems to notice that anything's going on. Apart from our success, of course. But the supernatural stuff—nothing."

"Did you know Caitlin would be travelling with you?"

"No. It was only when we were ready to leave Inverness that she announced she was coming, too. I was shocked. She's not part of the circus, and I asked why. She said if I wanted to keep our success that she had to, and Rafe and Mairi were keen, so I agreed, and she's been with us ever since."

"Tell us about the deaths," Alex said.

"They started as soon as we left Inverness, but I didn't associate them with us for weeks. It was only when I noticed that Caitlin was behaving more oddly than usual that I asked what was going on, and Rafe told me, but not at first. I had to ask again and again."

Corbin's voice started to rise with panic, and Alex tried to reassure him, keen to keep the story coming, although it seemed to Avery that Corbin wouldn't stop now. He'd had no one to talk to and no one to help him, and now that they were listening, he needed to tell them everything. "It's okay," Alex said. "How odd did Caitlin become?"

"She became short tempered, angry, distant, odd. Other performers started to complain about her. I knew it had to be bad, she kept to herself most of the time, so if others had noticed—" He broke off, his meaning clear. "Her mood could last for weeks, and then she'd be fine again. I threatened to make her leave at one point when she became so bad. I thought to hell with the success, and that's when Rafe told me I couldn't. Caitlin is tied to the heart of the ritual. She's what Hecate wants most. She carries Empusa."

"Who?" Alex and Avery asked in unison.

"Oh, that's bad news," Shadow said, her hands moving to her daggers and resting on the hilts. "You have an Empusa in your company?"

Corbin looked flustered, "You've heard of her?"

"I've heard of *them*. They are shape-shifting females who consume young men. They're a type of Lamia. They're dangerous, violent, slippery, and tricky to kill."

Avery's thoughts reeled. "Are you saying Caitlin is an Empusa?"

Corbin shook his head. "No, she carries one within her. At the moment they are two separate beings, the Empusa within Caitlin's body. She kills through Caitlin, when she needs to feed." He shuddered as if he couldn't believe what he was saying, and then looked at Shadow. "You sound like you think there's more than one."

"There are, where I come from."

"But Rafe describes her as *the* Empusa, and so does Caitlin, as if there's only one. It is Hecate's wish that she becomes real. That's what she demanded for giving us the Raven King and Green Man—what you call Otherworld magic. But I swear I didn't know this for weeks, and there's *nothing* I can do!"

There was more to this, there had to be. Avery asked, "What does Caitlin get out of this?"

"Youth and immortality. She's getting steadily younger, day by day. More youthful, stronger, fitter."

Shadow rolled her eyes. "Longevity is not all it's cracked up to be."

"Says the woman who is a fey immortal," Alex pointed out.

"Not immortal, just long-lived, so I should know, right? It's fine when you're surrounded by others like you, but sucks when you outlive them."

Corbin barked out a laugh. "Try telling her that. I have learned that they—the Empusa and Caitlin—will become one, but something has to happen first."

Avery met Alex's eyes as understanding dawned, but it was Corbin she addressed. "Me dying at the standing stones as a crossroads sacrifice has to happen. No wonder she's angry. I'm the end point of her ritual."

Shadow added, "And that's why we couldn't find her last night, Alex. She was out, hunting."

Corbin took several deep breaths and he started to shake. "I feel sick. Men are dying because of what I agreed to. I've been a fool."

Shadow pulled one of her daggers out of its leather sheath and balanced it with the tip on the end of her finger, effortlessly. "Has your circus been struggling for a while?"

"Yes, actually, how did you know?"

She didn't answer. "And did you find Rafe and Mairi, or did they come to you, like a miracle?"

His shoulders dropped as he saw where she was leading. "They came to me."

Shadow twirled her dagger round her fingers, spinning it so quickly that they all watched, mesmerised, until she caught it in her palm and threw it at an ornately carved wooden column, one of the many running down the sides of the church. The dagger point landed dead centre on the carving of a Green Man. She smiled, satisfied, and then looked at Corbin. "You've been played. They make lots of money—and so do you—and she gets youth and beauty and power. I think this has less to do with what Hecate wants than what Caitlin wants."

Corbin's expression changed from fear to confusion and then rested on anger. "How do I stop them?"

Shadow grinned. "That's better. We break Caitlin's link to the crossroads. Or just kill her, which would solve everything."

Sixteen

"There'll be no more killing!" Alex said, looking at Shadow like she was insane. "This isn't the Wild West."

Shadow walked over to the pillar to retrieve her knife. "I have no idea what the Wild West is, but in my world, that's what we do."

"It's not your world, either! It's ours, and there are consequences to killing."

"There are bigger consequences for her remaining alive and becoming an Empusa," Shadow reasoned. "If she becomes one, she could disappear, change form constantly, and we'd never find her."

Avery was outraged. "And I would be dead! I'd like a solution that doesn't involve my death."

"And so would I, obviously," Alex agreed.

As Avery watched Shadow and Alex arguing about how best to corner Caitlin, she huddled inside her jacket, wishing she'd worn something thicker and warmer, and also wishing she'd had more sleep. She was reluctant to use her warming spell; it seemed an unnecessary use of her power. The rain was heavy, drumming on the roof of the old church, and inside it felt damp and cold. One good thing about the cold was that it kept her awake, but she had a feeling she'd need to sleep that afternoon. All these late nights were catching up with her, and the pull of the standing stone didn't help.

Shadow suggested she was best suited to the job. She stood with her hands on her hips, looking at Alex. "I'm fey, and therefore stronger and faster than you."

"I'm a witch, and therefore better than you at tackling magical enchantments."

Shadow smirked. "That does not wash with me."

Avery held her hand up. "Can I interrupt? Corbin, I have a question. Does Caitlin carry something with her all the time, like a necklace, or a ring, or some kind of object that she has in her pocket? Anything at all that you've noticed seems significant to her?"

Corbin had been leaning back in his pew, looking out of one of the stained glass windows, seemingly miles away, but he turned to her and frowned. His face was grey and lined, and his fear and frustration seemed genuine. Avery hoped they were right to trust him. "She wears an ornate ring on her finger. It looks as if it should interlock with another, if you know what I mean. Anyway, she twirls it constantly. Why?"

"She's not a witch, therefore she doesn't wield magic, and she can't create spells. All of her magic comes from the ritual she performed. So, how can she carry the magic of the crossroads with her? A spell I found suggests there is a way to do it, but it involves two linked objects. That ring could be it. We need to get it off her."

Corbin ran his hand across his face, as if he could wipe his problems away. "I can't believe I've done this. I've been stupid, greedy."

"You wanted to save your circus, it's understandable," Avery said, feeling sorry for him despite her predicament, but not really sure it was that understandable at all.

Shadow wasn't so kind. "Anyone who embarks on a deal that relies on magic—with someone you don't know—is insane. If we can end this, just promise me you won't do this again."

Corbin looked at her, incredulous. "Are you kidding me? Of course I won't."

Shadow pursed her lips. "Avery, do you think removing this ring will stop the magic?"

"It will, in theory, break her link and sever her power. Meaning, she is no longer impervious to our magic. She would no longer carry the Empusa, and it should also break my bond to the stone." She shrugged. "I'm not sure if removing the ring will be enough. We might have to destroy it, somehow."

"I'm not convinced," Shadow said. "I'd still rather kill her."

Alex ignored her. "Corbin, you know Caitlin's routines better than anyone. How do we get to her to get that ring?"

"When she sleeps?" He shrugged. "She watches everything and everyone. I don't know if you can get close to her. Her caravan is next to Rafe and Mairi's, which offers her extra protection, but I don't think she needs it."

Alex considered his suggestion for a moment. "It will be too quiet. If she resists, it could get loud. We'll wake everyone up, people will come running, and Rafe and Mairi will interfere. Is there another time when the camp is otherwise occupied, and the noise will go unnoticed?"

"It would have to be either during the performance or straight after it." Corbin weighed the options. "Probably right at the end. It's chaos. The crowds take a while to leave. Some of them get autographs, then many head to the stalls and games. The team hangs around in the Big Top, just talking through performance issues, tidying up, celebrating, and unwinding. People can hang around in there for a while before they head to the showers. There's no good time, but that's the best."

Alex looked hopeful, finally. "Great. Obviously we'll protect you and anyone else if they get involved, but hopefully that won't be an issue."

"Okay." Corbin paused, looking awkward. "And look, I need to tell you something else."

All three looked at him suspiciously.

"What?" Shadow asked.

"There's been a man hanging around the circus for the last few performances, from about two or three towns ago, wherever we were then. I lose track. I've noticed him because he comes alone."

"Why does that matter?" Alex asked.

"People generally don't come to a circus on their own, repeatedly, and there's something about him I don't like. It's the way he watches us all. He's tall, grey hair, in his forties, wears bike leathers sometimes, other times just jeans and boots. But he's imposing."

Warning bells went off in Avery's head. "I've seen him, too. In the town—twice now. The first time he was watching Caitlin, and the second time, my shop. He's intense looking, but I didn't sense any kind of magic power about him. It has to be the same guy."

"I think he's searching for something," Corbin said. "But don't ask me what."

Alex exchanged a nervous glance with Avery. "Have Rafe and Mairi noticed him? Is he with them?"

"I don't think so. They don't spend as much time in the tent as me, or around the grounds during the performances. They stick to managing the staff."

Avery couldn't believe her ears. She didn't need something else to worry about. "What makes you think he's searching for something?"

"Because he's so relentless. Initially I was worried one of the females had a stalker, but it's not that. I've asked around, just casually, but no one seems to know him."

"Bollocks!" Alex said. "Who the hell is he and what does he want?"

Corbin looked at the floor and then at Alex. "I don't know. I'm starting to feel hemmed in by forces beyond my control."

"This is getting interesting," Shadow said, the only one who looked excited by the news.

Alex looked up at the ceiling as if divine intervention would strike. "I'll update Newton, in case it helps him find out anything about him. Which I doubt."

Avery rose to her feet and started to walk up and down the aisle to warm up. "Great. A mysterious man who could make things worse, and we have no idea how to get that ring from Caitlin. I'm going to pretend that man doesn't exist for now, and think only about her."

Alex sighed. "Can I suggest we get out of this freezing church and regroup later? Then we can think of a plan, which doesn't involve killing someone!" He looked at Shadow pointedly.

"If you have no stomach for it, I'm fine with handling it," she told him.

"I'm not fine with you doing it, either!"

"You aren't my moral protector. This is the way the world works where I come from. Many of us carry weapons—swords, daggers, bows—all the time. This system of *police* you have doesn't exist." She said the word as if it tasted like poison. "We manage things ourselves."

"At some point, you have to learn to live in our world, like it or not." Alex turned back to Corbin, ignoring Shadow's sceptical expression. "How do we keep in touch with you?"

Corbin stood up as he prepared to leave, and fear crept into his eyes again. "You don't. I'll keep in touch with you. I told you, she's uncanny. I feel she sees through me. I'm already worried that if she asks me something, I won't be able to keep my mouth shut."

Alex looked at Avery. "We need a spell, something to help him."

Corbin backed away, alarmed. "No! I've had enough magic!"

As scared as Corbin was, Alex was right, and Avery tried to reassure him. She held her hands up, palms out. "This is only to protect you. A small spell that will seal your lips about this meeting. If she asks you anything, you'll deny it. You'll say you went for a walk."

"In this weather?"

The rain was now falling heavier than ever.

"Say you set out across the fields to the beach, and the rain came in. It's true enough. It wasn't that bad earlier," Avery said. "Did she see you leave?"

"No," he admitted. "She was sleeping heavily. Probably after her feed last night."

"Good. With luck, she's still sleeping. We've only been here for an hour. I have just the spell, unless..." She looked at Alex. "You have one?"

"I do, you should conserve your strength. Corbin?"

His shoulders dropped. "All right, then."

Alex stepped close and began to cast the spell, his fingers weaving shapes in the air. For a second Corbin's eyes glazed, and then he blinked and focussed.

Alex dropped his hands, satisfied, but offered one final word of advice. "Okay. Done. But don't speak of today to anyone. Let her ask if she needs to. Hopefully, she won't. Can you try to call us tonight, just so we can update you?"

"I'll try. If I'm still alive," Corbin said ominously, before heading out the door.

$$+ \quad + \quad +$$

"You were right," Avery told Dan when she returned to the shop at lunchtime, Shadow at her side.

"I was? About what?"

"About Corbin. He did want to help us."

"Really? Go me. I am useful, after all." Dan preened slightly, and was rewarded when Shadow smiled at him.

Shadow said, "I think you're very useful. I wanted to know if you thought I could use this crossroads magic to go home?"

His face fell. "Why are you asking me? I don't know about that, but I'd guess that as a boundary, the lines between our worlds are blurring, enough for your fey magic to cross, but not enough for you." He looked at Avery, throwing her a look that appealed for help. "Am I right?"

Avery tried not to show her impatience, but her tiredness meant she showed it anyway. "Yes. I keep telling you, Shadow, the magic that brought you here opened an actual portal—a real portal, not just a blurring of boundaries and a seep of magic! You know this!"

Shadow glared at her. "But an Empusa has crossed. That suggests it is closer to a portal than not!"

"A Medusa?" Dan asked, horrified. "You two kept that quiet!"

"Not a Medusa, dummy," Avery said. "An Empusa, which according to Madame here, is some kind of Lamia, and a man-eating monster. And it hasn't crossed, like through a portal. It is actually the spirit of one, summoned by Hecate. That's different."

Dan glanced around, checking that no one was close enough to hear this strange conversation. "I've heard of Lamias. You're talking Greek myth now. Give me a moment." He ran to the myth section and darted back within seconds, bringing a selection of books. He selected one and flicked through it until he came to a stop, and then looked at them, grinning. "The Empusa is a servant of Hecate, one of several who are worshipped at crossroads. It's reputed to have a leg of copper, and is a shape-shifting female."

Shadow looked triumphant. "Told you she was a shape-shifter. Never seen one with a leg of copper, though. And we have more than one of them in my world. And," she jabbed a finger at Dan, "I'm not from Greek myth. I think you'll find all creatures belong everywhere. Maybe just their names change sometimes."

"Yes ma'am," Dan said, a new note of admiration in his gaze.

"But that must be what Corbin meant, when he said The Empusa," Avery said, excited. "Maybe she's the mother of all Empusas."

"Well, that does not sound good," Dan declared, turning back to the book. "But maybe I can find out more about it."

"Ask me! I know," Shadow said, joining him behind the counter.

Avery left them talking, and headed to the back room to see Sally. She put the kettle on and said, "Break time."

Sally looked up and smiled, left the computer, and joined her at the table.

"Thank you. How are you bearing up?"

Avery decided to confess. "I'm not, really. I've been sacrificed to Hecate, and my magic is draining away. Every time I close my eyes, I see that damn crossroads. My hand itches where the stupid mark is, and if it weren't for Caspian, I'd be dead by now. I'm exhausted and pissed off, and it's really hard to stay positive right now. And I feel I owe Caspian. I'm not sure I like that, either. Alex certainly doesn't." Now that she'd declared all, she felt tearful.

Sally grabbed her hand. "I'm sorry, Avery. This sucks, and I'm scared for you, too. I think we're all trying to make light of this, because it makes us feel better. But Alex would do anything for you—anything. That includes tolerating you being magically linked to Caspian."

Suddenly Avery realised the root of her fear. "I worry he'll leave me over this. That me and Caspian will end up in some weird relationship."

Sally frowned and squeezed her hand. "Is that what you want?"

"No! Alex and I were talking about moving in together. He suggested it! That's what I want. I don't want Caspian."

Sally smiled softly. "You idiot. Then that's what will happen. Things are scary now because you can't control what's happening. You were taken against your will, your palm marked with fey script, and you doubt your magic for the first time—ever. But don't. You'll work it out. You always do. Tell me what you found out this morning."

Avery relayed their conversation with Corbin, and then said, "So, we have a rough plan. But we need the help of the Raven King and the Green Man, too."

"But the Raven King comes to Corbin, right? He inhabits him, gives him power, isn't that what you said?"

Avery nodded, her thoughts woolly and confused.

"It sounds like Corbin thinks he's powerless, too," Sally went on, "but he's not. He becomes the Raven King—in short bursts, admittedly—and he desperately wants out of this arrangement. If you ask me, you've got some pretty big guns on your side."

As Sally's words registered, Avery started to feel hopeful, and the fog in her brain started to clear. "By the great Goddess. You're a freaking genius, Sally. You and Dan. What would I do without you?"

Sally winked. "You'd have to work a damn sight harder than you do now, that's for sure. Now, get up those stairs, hit those books, and make it work!"

Seventeen

All afternoon Avery worked hard, looking through her grimoires and other books for a way to defeat Caitlin. She eventually fell asleep on her attic sofa, wrapped in a blanket with the cats curled around her, while the fire smouldered and her incense burned. It was the image of the crossroads that woke her.

Once again it was dark and a full moon shone above her, casting its bright white light all around, and throwing shadows on the ground from the standing stones. Three of the stones' scripts glowed with a fiery gold light, except for the one closest to her. It beckoned her, and she felt its insidious pull. She stepped closer and closer, her palm raised, ready to place it on the stone, but the voice in her head was shouting at her to pull away. For a few seconds she couldn't place it, and then realised it was her own voice, from somewhere deep inside, warning her to run.

She dropped her hand, clenched it into a fist, and backed away. She turned, trying to get her bearings, anything that would help pinpoint exactly where she was, but other than the stones and the moors, there was nothing. Surely, she thought, now that they knew it was close to Lochend, it couldn't be hard to find four standing stones in one spot. She took a deep breath, inhaling the smell of something sweet and flowery that merged with the scent of grass and earth.

Drumming started again, a solitary drum that beat slowly, ominously, and the centre of the crossroads became shrouded in mist. She knew what this meant. Caitlin was coming back. She tried to run, but her feet felt as if they were bound to the earth. Caitlin's misty form solidified and she smiled, her eyes filling with a feral glint as she saw Avery. Corbin was right. She looked younger than she had even days before.

She spoke with a low rasp, her Scottish accent hard and accusatory. "I felt you here. It's time. You need to stop resisting. It won't hurt."

She stepped towards Avery.

"No," Avery answered, retreating as her heart thumped and her mouth went dry. "You will not win. I will stop you."

Caitlin threw back her head and laughed, and for a second her features distorted, showing something else beneath the surface of her skin. Something inhuman. "You're too late. And who will rescue you? You're alone."

Avery felt something at her back, something cold and immovable, and she looked around, alarmed to find the standing stone behind her. How had that happened? She had put distance between them.

Once again, everything whirled as she felt her magic drain away.

And then she heard another voice, shouting desperately. Avery, wake up! Something stung her cheek, and she lifted her hand to it, feeling its heat, and then a surge of magic filled her and the last thing she saw was Caitlin's anguished face as she ran at her.

Caspian's pale face was in front of hers, and she felt his hand across her face again, stinging her cheek with a resounding slap.

"Ouch! What the f—"

Caspian looked terrified and appalled all at once. "Sorry, Avery. You wouldn't wake, I shook you, and then I thought slapping you would work."

He sank to the floor as she struggled to sit up, the blanket falling from her shoulders.

"Shit. I was there again. And so was she." She stared at Caspian as the full implications of what had happened hit her. "I could control the pull of the stone for a while, and then she appeared, and I was so disorientated! The stone was right behind me, but I moved away from it, I know I did." She stopped talking, realising she was rambling incoherently, and took several deep breaths. "How are you here? How did you know?"

"Our magic, remember? We're linked, which means I am linked to the crossroads, too. I felt its pull, and I knew you were in trouble. I used witch-flight to get here." He rubbed his face and laughed unexpectedly. "I was in the middle of a meeting and literally ran out of the room. They'll think I'm insane."

Avery's eyes widened with surprise as she noted his smart suit and crisp white shirt. "Oops. Sorry. But thank you, I think you just saved my life—again. I mean, really, thank you. I'm sure this wasn't what you signed up for."

"I knew exactly what I was signing up for, and I'd do it again in a heartbeat." His eyes met hers, holding her gaze for a fraction too long to be comfortable before he stood up, brushing down his trousers and straightening his lapels. She tried to stand too, but her legs felt weak, and he gestured for her to sit again. "Stay there. Do you want some water, tea, whiskey?"

"No, I'm fine. I can get it myself. I just need a minute."

He nodded, his dark eyes unfathomable. "All right, I should probably go. I need to fly back into the bathroom cubicle, like bloody Superman. Let's hope no one else is there."

"Are you sure you have the strength?" she asked him, concerned.

"Yes. The pull was weak for me. Briar has given me tonics too, to bolster my magic. Just promise me you won't go back to sleep again."

"No chance. We're meeting tonight—we have good news about Corbin."

"Great. Seven?"

"Right here. Well, downstairs."

"Later then, Avery," he said softly, before disappearing in a whirl of wind.

Avery's head fell back on the pillow as she contemplated her near miss, and Caspian's undeniable feelings for her. Crap.

✝ ✝ ✝

Alex took a long look at Avery, and then brushed his hand across her cheek. "It still looks red."

"It still hurts. But it saved my life."

"If he touches you again, I'll kill him."

"Alex! Didn't you hear me? He saved my life. *I should be dead!*"

His long, dark hair was pulled back in a half-pony, and his chin and cheeks were grazed with stubble. As usual he wore an old band t-shirt, jeans, and boots. He couldn't be more different from Caspian. His shoulders dropped, and his aggression disappeared as he pulled her close, hugging the breath out of her. "I'm sorry. It should be me saving you, not him." His voice was rough next to her ear.

"You did. You cast the spell that linked our magic." Avery slid her hands around his waist and pulled him closer, savouring his warmth. "If you want to kill anyone, it should be Caitlin."

"True." He released her. "We need to find her tonight. The sooner we end this, the better."

"I don't want to sleep again. Despite Caspian's magic and Briar's tonics, I still succumbed to the magic." They were standing in Avery's kitchen, waiting for everyone else to arrive, and she had just updated Alex on her day. She poured herself a glass of wine, slid a beer towards him, and then leaned against the counter. "Have you had any ideas?"

"Other than isolate her and try to get that ring from her? No."

"I think we'll have to do more than steal it off her."

"We can destroy it. We have spells that will destroy jewellery or melt metal, especially El. It will be easy for her."

"I have a feeling that won't be enough. She told me I was *too late*, when

I told her I'd win. Maybe we are?"

He tried to reassure her. "Then why does she still need you dead, sacrificed? It's not over yet."

The door slammed and they were interrupted by Briar shouting, "We're here."

Avery and Alex headed through to the living area to see Briar had arrived with El and Reuben. Reuben was carrying half a dozen pizza boxes, and the smell of spicy tomatoes, cheese, and meats filled the room.

"That smells amazing," Avery said, pointing at the dining table that was already stacked with plates, knives, and forks. "Drop them there, please."

He grinned. "No problem." Then he paused and frowned. "Avery, you look pale. What's happened?"

She shrugged, self-conscious. "I had another episode this afternoon, but I'm okay."

"No, you're not," Alex said gruffly. "You almost died. Again."

Briar left her bowl of salad on the table, and raced to her side. "How?"

"I dozed off on the sofa upstairs, and well, I ended up at the crossroads. If it wasn't for Caspian, I'd be dead right now."

At that point, the door slammed below them and the chatter of voices announced that Shadow, Newton, and Caspian had arrived at the same time. Caspian appeared at the top of the stairs first, and stopped. "Why are you all looking at me like that?"

"Sorry," Briar said. "We've just found out Avery nearly died and you saved her."

"Ah, that." He looked uncomfortable at the attention, and moved into the room to make way for Shadow and Newton behind him. "That *was* the purpose of our magical link."

Newton looked confused. "What's happened?"

Avery sighed, as uncomfortable to be the centre of attention as Caspian. "Grab pizza, everyone, and we'll fill you in."

For the next few minutes there was a flurry of activity as everyone poured drinks, plated up food, and found seats either around the table or on the sofa. By the time she and Caspian had finished telling everyone about the afternoon, the mood was sombre.

"We can't let this carry on anymore," Reuben declared. "We have to act tonight."

"But are we even close to being ready?" El asked. "Don't get me wrong, we have to do something, but Avery has already told us that magic won't work on Caitlin. What are our options?"

Shadow shrugged. "It's simple. I'll kill her."

Newton looked appalled. "You will not!"

Shadow was unimpressed. "Your laws don't apply to me."

"They bloody well do! I can lock a fey up for murder just as I would anyone."

She smirked. "You could try. Gabe had to use an iron cage to keep me in."

An ugly flush of red started to spread up Newton's neck and his face. "You will not kill anyone. You're in our world now, and I do not condone this."

"That's just what I told her," Alex said.

Briar intervened. "No one condones it. Shadow, we're going to try other options." Then she paused as she looked around. "I presume we have other options."

"Perhaps you should hear what we found out from Corbin first," Shadow suggested. "Our options are small."

Newton jabbed a finger at Shadow. "This is not over!"

She shrugged and reached for another slice of pizza. "Someone update him, please."

"Allow me, Madame," Alex said sarcastically. He started to relay their morning meeting with Corbin, and the energy in the room started to lift, until he mentioned the Empusa.

"A what?" Briar asked, frowning.

"It's a shape-shifting female who likes to feed on young men," Shadow told them. "I've been researching them this afternoon with Dan. I originally thought they were a type of Lamia—we have them in our world, too. But it seems they're sisters...sort of."

El looked baffled. "What's a Lamia?"

"Both the Lamia and the Empusa are either daughters of Hecate or her servants, depending what source you read," Shadow explained. "The Lamia is half-snake, half-woman, and again, she likes devouring young men. The Empusa also takes the form of a beautiful young woman, but she has a copper leg and donkey's leg."

Reuben looked horrified. "Sorry for pointing this out, but a woman with a donkey's leg does not sound that beautiful to me."

Shadow tossed her hair seductively, and a shimmer of sensuality passed over her, making her look dazzlingly beautiful. "She will use her magic, just like this. Her powers to seduce are legendary. You wouldn't even notice. And besides, she shape-shifts. She could look like anything! Even El!" She shook away her glamour, leaving the others momentarily silent.

Reuben looked suspiciously at El, and she shook her head. "Idiot." She turned back to Shadow. "But at the moment she's inside Caitlin?"

"Yes. Some accounts say they followed Hecate from the Underworld. They are commonly called demonic vampires, and both are associated with crossroads. But, like all legends, there are lots of stories and little fact. Most commonly, they are thought to be spirits or wraiths, which also sort of fits, because they came from the Underworld."

Newton groaned. "So Caitlin willingly allowed an Empusa into her? Why?"

Alex laughed, incredulous. "Because it's a sure fire way to achieve youth and immortality. We think that's what this is about—Caitlin's wish for youth. This has nothing to do with Hecate wanting her daughter or servant to walk the Earth."

"Hold on," Newton said, holding up his hand. "So this Caitlin is the woman who you keep seeing, Avery?"

She nodded. "It seems so. I guess you can stop searching to find out who she is."

"How old is she?"

"Well, she looks to be in her thirties now, but Corbin said she was an old, wise woman."

"I guess that fits, then. The only Caitlin I could find was Mairi's great-grandmother, and initially I dismissed her as being too old, but now it makes sense."

"Mairi's great-grandmother?" Avery asked, astonished. "I suppose that also explains the feeling that the spell has gone on a long time, and that the crossroads is sort of timeless. Maybe it was something she once started and had to stop?"

"Well, we may know who she is, but that doesn't help us stop her," Newton said, sighing.

Reuben looked troubled. "So if she's already hunting, and getting younger, why does she need Avery as a sacrifice?"

"To complete the transformation," Caspian said. "At the moment, it inhabits her. I believe she wants to become one with it. Once the final standing stone has an elemental Air witch, she will no longer need the boundary magic. Which brings me to the important question. *How* does she access that power?"

"By a ring she wears," Alex told them. "She must have its counterpart at the crossroads. It would work like the spell that Avery found."

"I've told Avery I can take us to the actual place," Caspian said. "We can try to find the ring there. That would save us from needing to take her on."

Alex glared at him. "No way! It could be a disaster. It's in Scotland, anyway. How are you going to get there?"

"Witch-flight."

Reuben choked on his beer. "Is it even possible to go that far—to a place you haven't seen?"

"Yes! And I have seen it. I got a glimpse of it, from Avery. And she's seen it several times. And that's how Avery got back from there the first and only time she went there!"

Alex was really angry now. "And it made her really sick to travel that far! Are you for real? You know the threat that place poses to Avery. That's where it wants her to be! It's dangerous enough with just a psychic link!"

"I am well aware of that," Caspian said evenly. "I saved her from it this afternoon. But she won't survive another night if she sleeps. Neither my magic nor Briar's tonics are working. The standing stone is too strong. Hecate's magic is too strong. Avery could manage one night without sleep, but two or more? Unlikely."

The room fell silent, broken only by Alex's chair scraping back across the floor as he left the table and paced around the room. "This is shit."

"Just wait," Avery said, desperately trying to calm everyone down. "Corbin is on our side."

"At least someone is," El sighed.

Avery continued, "And so are the Green Man and the Raven King. Both Sally and Dan have pointed out valuable things to me recently, and so did Corbin today. Both the God and the nature spirit have been bound against their will. Corbin knows it! He feels it. During every performance, the Raven King inhabits him and they become one. He feels his frustration and annoyance. Which means, the enemy of our enemy is our friend! They will help us stop Caitlin!"

After a brief silence, in which everyone glanced at each other speculatively, Briar said, "It certainly seems logical, but it also sounds as if Corbin has little control of it. For example, how can he help if he's being the Ring Master? We were thinking of going during the performance. Which doesn't leave us a lot of time, by the way," she said, glancing at her watch. "It's after eight now. Corbin only feels the Raven King during the performance—we think. We need to find out if he can channel him at other times...and if he even likes the idea. And how the hell do we enlist the Green Man?"

"And importantly, how do we isolate Caitlin from the rest of the performers?" El pointed out. "Her gypsy caravan might be at the back of the field, but it's still close to the others. We know that there are always performers around, or their security. They could very well be dragged into this."

Shadow added, "And what about Rafe and Mairi? As far as we know, they're regular human people, but what if they're not? We need to know. Although," she shrugged, "I'm sure I could handle it, anyway."

"Wow," Newton said, aghast. "Your ego knows no bounds!"

"I am fey, that says it all," she declared.

Despite her exhaustion, Avery tried to quash a giggle. That saying would end up on a t-shirt someday soon.

"Have you investigated the other circus members?" Reuben asked Newton.

He nodded. "I haven't mentioned it because we didn't find anything of significance for any of them. They are all exactly who they say they are. We looked into the management again—which includes Rafe and Mairi—particularly closely, but again, nothing. They come from Inverness, they've held management jobs all over the place for years, and as Corbin told you, joined his circus a couple of years ago. Nothing untoward has been associated with them. However, that's not to say that Rafe and Mairi haven't got some kind of magical *something*." He grimaced. "Our investigations don't cover that."

Alex caught Avery's eye. "We have something else to share, too. The man Avery has seen in White Haven, the one outside the shop, has been hanging around the circus, too. Following their tour. Corbin thinks it's suspicious."

"Just great!" Newton said. "I'm doubly worried about him now."

El sighed. "Okay, it seems we're not as ready as we need to be. Which means attacking tonight sounds increasingly stupid. Agreed?"

There was a mumble of grumbling and nods, except from Alex and Caspian, who together said, "What about Avery?"

They looked warily at each other, and then back to the group.

Avery answered, "I agree. It's madness to go tonight. Someone needs to contact Corbin and ask if he can manipulate the Raven King, and prepare him for tomorrow night. And then we need to work on spells, plans, anything to lure Caitlin away. We can try first to disarm her to break her crossroads connection before we have to visit there. But if it fails, I will go with Caspian."

"And what about tonight, Avery?" Alex asked. He had stopped pacing, and instead leaned against the wall, watching her.

She pushed her wine glass aside. "I guess I live on caffeine, find a spell to keep me awake, and then spend all night carrying on the spell searches I started this afternoon. I'm guessing that we'll only get one shot at this before she dives for cover. She's comfortable now. She thinks she holds all the cards—well, other than me frustrating her. Everything else is going to plan. Let's do it right and wait until tomorrow." She looked at Newton. "The death last night? Was that her?"

He nodded and became very official. "It looks like it. Once again, the victim was a young man. There are no obvious causes of death, other than his organs looking withered and older than they should. It's certainly not a normal death. I'm fielding a lot of questions at the station, and have loads of pressure on me to solve this."

"I saw it on the news," El told them, looking grim. "There's a lot of speculation—although of course they didn't mention details. However, they did refer to the caves under West Haven, and the investigation. They are wondering if they're linked."

"Makes sense," Reuben said. "Caves of bones, young men dying, on the back of those gruesome deaths before Christmas. This doesn't make White Haven look good."

"James said he's heard rumblings of concern about black magic from his parishioners," Avery told them. "He said it was only from a few people, but this is a small place. I'm worried it will set off something bigger."

"Like a witch hunt?" Briar asked, eyes-wide.

Reuben groaned. "It's the twenty-first century, Briar. Chill out. If anything, those rumours will make this place more attractive."

"It's not hampering my sales yet," El said.

Briar shuffled uncomfortably. "Nor mine."

"Avery?" Reuben asked.

"No, not mine, either," she admitted. "But it might. Rupert is planning to do ghost tours of White Haven, apparently. That might add a new dimension of interest."

Reuben was still dismissive. "Loads of places do that. And besides, he's an idiot. Let's focus on tomorrow. What can we do to prepare?"

Alex joined them back at the table. "Corbin said he'll call me later. I can update him on our plan, and question him about the Raven King. I'll call you when I know more. He'll be performing now." He looked across to El. "We need spells to destroy jewellery, or magic in jewellery, or anything like that! And say Caitlin turns into the Empusa while we're attacking her. What then? What are its weaknesses?"

At this point, Shadow grinned. "I bet a blade of pure dragonium will do the trick."

"What the hell is that?" Newton asked.

"A very special metal with very special properties, and I happen to know it is the only metal able to slay a Lamia, so it's likely the same will apply here." She stared at Newton, hard. "I presume you have no problem with me slaying the Empusa?"

He squared his shoulders. "Only as last resort."

She raised an eyebrow. "So you're planning on taking an Empusa into custody?"

Newton thumped the table with a clenched fist. "Bollocks! All right, then. Yes!"

"Thank you," she said silkily.

El leaned forward, her eyes alight with curiosity. "You have a sword of pure dragonium? I've never heard of that. Is that something to do with *dragons*?"

"It most certainly is," she replied enigmatically.

"There are dragons in your world?"

"Of course! What a stupid question." Shadow looked incredulous at everyone around the table, as they had all paused mid-bite or mid-drink to look at her, astonished.

El ignored the jibe. "How do you happen to have such a marvellous sword?"

"I made it my business to have one when I discovered how useful they are. It's back at the farmhouse. It gets a bit tricky carrying it around all the time."

"Awesome," El said, clearly excited. "I need to look at that sometime."

Shadow merely shrugged. "Sure, sister."

Wow, Avery thought, *Shadow just kept getting more and more interesting*. She dragged a box of pizza towards her, deciding she needed another slice if she was to keep going all night. "Newton, you know you can't come tomorrow, right?"

He grimaced. "I had a feeling you were going to say that."

"You know the rules. If it's not official police business, you're out."

"And what about you, missy?" he replied. "You're out, too."

Avery bristled. "We'll see about that."

Eighteen

"D o you have a death wish?" Alex asked Avery once the others had left.

"Of course not! But equally I am not about to be left out of the fight."

"If Caitlin sees you tomorrow night, you could end up back at the crossroads in seconds. The real place. And you wouldn't be able to fly back, because you're too weak, and you would be alone. And then dead."

The more Alex talked, the crosser he became, and he glared at her.

She glared right back. "But that's where I need to be. She doesn't know that I know we have to break the crossroads link and sever her power."

"But that supposes that our idea is right. We don't know that for sure, not really. And when you're there, you're automatically weaker. And you won't be with Caspian if you get into trouble."

Avery sighed. "What worries me is that Caspian says he can take us, but what if he's wrong? He's weaker because of his connection to me. And you know how witch-flight works. You need to know a place well—he doesn't, despite everything he's saying. If you can't get close to her to take away the ring, then we *have* to get to that place! *I* have to!"

Alex fell silent, watching her speculatively. "You're saying, the very thing she wants to do will be the very thing that ends this. That it will work against her."

"Yes."

He closed his eyes briefly, and then looked into hers. "Bollocks. It's logical, but risky. Hugely risky!"

"Will you help me to keep awake, and find a spell to locate the ring in that crossroads? And while we're at it, a spell to destroy it or deactivate it?"

"Of course I will." He walked across to her, and pulled her close, nuzzling his lips to her neck. "I'll do anything to keep you alive. I'd go with you too, but I'm pretty sure that's not possible."

"I know you would," she mumbled into his chest. "Thank you."

After one final squeeze, he released her. "Right. An energising tea coming up, and then a spell to keep us both awake."

"No! Just me. You should sleep while you can."

"Nope. We're in this together."

He headed to the kitchen and she went upstairs to her attic. The first thing she did was select incense that would keep them alert. She already had some special mixes prepared, including a few she'd bought from Briar. She found the one she wanted and started it burning in the corner. She said a spell to accompany it, and within a few minutes started to feel their benefit.

She threw a log on the fire, and with a word lit the candles placed around her room. Avery then took a few deep breaths to ground herself, releasing them slowly. *Right*. She was ready for this. *Wait for it, Caitlin. You don't know who you're messing with.*

She pulled her old grimoire towards her and found the spell Helena had shown her that detailed the crossroads link using a talisman. She was still studying it when Alex appeared with their drinks.

"Extra strong," he said, placing it on the table.

She took a sip and sighed with pleasure. "Delicious. Thanks. Right, look at this spell. What we need to work out is how to break the connection. I assume it will be simply a case of finding said talisman and digging it up. Agreed?"

"Agreed. But you'll be too weak to fly back with it, and as long as you're still there, the talisman will still work, so you will need to destroy it." He stared at her. "I still don't like this. What if the standing stone's power saps your will when you arrive? You'll never have a chance to even find the ring."

"One problem at a time. How do I destroy it?"

He thought for a second, and then grinned. "I know what we can use."

She narrowed her eyes at him. "You sound excited. Go on."

"El made a knife that could cut through any metal, remember? It was part of those objects we made for Ben and the others."

Avery nearly spilled her tea with shock. "Of course! I'll ring her."

She grabbed her phone and flicked through to El's number, relieved when El answered quickly, asking Avery, "Are you okay?"

"Fine. Do you remember that knife you made for Ben, the one that cut through any metal? That's what we need to destroy the ring."

El laughed. "Strange you should mention that. Guess what I'm working on right now?"

"You're in your workshop making a knife!"

"Too right. You're not the only one pulling an all-nighter. You'll need a holster for it, but Reuben is on that. It's a long and complicated spell, and I'm annoyed with myself for not making another one straight away, so I'd better get on with it."

She rang off and Avery turned to Alex. "I'm getting a knife!"

"Excellent. Now we have to work out what to do about that standing stone."

"Something to block its pull."

He nodded. "And something to protect you against Hecate's influence." At her obvious confusion, he continued, "Hecate can point you in the right direction, or make you lose your way—Goddess of the Crossroads, remember? If she acts against you, and she might if her plans for her Empusa are thwarted, you need to be able to fight that, too."

Avery nodded. "So I need a spell to see through glamour, to find the true way."

"And wear silver. Lots of it."

Silver had many positive properties. It offered protection from negative energies, stimulated psychic awareness, increased perception, amplified certain gemstones, and was particularly identified with the moon. "Well, that's easy enough. I have a lot of silver jewellery. And I've got the necklace El made for me. Maybe I should pair it with another one, with chalcedony." Chalcedony was a gemstone known for its calming and energising properties, its ability to absorb negative energies, and confer protection from abuse and conflict. Combined with silver, these properties would be multiplied.

"Have you got one?"

Avery pointed to her shelves, which held a small selection of gemstones, not anywhere near as many as El, but she did stock the main ones. "Yep, and I have some silver wire I can bind it in."

"Good. You should wear it now. And," Alex added, "I've decided I'm going to do some scrying tonight."

"On who?" she asked, heading over to grab the gemstone.

"Caitlin."

Avery paused, hand on the basket of stones, all cleansed on the day she had bought them. "Is that wise?"

"Why not? No reason to think she would know. I want to double check that what Corbin says is right. If I can watch her for while, and confirm the ring is the talisman, I'll be much happier."

"Okay." Avery searched the basket for the chalcedony, and found the biggest piece she had. It was coloured a waxy greyish-blue, and was about 3 centimetres in diameter, in a rough, misshapen circle. She warmed it in her palm as she returned to the table. "What are you using to scry?"

"I've brought my silver bowl with me. I'll set up in front of the fire, and turn the lamps off there. The darker the better. I'll do it now, if that's okay?"

She smiled. "Of course. I'll start on a spell to keep us awake first."

He headed over to his bag that was on the floor, crouched down, and pulled out the materials he needed. After a few seconds he called over. "You know, I like this. Not under these current circumstances, but in general."

Avery paused, her hand on her grimoire. "What do you mean?"

"Us, working together on spells in your attic. It feels right. When I move in, this could be our new normal."

Avery felt a warm flush of pleasure race through her. "This *will* be our normal. I like it, too. When's it going to happen?"

"As soon as this crap is over."

She beamed at him. "Good. And you can bring your gorgeous sofa. We'll put mine at your place."

Now he smiled at her. "Really? I do love my sofa."

"Really. And you can put up more shelves for your stuff, over there," she said pointing to a patch of wall. "And whatever else you want to bring, we'll find room for. It will be our home, not just mine."

"You're on. Now get on with your spells," he instructed, blowing her a kiss.

She turned away grinning, determined that Caitlin, Hecate, or a demonic, vampire man-eating Empusa would not stop her domestic bliss. She placed both of her grimoires next to each other on the table, and then scribbled a list on a piece of paper of the things she needed to find. She knew all too well how easy it was to lose track when she started hunting through her spells. They sent her down a rabbit hole.

First was the spell to keep them awake, and she found one quickly. It was a simple incantation that needed something personal from both of them. She took a pair of scissors and snipped some of her hair, and then snipped some of Alex's. She placed the locks in a small metal dish with a simple concoction of dried herbs, and then said the incantation as she burnt them. The acrid fumes filled the air, and Avery wrinkled her face in disgust. *Ugh.* The smell alone was enough to keep her awake. But as the ingredients burnt away to a fine powder, she felt a renewed energy flow through her, and combined with everything else they had set up, she thought she'd be awake for days.

"Wow!" Alex called over. "I can really feel that."

"Good. Me, too. I think we'll crash later, but frankly, that's fine."

He turned back to his preparations, and she returned to her books. She realised that her mind was focusing sharper than it had done in days, and ideas fired quickly. She searched for blocking spells, which were stronger than protection spells, more specific. There were spells to deflect ill-will, curses, and hexes. None of them were specific to her needs, but there were some that could be adapted, and she reminded herself that adapting spells was something she was good at. This was a fact she'd almost forgotten in recent days as her magic had been sapped by the stones. She found a spell that talked about cursed objects and decided that would be her best bet. And then the itch in her palm made her open her hand and stare at the mark again.

The fiery mark beneath her skin was more visible in the low lighting. She had fey script on her hand. *How weird was that?* She wondered what type of stone the standing stone was made of, if even knowing that would help. *Probably not.* And there was no way she could find that out now. And how did *fey script even end up there?* There was so much that she still didn't know about magic. It was this that made it so dangerous, and also so attractive. There was always so much to learn. A lifetime of study couldn't encompass it all.

As Avery stared at the mark, it suddenly seemed incredibly important that she know more about it. She glanced over to where Alex sat cross-legged on the rug in front of the fire. His head was bent over the silver scrying bowl, now filled with water. He was unnaturally still, which meant he was already in his trance.

Grabbing her phone, Avery headed downstairs to the living room to call Shadow. It rang for a while before she finally picked up, and when she answered, Shadow was breathless.

"Avery. Are you all right?"

These were the first words anyone ever said to her now, and it wasn't casual. It was always in a worried, panicked, *has something happened* voice.

"I'm fine," she said, mustering her patience, and reminding herself to be grateful for her friend's concern. "Are you? You sound out of breath."

"I've been fighting with Gabe."

Now Avery was alarmed. "*What*? Why?"

"Sparring with swords. He's insisting on using proper ones, which I told him was hazardous for his health, but he won't listen to me. I've almost taken his life, twice. "

Avery heard Gabe shout in the background. "Once, you liar!"

"And why are you sparring?" Avery asked, as she headed to the kitchen to brew more tea.

"Just making sure I've not grown rusty in the last few weeks." She sounded smug. "I haven't."

"So you're sure you'll need to use it?"

"I hope I will. Anything you need, Avery, or was this just a late night chat? I need to get back to teaching Gabe how to fight."

"I wanted to know what the script on my hand says, exactly."

"I've told you. It means you're sacrificed."

Avery bit back her impatience. "But is that what it *says*? Words mean everything in magic, and they have multiple meanings."

Shadow huffed. "Send me a picture so I can check."

Avery took a photo with her phone and pressed *send*, and there was a pause for a moment.

"It's a word. It looks short, but the translation is 'soul-yoked,' which generally in fey understanding means you're connected until death. That's why I said you were sacrificed. And remember that the stone called to elemental Air as a sacrifice to Hecate. It's not a good word, Avery."

"Okay, thanks Shadow. Good luck with Gabe."

She laughed. "It's not me who'll need the luck."

Avery hung up and walked upstairs with a fresh pot of tea, pondering the meaning of *soul-yoked*. While it might feel ominous to Shadow, she wasn't convinced. She was connected to a standing stone that was dedicated to elemental Air, and that stood on a crossroads dedicated to Hecate. Hecate was a powerful Goddess, and like all Gods served their own purposes before anything. But she was a Goddess known for her love of witches. And Avery was a witch. A powerful witch. If anything, Hecate should do *her* bidding, not Caitlin's.

Alex was still bent over the water in front of the fire, so she took a sip of tea, pulled Helena's grimoire closer, and cast a spell to search for spells that invoked Hecate. The pages ruffled and then started to turn of their own accord, falling still at certain points, which allowed Avery to mark them with paper. When the spell had finished, there were at least a dozen spells to investigate, and like many in Helena's book, they were very old and written with tiny script in arcane language. Fortunately, months of studying them had allowed her to become familiar with the language used, so she could quickly work out which ones were worth investing more time in. After a while, she whispered, "Bingo." *There it is. A spell to invoke the Crossroads Goddess.*

She quickly started to make notes, translating it into modern English, and checking her ingredients on the shelf. At this stage she wasn't sure she wanted to summon Hecate, but she needed options, and this was one of them.

The silence of the room was broken by a log cracking and hissing in the grate, and she walked over and topped it up with another, checking on Alex while she was there. She crouched down and saw that his eyes were transfixed on the water. The round, shallow bowl was about 12 centimetres in diameter, and a ripple continuously passed across the water's surface, which in this light looked black. Avery couldn't see a thing in it. Satisfied that Alex seemed fine, his breathing deep and even, she returned to her list and realised she still hadn't found a blocking spell, but would she need one now? Could she subvert the stone's power and use it for herself?

Ultimately, Avery needed a finding spell, something that would help her locate the talisman buried at the crossroads. She glanced at her watch. It was nearly midnight. She'd better get on with it.

✝ ✝ ✝

Avery was just starting to get worried about Alex when he finally stirred from his trance.

He stretched and rolled his shoulders, blinking to clear his vision, before finally turning to face her. "How long was I gone?"

"Nearly three hours."

"Wow. No wonder I feel stiff."

Avery poured him a glass of water and took it to him. "Did you have any luck?"

"I certainly did." He winced. "Unfortunately, it's more complicated than it looks."

All of Avery's enthusiasm started to fall. "Why?"

"There's more tethered to that crossroads than we thought. But it's okay," he reassured her. "Forewarned is forearmed."

She sat next to him on the rug, holding her hands in front of the fire. "I need to be convinced. Go on."

"I started to watch the whole circus, at first. It took me a while to zero in on Caitlin. It was pretty interesting, eavesdropping on their conversations. There seems to be some dissension in the ranks." He looked at her, one eyebrow raised like Spock.

"Not such happy campers, then? Who causes the problems?"

"Rafe and Mairi. It seems they are getting a little bit too bossy and have been for a while, and they're undermining Corbin. I get the impression most people really like him, especially as he's making the circus so successful, so when they undermine him, it doesn't go down too well."

"They don't think Rafe and Mairi help with the success?"

"They know they do, but because their attitude sucks, they overlook it. And of the few I overheard, no one likes Caitlin. They think she's odd and wish she'd leave."

"Do they notice that she's looking younger?"

He shook his head. "Not that I could tell. Maybe they don't see enough of her."

"If we manage to stop Caitlin—no wait," she corrected herself. "When we stop Caitlin, what will Rafe and Mairi do?"

"That's a good question. Fight? Argue? Run? Who knows! But I do know how she's harnessed the Green Man and the Raven King. She has totems of both of them. A bundle of leaves and wood all bound together, which must represent the Green Man, and a bundle of feathers, claws, and skull of a raven."

"Do you think the same totems are buried at the crossroads?"

"I'm not sure. She never spoke about them. I just saw them in her gypsy caravan. She's got them on a small shelf, laid out a little bit like an altar. And I saw a bit more of the Empusa that lurks within her. She is one scary-looking creature."

Avery was shocked. "How did you see it?"

"In the mirror. Caitlin seemed to call it somehow. As she looked at herself, her features changed. I can understand why it's called a demonic vampire. Its face is barely human; high cheekbones, dark eyes that were all pupils, and big, sharp teeth. I could just see it beneath Caitlin's skin, and for a second, it became clear." He shuddered. "Its shape-shifting ability must be good, because no one would be seduced by that. I can't believe there is something in existence that is both demon and vampire. Just our bloody luck."

Avery frowned. "There are layers to this. It may take more than just finding the other half of the ring to break her link. Do you think Rafe and Mairi are bound to it, too?"

"Not that I could tell."

Avery stared into the flames, pondering the complexity of the situation. "You'd think Mairi would be appalled at her wanting to become an Empusa. I don't get that at all. What does she get out of it?"

"I don't know and I don't care," Alex said. "As long as we stop Caitlin, it doesn't matter."

Avery wasn't convinced. She hated unknowns, and wanted to reduce the variables as much as possible. "Did you see Corbin? Was he safe?"

"I did, and he was. It seems the animosity between Corbin and the other three is simmering, and Corbin is keeping his distance anyway. So far they don't seem to know about our meeting." Alex broke off, looking at his watch. "He never phoned me. I guess it's too late now. Maybe he'll call tomorrow."

"He might think it's safer then, especially if the others sleep in late."

Alex changed the subject. "How have you got on?"

"Good. I have a selection of spells to use, including a finding spell, especially for something underground. It might not be as good as something Estelle would have done, but it should work. And I think I have something that might bring Hecate to my side."

"That sounds dangerous."

"This whole thing is dangerous."

He rose to his feet, pulling her with him. "Come and show me, and then seeing as I'm feeling very alert and energetic, I've thought of other ways to pass the night."

"Alex Bonneville!" Avery exclaimed, pretending to be shocked. "What are you suggesting?"

"Sex. And lot's of it. So let's get this other stuff out of the way quickly."

✝ ✝ ✝

Alex came down to the shop with Avery the next morning, both of them bounding downstairs, full of energy.

Dan was unpacking some new stock on the shop floor, and he eyed them suspiciously. "What's going on? You look surprisingly alert. And you, Avery, are never alert at this hour."

"We've got some pretty hard core spells going on to keep us awake," Avery explained. "As well as energising teas, and incense. I feel wired!"

"And we had hours of sex," Alex told him.

Avery slapped his arm. "Alex!"

"We have sex, Avery. Everyone knows it."

Dan groaned. "Yes, I know it, but I don't need to be reminded of what I'm not having." He rose to his feet, picking the empty box up with him, and headed to the front door. "I'll open up. Why have you pulled a Barry Whiter?"

"A what?" Alex asked.

"An all-nighter."

"Ah, of course. Avery can't sleep or she'll end up back at the crossroads, which strangely is where she now wants to be. So, obviously, I kept her company."

"Like the gentleman you are," Dan acknowledged. "Plotting Caitlin's downfall, I hope."

"Of course, along with other things."

"Enough, thank you!" Avery said, glaring at him.

Alex blew her a kiss and continued. "Anyway Dan, you and Sally have to keep an eye on her today, and make sure she renews that spell to keep her awake. Tonight's the night."

Immediately, Dan stopped joking. "Are you ready? Really ready? I don't want my favourite boss to die."

"We're ready," she reassured him. "Or as ready as we possibly can be."

"So when is it all happening?"

"After tonight's performance, we hope," Alex told him. "I'm waiting to hear from Corbin."

"Anything I can do?" Dan asked.

"Just your usual," Avery said. "And if you think of any useful bit of lore or myth that might help, just say so. And keep the coffee coming."

He saluted her. "Yes, boss."

This was going to be a long day.

+ + +

While Dan and Sally were at lunch later that day, Avery relaxed on the stool behind the counter, reading one of the books Dan had brought in on myths and folklore. Her solitude was disturbed when the bell rang over the door and a man walked in.

But not just any man. It was the American, and Avery felt a tight tangle of worry start in the pit of her stomach.

He stood just inside the entrance and looked around the shop, and for a second he didn't see her, allowing her the time to study him properly. He was tall, lean, and somewhere in his forties, Avery guessed. His hair was dark and shot through with grey, and it was swept back at the temples, revealing a clean-shaven square jaw, and he wore scuffed jeans and a motorbike jacket.

As if he felt her gaze on him, he turned and saw her behind the counter. For a moment he paused, and she had the feeling he was assessing her too, and then he walked over.

"I think it's time we had a chat," he announced.

There was something dangerous about this man. Avery couldn't detect magic, but she was pretty sure he was familiar with it.

"You're probably right. You can start by telling me why you've been watching my shop."

"Because I think you're searching for the same thing that I am."

An Empusa? She doubted that.

"I'm sorry," she said, "you're going to have to enlighten me."

His lips tightened into a thin line. "Playing it like this, are we?"

Avery stood up, shoving the book beneath the counter. She kept her voice low, because she knew there were customers browsing the shelves, but this man was infuriating. "Don't you dare come into my shop and accuse me of playing games, you arrogant prick. What do you want?"

"I want the Ring of Callanish."

"I don't even know what that is!" Even as she said it, she had a horrible feeling she knew exactly what it was.

His eyes were as hard as his voice, and leaned over the counter so that they were almost nose-to-nose. "I think you do, and I think it holds your fate. Want to talk now?"

"You're talking gibberish. Who are you?"

"You know that I'm not talking gibberish, Avery. Can't we be civil?"

Avery was itching to hex him. Her magic was weakened, but she could still do that. However, this was not the time, and she was intrigued. "Civility starts with greetings and introductions. We seem to have skipped that part."

He drew back, but Avery didn't move. "I'm a collector, and I work with other collectors, and we want the ring that's at that circus."

"Name?"

"Harlan Beckett."

"And you know my name how?"

"I asked around. You're very well known. Now, the circus. I know you're investigating there. We can't get to it, but I think you can."

"I beg your pardon? You're still talking in riddles, and I need more than that."

"I am a collector, admittedly of unusual things, and sometimes it's a dangerous job. The woman up there who wields the Ring of Callanish is more dangerous than most. She's summoning things that soon she won't be able to control. But you know that. Do you want to talk now?"

Avery studied him. He seemed serious, and there was an urgency to his tone, a desperation he was trying to hide. Maybe they could help each other. It was worth talking to him, at least.

"Why are you coming to me?" she asked him, softening her voice.

He glanced around at her shop, and then looked out of the window before looking at her again. "White Haven has gained quite a reputation lately, more than it's ever had before. The events at Old Haven Church, The Walk of the Spirits, the latest deaths at West Haven and the caves... We make it our business to follow up on things like that. They led us to you, and some of your friends. I may even be able to help you."

Avery saw a customer heading her way with a couple of books to buy, and she made a decision. She needed to talk to him, it would be stupid not to, but she didn't want him in the back of her shop.

"There's a cafe down the street, Sea Spray Cafe. I'll meet you there in 15 minutes."

Nineteen

When Avery arrived at the cafe, she saw Harlan seated at a table next to the window, and once she'd ordered her coffee, she sat across from him. He'd taken his jacket off, revealing a long-sleeved cotton t-shirt, the sleeves of which he'd pushed up his forearms. They showed a tattooed script that ran up the inside of each arm, but Avery didn't recognise the language. His arms were corded with muscle, and beneath his shirt Avery could see the swell of muscle across his chest and shoulders. This man knew how to fight; she could see it behind his eyes. But at the moment, their predominant emotion was relief.

"I wasn't sure you'd come," he told her.

"I wasn't sure either, but in the end, you had me sufficiently intrigued. So Harlan, tell me more."

"Caitlin Murray has harnessed the power of the Ring of Callanish. She's using its power to summon crossroads magic, and she's left a trail of deaths across the country."

She nodded. "We know that. I didn't, however, know the ring had a name."

His eyes narrowed. "It's the ring I'm interested in the most. We will pay you a good price for it if you'll help us get it."

"Who's *us*?"

"My colleagues. There are a few of us, and we all search for items that have a rich mythical and magical provenance, and sometimes we sell them on."

"Sometimes?" Avery allowed herself a small smile. "I know a black market organisation when I hear one."

"There's nothing black market about it. It's not illegal," and then he paused as he met her eyes, and added, "most of the time. But, I will admit, it's not a regular market."

Avery waited while the waitress placed her coffee in front of her, and then asked, "What's so special about this ring?"

"It conducts magic particularly well. It's been around for centuries, rumoured to have been forged by a sorcerer to enhance his spells. The years have added potency to its myth and power. It's particularly interesting because it breaks into two parts, and she has chosen to use it most effectively. It had been thought to be lost, and then all of sudden—" He spread his hands wide. "It reappears in the hands of Caitlin and the Crossroads Circus."

"Isn't Callanish a famous ring of stones in Scotland?"

"It is."

"Is that what it's named after?"

His eyes were amused as he looked at her. "We think so."

Avery sipped her coffee and asked, "How do you *know* she has that particular ring? She keeps to herself, and barely leaves the grounds."

"A buyer alerted us to the unusual events that have followed the circus. He suggested the ring was the source—it seems he's been looking for it for a long time. I was assigned to find out if that was true, and if so, who uses it." He sighed. "I've studied that circus for weeks. You're right. She keeps to herself, only venturing out at their arrival in each new place, as if she's searching for something. I spotted the ring upon her finger, but have been unable to get any closer. And I admit, I was curious. What is she using such a powerful ring for? And then I found out that White Haven was on their event list, quite a recent change to their schedule. I imagined the circus wanted to take advantage of this place's reputation, too. I followed them here, and watched her do her usual visit to the town on her arrival, but this time her visit was short." He fixed his pale grey eyes on her and drummed his fingers on the table. "She found you, and I wondered what was so special about you."

"Nothing at all," Avery said smoothly.

He shook his head. "I thought we were being honest? You are a witch. I know how to recognise those who wield magic. It's my job to know it. And you're not the only one here, either. I've brought some products from Charming Balms, and jewellery from The Silver Bough. I've studied them carefully. I've been in your shop when you weren't there, and I've had a drink in The Wayward Son. I know magic when I see it. But, it's *you* who she wants."

That was unnerving. She considered denying everything, but it wouldn't achieve much. "You're right. She wants me because I control elemental Air. It seems she needs me, my power."

"To do what?"

"To complete her ritual."

He looked as if he was going to ask more, but instead he said, "So you believe me?"

Avery sat back in her chair and looked out of the window as she considered what he'd said. The ring would explain the potency of the crossroads magic, and when that mixed with the remnants of their magic that still drifted across the town from the events of the previous summer, it would create even more power.

She looked at Harlan to find him watching her. "I believe you. It makes sense. However, we've come up with a plan to stop her, and you won't like it."

"Why?"

"We're going to destroy it."

"Impossible," he said softly. "It's not just any ring, remember?"

"I'm not just anyone, either. I have a weapon that will destroy any metal."

Harlan's eyebrows shot up. "How did you get that? Oh wait, your friend from The Silver Bough?"

"You have been busy."

"I'm thorough. It's my job." He crossed his arms in front of his chest and leaned back too. "But it won't work. The ring is too strong. Sorcerer-made, remember?"

Avery's confidence faltered. "Is that a fact, or a theory?"

"A theory, but a good one. The legends suggest that the sorcerer used crossroads magic himself, that the ring was specifically designed for it, so it is particularly suited to this situation."

"If you think we can't destroy it, how were you planning on stopping her?"

"Well, that's where it gets tricky."

Avery let out a barely there laugh. "You don't know, do you?"

Harlan straightened his shoulders and an edge entered his voice. "Actually, yes I do. If the two halves of the ring are joined back together, it should break the bond with the crossroads, stripping her of her power. However, the particular details of this ring are lost in time, so this is also a theory."

"Didn't you say you did this for a living?"

"Yes. And I'm very good at it. However, Caitlin has thought this through well and is particularly well protected."

"I agree with you there. However, I'm not sure I agree with your ring theory. First you'd have to get it off her finger, second, putting them together could just make one gigantic spell." She frowned at him. "Does this mean you know where the other half of the ring is and can get it?"

He had the grace to look sheepish. "Actually, no. It's in Scotland. I think we both know that. It's where she's from, but we cannot find the crossroads. I have colleagues up there now searching for it, but they've had no luck."

"Are they looking outside Inverness?"

"Yes, along the shores of Loch Ness, and according to the locals there is one there, somewhere, but it's proving impossible to find."

"She must have managed to hide the crossroads, using the magic it generates. Using Hecate."

"Boundary magic," he said.

"I've been there," she confessed, "but it's sort of stuck in a stasis, or at least that's what it felt like."

Harlan leaned across the table. "How have you been there?"

"She took me there, and it wasn't by choice. I escaped by the skin of my teeth."

"How?"

Avery sighed as she weighed her options. She had only just met this man, and here she was sharing things that most people would have her locked up for. But it was clear that he was no ordinary man.

She lowered her voice and answered him with a question. "It doesn't bother you that I'm a witch?"

"I know magic, and I know other witches. No, it doesn't bother me. It's what I do. Not many places, however, have as much magic around the town as here."

"Probably not," she admitted. "We had a *thing* last year."

"A *thing*? Care to elaborate?"

"Not really."

Harlan laughed, and it made him look far less menacing. "Fair enough. But the Green Man is strong here. Your spring has arrived early. And the Raven King is here, too. I can feel him. You have a lot of ravens in town at the moment. That hasn't happened anywhere else I've been."

"I think that's probably to do with the *thing* that happened. It should work to our advantage."

"I presume you won't elaborate."

"I'd rather not."

"You haven't told me how you escaped from the crossroads."

"I flew out of there, on my broomstick."

He laughed loudly. "You have a sense of humour! I like it. But, I think you mean witch-flight."

"You are surprisingly well-informed."

"My job, remember?"

"You seem to know a lot about me. What about you? What's an American doing in England? Not enough myths there?"

"There are plenty there, but it's a long story. I tend to move around." He eased back in his chair. "Where does this leave us, Avery? We both want to stop Caitlin, but we have different ideas of how to do it. And at this moment, you have far more ability to succeed than me. But, I would like that ring."

And that was the rub, Avery thought. She wanted to destroy it, they all did; no good could come of it. *But what if they couldn't? What if he was right?* And even if he was, they'd be better at keeping it safe than giving it to him.

"Say you're right, and we can't destroy the ring. What will you do with it?"

"I have a buyer."

"I'm not sure I like that option. What if your buyer decides to do something equally dangerous with it?"

"I doubt he will. He's a collector. It will probably be displayed in a deep, dark personal vault somewhere. And I'll pay, remember?"

"I don't need your money, Harlan."

Anger flashed behind his eyes. "So, what now?"

Avery's mind raced. She needed to speak to the others. They were going to stop this tonight, and they had a plan...of sorts. If she couldn't destroy the ring, they had to try his suggestion. It might even work. But whatever happened, they certainly didn't want him with them. He had his own interests at heart and would only jeopardise theirs.

"Harlan, it's been good to meet you, but I'm not sure we can help you. I don't think any of us will want that ring going somewhere else, and I will try to destroy it before I try anything else."

He stared at her for a moment and sighed, before sliding a business card across the table. "I appreciate your honesty, and I certainly don't want to antagonise you. But I'll be honest, too. I want that ring, and I will try to get it, so if you won't help me, I'll try another way. You have my number if you change your mind."

And with that he stood, grabbed his jacket, and left.

Twenty

"**W**hat's happened now?" Dan asked when she arrived back in the shop.

"Is it that obvious?"

"That you look annoyed and distracted? Yes. And Sally said you had a mysterious assignation with a strange man."

"I said no such thing!" Sally exclaimed as she joined them. "You're such an exaggerator. But seriously, who was he, and where did you go?"

Avery groaned. "There's a new player in town—the American!"

Dan whistled. "The guy who was watching the shop?"

"The very same! He's a collector of arcane things, and guess what he's here for?"

"Something circusy?" Dan asked suspiciously.

"Too right." She told them about her meeting.

Sally frowned. "So he thinks Caitlin has a powerful ring?"

"Yep. He's seen it, and is convinced that it's the one he wants. And he clearly knows a lot more about us than we do about him. But, we have Newton, and I have his card and his name, so I'm off to make a phone call."

Avery headed to the back room, and stuck some bread in the toaster while she made the call. Newton picked up quickly. "Are you all right?"

"I'm fine. I'm juiced up on spells to keep me awake. Look, I had a strange meeting today. Have you got time to chat?"

"Sure. How strange?"

"I met the American man who's been watching my shop and the circus.

He's called Harlan Beckett, and he works for The Orphic Guild. They collect arcane artefacts for private buyers. He wants Caitlin's ring, which is apparently famous in the paranormal world, but I hadn't heard of it. I wondered if you could find out anything about him?"

"Excellent, no problem. At least we have a name. Did he threaten you?"

Avery thought for a moment as the toaster popped and she buttered her toast. "No, not really. But he made it clear he wanted the ring, and I made it clear he shouldn't have it, so we have opposing agendas."

"Tell me what he looks like."

Avery gave him the best description she could. "We're meeting tonight in the pub, before we go to the circus if you want to join us."

"I've been thinking I should come to the circus with you," he said. She could hear voices in the background, and they went quiet as he seemed to move rooms.

"Are you sure that's a good idea, Newton?"

"No. But I'm coming anyway. Tell Reuben to bring his shotgun and salt shells. See you later."

Despite all their planning, Avery felt increasingly nervous and under-prepared. She carried the plate of toast to the table and sat down, brushing aside boxes of books and incense. There were too many variables—Corbin, boundary magic, Hecate, the Green Man, and the Raven King, trying to isolate Caitlin while keeping the circus safe, and Shadow. She hated to have doubts about her, but they barely knew her. She said she wanted to help, but Avery knew she had her own agenda, too. She wanted to use the boundary magic to get home, even though they had told her it wasn't like the portal that had brought her here. She was headstrong and stubborn. And now there was Harlan who knew far too much about them, and Avery had the sinking suspicion that Shadow's agenda was more closely aligned to his than their own. Hadn't she talked only recently about treasure hunting, and how she used to do that in her own world?

The toast tasted like cardboard, but she forced it down anyway into her churning stomach. What was the matter with her? They could deal with this. They had before. Except, she reminded herself, her own life hadn't been at risk before. Not like this. Not soul-yoked to a mystical standing stone that wanted her essence, her power.

She pressed her palms to her eyes and closed her eyes tightly, and immediately the crossroads was there, eerie under a full moon, the mist writhing across the ground. Shit! Her eyes flew open, and she was relieved to find she was still at the shop. Time to renew her spell and keep herself awake.

Before she could move, her phone rang, vibrating across the table, and she saw Shadow's name light up the screen. Now what?

"Hey Shadow, everything okay?"

"I'm going to head to the circus on my horse, so I'll meet you there," she announced. "Remind me, what time are you going?"

"We'll arrive just before the show ends. The stalls will be open for another hour or so, so we'll blend in with the crowds post-performance."

They had theorised that with the hustle of people leaving, the stalls still full, and the circus performers busy celebrating in the Big Top, that it was the best time to isolate Caitlin.

"Good. I'll text you, but maybe we should meet in the far corner of the castle, under the walls. It will be well away from the main place."

"Where we put the camera? Sure," Avery agreed. "How will you disguise your sword?"

"Fey glamour. It will be sufficient for a few hours."

A horrible suspicion entered Avery's mind. "Any reason you don't want to meet us at the pub?"

"None. I just thought it was a good way to do extra reconnaissance on the way. In the fields behind the circus is where I feel the Green Man the most."

"Okay, we'll see you there. But don't do anything crazy!"

Shadow laughed impatiently. "Course not. Laters."

Avery hung up and looked at the phone for a long moment, perplexed as to how quickly Shadow had picked up English slang and idioms. Maybe it was a fey thing, and her strange magic. Shadow was smart and quick-witted. Not much escaped her. But more importantly, Avery's paranoia was back. Was she imagining things, or did Shadow sound cagey? If Harlan knew about the witches, he must know about Shadow and Gabe. It sounded like he'd been watching them long enough. Had he just made Shadow a better offer? Avery rose to her feet. Well, whatever happened, it was ending tonight, one way or another. Time to renew the energy spell.

✝ ✝ ✝

When Avery joined Dan and Sally back in the shop, she felt freakishly alert again, like she'd had too much caffeine. The spell was effective, but the side effects were unpleasant. Both of them looked at her, worry written all over their faces.

Sally's hands rested on her hips and Avery realised she was about to be lectured. "I think you should delay this again. It's too dangerous."

"It's too dangerous not to!" Avery said softly. She pointed towards the windows and the street beyond. "You've seen what's happening. White Haven is unseasonably warm, and that's because the Green Man is here. Now, don't get me wrong, I love the Green Man, he's a nature spirit and he's doing his thing. But it's not right! It shouldn't be spring now. And there are ravens everywhere, not just at the castle." As if to prove her point, two appeared on the eaves of the shop opposite, cocking their heads to look at her. "They prove the Raven King is here. I can feel the flap of his wings over the town and the castle. They're feeding off our magic, too!"

Dan watched the ravens and then looked at her. "I presumed that was the case. The crossroads magic is mixing with yours."

"Sort of. It's the only explanation. Harlan said this hasn't happened anywhere else—well, not to this extent. And the longer this continues, the stronger it will get." Avery's voice rose with exasperation. "And I can't sleep, or I'll end up at that bloody crossroads. We can't wait."

Sally's shoulders sagged as the reality of the situation hit her, but Dan said, "I looked up that ring, admittedly in the few resources I have on hand, but I found nothing. However, I'm sure you've heard of Callanish and know where it is?"

"I know that it's a ring of stones in Scotland," Avery admitted.

"Callanish is a village in the far north of Scotland, on the Isle of Lewis. It's famous for the standing stones there, which predate Stonehenge by about five hundred years." He showed them the images he'd found on his phone.

"Another group of stones?" Sally exclaimed.

"They're arranged in a circle and a cross, and as usual there are legends associated with them. Nothing about a sorcerer, though. Not that I could find, anyway."

Avery groaned. "Damn it. They're too far north to be where I was, and they look different, but that is interesting. Perhaps the ring was made for that site and Caitlin has made it work for her. After all, a cross within a circle is a sort of crossroads. Thanks Dan, that's good to know. Anyway, I'm going to go and do some restocking, just to keep me busy," and she turned and headed to the back room to collect some stock.

In the end, the afternoon passed all too quickly. As she finished locking up the shop and said goodnight to Dan and Sally, Sally enveloped her in a big hug. "Please don't do anything stupid tonight!"

"Of course not! Have a little faith."

"I have lots of faith," Sally said softly, as she released her from her iron grip. "But I know how you push yourself. Just be careful." Her face was etched in worry.

"I promise I'll be very careful, and you'll see me tomorrow, safe and sound."

Uncharacteristically, Dan hugged her, too. "Yes, please be careful. I'll buy coffee and cakes tomorrow if you make it." He flashed a grin. "Kidding. You will make it. You'd better, I can't put up with Sally alone. Although, there will be more of Sally's delicious cake for me..."

"Dan!" Sally slapped his arm. "You'll be lucky if you get any more of anything from me." She had another long look at Avery. "Okay, I have to go or I'll cry. I'll see you tomorrow."

"Yes, you will," Avery said, resolutely. "And thanks for your help, both of you. You've helped us a lot with your awesome suggestions." She waved them off, locked the door, and headed up to her flat, hoping that wasn't a horrible lie and that she wouldn't die that night. She fed the cats, giving them an extra big fuss, and then headed to the attic to collect all of her prepared gear. While she'd been restocking shelves, she'd used the time to memorise spells, and had written down a few on a piece of paper, just in case her memory failed her.

She dressed all in black—jeans, t-shirt, hoody, and a black leather jacket, and her knee-length, flat-heeled leather boots. She had a small black shoulder pack that she threw a selection of herbs in and another tonic from Briar, and then put some more silver jewellery on. She'd been wearing El's necklace and her own with the chalcedony stone all day. The stones felt warm against her skin, and she'd sensed their protection all day. After taking one last look around the room to ensure she had everything she needed, she headed to The Wayward Son where they were meeting for food and a final debrief, at Reuben's suggestion. He argued that you couldn't work on an empty stomach. No surprise there, Avery thought as she headed out the door. The day Reuben stopped being hungry was a day to really worry.

✛ ✛ ✛

"You met him on your own!" Alex said, appalled. His drink was halfway to his lips, but he slammed it down hard and his beer sloshed over the rim and onto the table. "Bollocks!" Briar threw a handful of paper napkins at him, and grabbing some herself, helped to mop up, while Alex continued to complain. "Why didn't you call me?"

Avery had just updated them on her meeting with Harlan. "I tried and couldn't get through. Besides, it's okay, I'm fine," she tried to reassure him but clearly failed. "I met him in the Sea Spray Cafe, surrounded by pensioners and families."

"Why did he come to you and not one of us?"

"Because he knows that it's me Caitlin wants."

The anxiety levels had already been high when they had all met, and now they were even higher. Caspian had joined their coven, and they were waiting on Newton and their food; as usual, they were sitting in the small room overlooking the courtyard at the back of the pub.

"Bloody hell, Ave," Reuben said. "We were only talking about black market stuff a couple of months ago. Do you think he's after things from us? You know, like the magical items we gave Ben?"

She shook her head. "I doubt it. He's after proper collectors' stuff, old arcane objects with history and provenance. But, I could be wrong. What is really worrying me is why Shadow isn't here. It's suspicious timing. I think she's Harlan's back-up."

All the witches exchanged nervous glances, and Caspian cleared his throat. "You're probably right, which means we have to make a plan to contain both of them, too."

El grimaced. "I'm not so sure. I doubt she'd double-cross us that quickly."

Reuben pointed a finger at her. "You were the one who said she had the bit between her teeth on this treasure hunting business. You can't change your mind now."

"I'm not changing my mind," she explained, "I just don't think she'd betray us—certainly not harm us deliberately."

"But if we stood in her way?" Briar asked. "And we don't know Harlan at all. Who knows what he's capable of?"

Before anyone could continue, Newton arrived and sat in the remaining empty chair. "I take it you've updated them," he said to Avery.

"Yup. That's why everyone looks pissed off."

"Give us some hope," Reuben said. "What did you find on him?"

"Very little. He has no criminal record, and no social media profiles. All I know for sure is that he arrived in the UK ten years ago and lives in London. He pays his bills and his taxes, and owns a motorbike, a Moto Guzzi V7, and a Mercedes SCL300."

"Those are seriously nice toys!" Reuben exclaimed. "He must make good money."

"And the company he works for?" Alex asked. He'd mopped up his spilt beer and had balled the napkins up in a pile.

"It's legit, but very hush-hush. Have you checked the website?"

"I did," Avery admitted. "It says very little. Just a page with the barest of information and an email address. It's all in black and grey with some fancy font."

"What's the name of the company again?" Caspian asked, pulling his phone out, ready to start searching.

Avery checked the business card. "It's called The Orphic Guild. Very mystical."

While Caspian searched, Alex persisted. "It must have an address?"

"Not on the site," Newton told him. "Just an email. I found the address through company records. Again, it's in London. A private residence."

"Is that unusual?" El asked.

Newton shrugged. "It depends on the business, so no, not particularly." He looked around at their disappointed faces. "Sorry. That's all I can give you. Whatever they do, they keep their noses clean."

Before anyone could comment, one of the bar staff came over, bringing their food, and they fell silent for a moment.

As soon as they were alone again, El said, "The dagger's ready, and I think you should carry it, Avery, even though we're hoping you won't need to go to the crossroads. It just means you will have to be close to Caitlin to destroy the ring."

"*If* we can destroy the ring," Avery said, reminding them of Harlan's information.

Newton looked unimpressed. "We still have to try."

Reuben grinned. "Can I start calling you Frodo after this?"

"No. Piss off," Avery said, and threw a chip at him.

He caught it deftly and ate it with a smirk.

"I still think you should keep well away from Caitlin," Alex said.

Avery grimaced. "I'll try, but I'm going, regardless. I have to, I just know it."

El pulled the knife from her bag and slid it across the table. "Here's my labour of love for the last twenty-four hours." It was a steel blade with runes etched down it, and it had a small hilt with a simple design, but as soon as Avery took it from her, she felt its hum of power. El reminded her, "It will pretty much cut through or destroy any metal."

"So we can destroy her ring, either here or at the crossroads."

"Yep, which should break her bond."

"Even though it's the Ring of Callanish?" Reuben asked. "If it's been made by a sorcerer, it may have extra levels of protection."

"It's still metal," El said.

Caspian took the dagger from Avery, examining it with admiration. "Nice job, El. Do you take commissions?"

El's eyes widened with surprise. "Of course. You thinking of anything in particular?"

He ran his finger down the blade. "I have a few ideas. I'll chat to you once all this is over."

"Sure," she said, nodding.

Caspian handed the knife back to Avery. "I feel confident we can get to the crossroads anyway, Avery."

Avery met his gaze. "Unfortunately, I think I'll be there on my own, despite our best intentions."

Alex watched her speculatively and then turned to Caspian. "We think Caitlin will send her there as soon as she can, just like the first time it happened."

"So I'll follow," Caspian reasoned.

Briar grimaced. "And we'll be in a lot of trouble if none of this works, because she'll still have the power of the boundary magic."

"At least I heard from Corbin," Alex said, looking very relieved he'd finally got in touch. "The good news is that he thinks he can call the Raven King even without the circus performance. He sounded nervous, though."

Briar pushed her plate away. "He would be. What if he can't? What if I can't call the Green Man?" Over food, Briar had announced that she thought she had a way to connect to the nature spirit, and use his magic to help them.

"If anyone can, it's you," Avery said. "Earth magic is your thing. You're a green witch, essentially. He should connect with you. And your place, more than anyone else's, has gone mad with spring growth."

As she said it, Avery glanced outside, and noted the climbing plants that clambered up the walls of the courtyard garden were already showing strong green shoots.

Reuben pulled something from his jacket pocket. "This is the holster I found for you. It's a belt that I got from Chi."

"Chihiro from the tattoo place?" Avery asked as she took it from him.

"The very same. She has a thing for knives."

Avery remembered Chi's cool beauty and stunning tattoos. She had an enigmatic edge to her. "That doesn't surprise me. Where does the blade go?"

"In the scabbard at the back. I'll help you fit it when we get there."

Briar picked at her food, deep in thought. "What if Shadow is with

Harlan? What can we do?"

Avery placed her fork down. "Harlan needs us, that's a fact. He can't get to Caitlin. And Shadow does not have the magic we have. I think they'll be opportunistic. If he's there, and I think he will be, he'll bide his time and strike when he see his chance."

"The chance Shadow might create for him," Alex said.

Avery shrugged. "Perhaps."

Newton groaned. "I hate all these variables!'"

"We'll work with what we've got, we always do," Reuben pointed out. He pushed his plate away and checked his watch. "We should get going. Final thoughts, anyone?"

Alex held his fingers up, counting off one by one. "We have the knife to destroy the ring. Corbin to call the Raven King. Briar to bring the Green Man. We've got spells to draw Caitlin away. Shadow has her sword to slay the Empusa. And Harlan bloody Becket, who could well jeopardise everything. Let's go."

Twenty-One

As soon as Avery stepped out of her van into the field below the circus, she felt the Green Man's spirit around her.

She turned to the others. "He feels even stronger tonight. Can you feel him?"

Briar nodded. "The Green Man? Absolutely. He's like a gentle tickle on the senses." She crouched and pressed her hands into the earth, closing her eyes briefly. A spark of light lifted from her fingers and hung in the air, almost like glitter, until it drifted away on the night breeze. She stood and smiled softly. "He's curious about us and our magic. Let's hope it means he'll come more easily to me later."

Avery thought she heard a laugh, a deep throaty chuckle, and her head whipped around, searching the darkness. "Did you hear that?"

All of the witches nodded, and Briar reassured her. "It's okay, it's just him."

Briar sounded so relaxed about it, but it felt odd. It was one thing to know that his spirit was strong, it was quite another to hear him.

"Belt time," Reuben said, pulling it from his pocket and dragging Avery back to practicalities. "It's a horizontal sheath that sits on the small of your back."

He passed it to her and Avery strapped the leather belt in place, along the top of her jeans. The sheath felt comfortable, but Reuben stepped forward and adjusted it slightly, and then taking the knife from El, slid it into place. "Reach your hand behind you. Can you feel the hilt?"

Avery felt the cool metal in her fingers. "Easy. This feels good." She pulled the knife out in one smooth movement.

"Just be careful when you slide it back in. It will take practice to do it quickly," he told her. "And watch your fingers."

She grinned at him. "I feel like an assassin."

"That's worrying."

The others had been watching as they gathered their packs, and Alex said, "Please be careful with that. I've seen you chopping vegetables."

"Thanks for the vote of confidence," she told him, but he just laughed.

Reuben rummaged in the back of the van and pulled out the shotgun. "Here you go, Newton, and some shells." He pushed the box into his free hand and Newton quickly loaded both barrels.

The group headed up the hill, cutting directly across the field to where they could see a break in the hedge, and the edge of the car park. The castle was lit up against the night sky, its golden light a beacon in the darkness, and a short distance away was the roof of the Big Top, the huge circus tent that currently looked like a fairy palace. They were halfway there when they heard a rush of wings, and instinctively they all ducked. The wingspan felt huge, and the wind rolled over them before heading back to the circus.

"The Raven King," Caspian murmured. "Do you think Corbin knows we're here?"

"Let's hope so," Alex said, pushing on.

They could hear the crowd in the tent laughing and cheering, but made their way to the series of stalls. There were a lot of people there, their excitement palpable. Avery glanced up and almost faltered. Above them, perched on the castle walls, were hundreds of ravens. *A Conspiracy, that's what they were called collectively, or an Unkindness. Both ominous words,* Avery reflected.

The witches strolled through the scene, taking their time as they kept watch for anything unusual, but the crowds were excited and noisy. Avery looked for Harlan, but she didn't see him. They passed the small, square space where some of the cast were doing ad hoc performances—fire breathers and jugglers, tumblers, acrobats, and the couple on stilts, dressed as giants. The excitement was infectious, and despite the fight ahead, Avery's spirit lifted.

Within ten minutes the applause from the tent exploded, and whoops and cheers mixed with the tinny music from the stalls. *Time to get in position.* They pushed their way through to the far end, and slipped one by one through a gap between stalls and behind generators, until they reached the empty space beyond. If anything, it seemed too dark after leaving the brightness of the circus. Over to the right, the Big Top was still lit up, and beyond that were the fields of the circus folk. Caitlin's van was at the rear of the final one, close to the hedge and a good distance away from the others. *An easy escape to get out and hunt,* Avery mused.

They headed to the far corner of the castle, well away from everything else, and beneath its thick, crumbling walls and sitting on a tumble of stone, they found Shadow.

"I thought you'd changed your mind," Shadow greeted, rising to her feet. Her huge sword was already in her hand, and her daggers were strapped to her thighs. Avery couldn't help but stare at her imposing stature. Shadow was dressed in a sturdy leather jacket and tight fitting trousers, the breast of the jacket layered like armour. Metal arm guards protected her forearms, and her long hair was tied back into a high pony tail; she looked ready to fight. Avery had a sudden flashback to the Wild Hunt and swallowed her fear.

"We agreed not to be too early," Alex said, ignoring her jibe. "If you'd have come with us, you wouldn't have had to wait."

"I wanted to scope the place out again, get a feel for it. Kailen is no ordinary horse, either. He is sensitive to fey magic, just like me."

Avery looked beyond Shadow. "Where is your horse?"

Shadow gestured behind her. "The far side of the field, out of the way, but he'll come if I need him."

There was no moon tonight; it was obscured by cloud cover, and once again a thick mist was rising. It made it impossible for Avery to see anything. If Harlan were out there, they'd never know. She sent her magic out anyway, hoping to feel something, but she couldn't, and she pulled her concentration back to the others.

"Do you feel fey magic?" Caspian asked Shadow.

She looked disappointed. "Not really. A trace, like a whisper on the wind. But I feel the nature spirit, and the Raven King himself. It's incredible to me that they can't!" She jerked her chin up, in the direction of the crowds.

"It's the nature of magic," Briar told her. "You know that. People will rationalise anything that they don't understand. Make excuses for it. And besides, they use lights and sound to enhance the show, so it's easy to explain away."

Caspian agreed. "True, the non-magical are always willing to look away from the truth of things."

"This is a great philosophical discussion, but now's not the time," Reuben said, rolling his shoulders and neck to loosen up. "Me and El will go and scope out the campsite, makes sure it's as quiet as Corbin says, and then we'll cordon it off. Meet us in five."

"I better get prepared, too," Briar said, and she left the group to stand in the field a short distance away.

Avery watched Briar slip her shoes off, wriggle her feet into the grass, and raise her hands to the sky, silently invoking the spirit of the Green Man, but Avery's attention was pulled back to the conversation when she heard Shadow's raised voice.

"What's going on?" Shadow asked, suspicious. "I thought we were luring her out?"

Alex's eyes were bright. "We're going to throw up a magical wall between Caitlin and the rest of the camp, and then we don't have to lure her anywhere."

Shadow started to look worried. "I thought magic wouldn't work on her?"

"The magic separates the camp, it's not attacking her. And besides, we're going to use it on her anyway. With luck and skill, we'll overwhelm her."

"But you said we had more space out here."

"This seemed simpler," Alex argued. "And besides, you get a chance to use your sword quicker."

"Why's that?"

"You keep reminding us you're fey, so here's your chance. Wield your mighty sword and we'll get the ring off her quickly."

Avery pulled the knife from the holster. "And then I'll use this to destroy it."

Shadow's eyes narrowed. "I preferred the first plan."

"Well, you should have been there for the second discussion, then," Alex said.

It was unlike Shadow to look worried, and it immediately raised Avery's suspicions. Harlan must be out there somewhere. She stared into the darkness again, and then stumbled as she felt a shift in the earth beneath her. Looking around at Briar, she saw that below her feet grass was growing, and Briar's feet were sinking into the earth.

Briar continued to raise her arms to the sky, and then stopped, bending swiftly and pulling bare earth into her hands. Avery's mouth fell open as she watched Briar smear the earth across her brow and down her cheeks, and rub her hands with it. And then astonishingly, Briar's eyes filled with a bright, green glow that pulsed softly and then disappeared. Power swelled in the air around her, and Avery stepped back as magic unfurled across the field. The Green Man had arrived.

Briar lowered her hands and looked across at Avery, but it wasn't the Briar that Avery knew. She spoke, her voice rougher, deeper than usual. "I am ready. I shall call the King." She turned to the campsite and raised her arms again.

Avery was aware that the others had grown quiet behind her, waiting expectantly in the deep, rich silence that had suddenly fallen. A thick wall of mist rolled out between them, the campsite and the stalls a short distance away. The thumps of the music and the shrieks of laughter disappeared, and the lights winked out as the mist grew ever thicker.

Reuben's plan was working. It had been his suggestion to use his magic to manipulate the mist, and it was a good one. But despite all their plans, Avery still felt nervous. She reached into her bag and drank one of Briar's tonics, wincing at its bitterness, and then renewed the spell that kept her awake. Despite it, she could feel that she was tired. Very tired. It was like the false high that caffeine gave, and she knew once the spell was gone she'd feel terrible.

Then Avery felt a shift in the air around them again, and the mist stirred in whirlpools. Alex spoke close to her ear. "It feels like a few nights ago, when we walked across the fields."

Avery nodded. "But much stronger."

Briar walked towards the campsite and they followed her into the mist that hung like a curtain. For a few seconds Avery could see nothing, and then it lifted slightly and the Raven King emerged.

Avery's breath caught in her chest. It was Corbin, but it wasn't. Just as Briar had changed, so had he. He was still dressed in his costume of black feathers, and as he lifted his wings, the mist eddied outwards in ripples. But his face carried an Otherness that was inexplicable. His eyes burned with a fierce orange light that pierced the darkness, and his face was transformed into cold, hard planes, his expression grim.

He waited for Briar to reach him, and then turned and led the way to Caitlin.

Caspian spoke from behind Avery. "I'm not sure we're leading this anymore."

"Quickly, we can't lose them," Alex urged as they picked up their pace and ran after them.

As soon as they entered the campsite, the mist receded, forming a thick wall to their right, and Reuben and El walked out of it, the spell complete.

Caitlin's gypsy caravan stood alone, the hedge behind it. Briar flicked her hand out, and the hedge started to grow higher. A writhing, tangled mass of branches reached out to Caitlin's van, thrusting through its walls, and driving Caitlin from its depths, and right behind her were Rafe and Mairi. While Caitlin exuded confidence, Rafe and Mairi looked worried, and almost cowered behind her, although they lifted their heads in defiance as they tried to hide it.

Caitlin stood at the entrance, the yellow lamplight illuminating her from behind and casting her face in shadow, and she laughed. "So, the Raven King and the Green Man seek to break free! You're both fools. And so are all of you!"

"Are we?" Briar asked. "I am already stronger than you could ever be."

In response, Caitlin pulled two objects out of her pockets, and walked down the short flight of steps to the small fire that burned in front of her van, where her expression could be seen clearly, and so could the rings that glinted on her fingers.

Damn it. Which ring was it?

Caitlin laughed, her voice rough. "You can't hurt me! I have the power of the crossroads!"

"Crap!" Alex said. "She's got the totems."

She made as if to drop the totems in the fire, but Reuben was too quick, and he hurled a powerful shot of water at her. Caitlin reacted quickly, deflecting it with a wave of her hand, but Reuben succeeded in dowsing the fire, and she hissed at him, like a snake. And it was then that Avery realised she was starting to change into the Empusa. The air shimmered around her as her shape began to transform, simultaneously closing her hands around the totems and crushing them. Immediately, Briar and the Raven King fell to their knees.

Caitlin grew taller as her face narrowed, and strong, high cheekbones and a long jaw emerged. Her eyes burned with fire, and as her mouth opened, she revealed sharp teeth like a shark. Her clothes fell away, revealing the glint of armour and the strange copper leg the legends talked of. Avery blinked, barely able to believe her eyes.

Shadow didn't hesitate. She raced forward, her sword drawn, covering the ground between them in seconds, and slashed at the Empusa. In retaliation, the Empusa pulled two swords out, their blades flashing with fire, and struck back. Shadow pulled her dagger free too, and a blur of steel whirled between them.

And then several things happened at once.

Alex raced across the ground, running for the totems that she had tossed to the side, while El ran to join Shadow, her sword burning with its blue flame.

Avery couldn't believe she was still there and not at the crossroads, and she turned, ready to help Briar, but Briar's hands were sunk deep into the earth, and the ground shook beneath her as she pulled power from it. She staggered to her feet and changed form too, her body wreathed in foliage as she grew in size. The hedge suddenly exploded into life, and Alex, who was scrabbling at its base for the totems, disappeared in a mass of branches. The clearing was becoming a wood. Saplings were erupting from the earth around them, rapidly maturing into trees, and branches swept through the air, reaching for them with clawing fingers.

Next to Briar, the Raven King dissolved into hundreds of birds as he scattered across the night, and the area around Caitlin's caravan descended into chaos.

Avery tried to move, but couldn't. She felt her magic draining from her, and she wasn't even doing anything. She couldn't fight at all, and she realised with horrible clarity that Caitlin was drawing on her power now.

Mairi and Rafe looked terrified, and ran from Caitlin as if running for cover, but Newton intercepted them, tackling Rafe to the ground. Mairi screamed and tried to intervene, but Reuben ran to help.

Caspian grabbed Avery's arm. "This is impossible. We need to get to the crossroads."

"But Alex—he's trapped!"

"There's no way we're getting to that ring here. Shadow and El between them can't even get close to her. We have to go!"

"But I can't even move. She's anchored me here." Avery was bewildered. "I thought she'd send me to the crossroads."

Caspian's face was pale. "You're magnifying her link. You're probably of more use to her here than there."

Avery swayed on her feet, suddenly dizzy. "Shit. I think you're right. What about you? Are you connected with her because of me?"

"Not yet, but it's only a matter of time. We're going, now!" He stepped behind her, pulling her close. "Work with me. Close your eyes and see the crossroads."

Avery was trembling with weakness, but she did as she was told and closed her eyes tightly.

Twenty-Two

Avery was at the crossroads. And she was alone. She'd left her friends battling the Empusa, Rafe and Mairi, and she had no idea if she'd ever see them again.

Where is Caspian?

The thick mist had vanished and once again the full moon was overhead. The crossroads waited as if with baited breath. Three of the standing stones were lit up, the fiery gold script speaking of the untold magic of the fey and of the witches whose powers the stones had taken. And the fourth standing stone was silent and grey, waiting for her.

Suddenly, a voice yelled at her, as if it was coming from the depths of a well, and once again she felt a sharp sting on her cheek and she cried out in shock. The voice was louder now. "*Avery! Come back to me!*"

She wrenched her eyes open to see Caspian's panic-stricken face inches from her own. As soon as she opened her eyes, he relaxed. "Sorry, Avery. That was a stupid suggestion, but it did help."

"What's happened? Are we here?"

"You tell me. We'd better be."

Avery felt dizzy and sick, but she forced herself to focus and look around.

They were standing dead centre of the crossroads, but now the stones were sentinel, dark and forbidding. The full moon was still overhead, casting the place in sharp relief, and a gentle breeze carried the scent of honey and pollen. The feeling of stasis was still prevalent there. The moon was like a malevolent eye watching them, and Avery had to remind herself that the moon was also her friend, not just Hecate's.

She sighed with relief. "Yes, this is it."

Caspian exhaled heavily. "Good." He fell to his knees, retching.

Avery dropped next to him, her hand on his back. "What's wrong?"

"Alex was right. That was far harder than I expected. Especially bringing two of us. I'll be okay. Just give me a minute."

She looked deep into his weary eyes, and listened to his laboured breathing. "Liar. This has half-killed you."

He glared at her. "I'll be fine."

"I'm sorry. This is my fault. Look what I've done to you."

"Caitlin, not you. And I volunteered."

She rummaged in her pack, and found Briar's last tonic. "Drink this."

"You'll need it."

"Not as much as you do."

"No," he said stubbornly.

"Take it! Right now you're weaker than I am. Be logical."

She thrust it at him, and he reluctantly took it, knocking it back in one go.

Avery stood up, trying to steady the shaking in her limbs. "I have to act now. I can feel it...the stone is pulling me." She looked at her itching palm, and the glow of the mark became stronger. "Bollocks. I have to find the ring."

Caspian nodded. "I feel it, too. Which stone is it?"

Unlike in her dreams, these didn't glow with a magical light. "I'm not sure."

But even as she spoke, the stone to her right started to glow, the carved script igniting with the fiery light.

Caspian gave a hollow laugh. "That one, I presume."

"Well, it can wait," she answered, desperately trying to ignore its pull. She'd got used to it now. "Move away."

Caspian dragged himself across the ground to the edge of the crossroads, well away from the beckoning stone, and Avery said the spell to find the ring, the spell she'd rehearsed all day.

Nothing happened.

"Damn it!" she shouted into the night.

"You're too weak," Caspian told her.

Avery didn't answer him, instead grounding herself and calling the wind to her, wrapping it close like a blanket. She felt it giving her strength, and she said the spell again, uttering it with conviction as she shaped the necessary signs in the air.

Again, her words tumbled across the moors, meaningless and spent.

Avery struggled to focus, her thoughts jumbled, as the script on the stones virtually ignited. She collapsed to the ground, her body shaking uncontrollably as her magic start to ebb.

"Draw on me!" Caspian shouted. "We're linked. Use it!"

"You're not strong enough!"

Avery looked around her at the stones and faint silver lines of the four roads leading away across the moors, and she felt despair and loss. She would die here, away from Alex, away from her friends, and they would die, too. Caitlin and the Empusa would win, and Hecate would once again have her crossroads sacrifice.

The loud screeching of a bird shattered her reverie, and she jerked around, seeing an enormous raven perched on a standing stone. It looked at her, its head cocked, and its dark eyes reflected the silver of the full moon. It screeched again, burning through her foggy thoughts, and she suddenly remembered all she'd planned that day.

Sacrifice be damned.

Avery was soul-yoked to a stone that channelled fey magic from beyond the boundaries of their world. That magic was now hers. She slipped her boots off and wriggled her feet in the loamy earth of the moor, and then stood on her trembling limbs. The moor started to spin around her, but she threw her arms wide and faced the standing stone, allowing it to feel her soul, opening herself up to its power. The tiny pull she'd felt before became a rope of sinewy magic, as old as the Earth itself. She grabbed it with her mind and pulled it back to her, and it was like flipping a switch. Power flooded into her so quickly that she felt as if she'd dissolved into it. Her feet left the earth and she turned slowly, her hair streaming around her.

This is power! This is magic!

Images flashed through her mind—strange faces and stranger places, beings whose lives were different from her own, from another place and time. The moors seemed to move, the earth rustling as if it was waking, and she heard the drums again, far in the distance.

They didn't frighten her anymore. They were the drums of the fey shaman calling to their Gods, and one of them was already here.

She uttered the spell to summon Hecate. It was time to remind her who she was.

Within seconds there was a rumble of thunder, the earth shook, and the sky ignited with forked lightning. A bright white jagged finger crashed down into the crossroads, and the earth sizzled. Avery could smell the ozone, but she didn't flinch.

A figure rose from the ground, mist-wrapped and wraithlike, until she finally revealed herself. A woman towered over her, regal, imposing, and draped in darkness. Stars whirled around her head, and snakes hissed at her feet. She was ageless—maiden, mother, and crone all at the same time.

"You called me, child?" Her voice was as a soft as a feather and as hard as steel, and the weight of worlds lay within it.

Avery was still hovering in the air, fey magic flooding through her. "Yes! I demand an apology! I have been summoned here as sacrifice to you! How dare you keep me here? I am a witch! I carry your power, as all witches do! Release me from this binding."

Hecate regarded her silently for a moment, her eyes narrowed, and Avery knew she was being judged. "I do not keep you here, nor do I ask for sacrifice. Others act in my name, but it is not of my choosing."

"You promised Caitlin the Empusa! She wields it now. She kills with it."

"The Empusa has always been a difficult servant...wilful, spiteful, eager to dabble in the affairs of men. This place," she gestured around her, "was always her place more than mine. It is the Empusa who controls your fate, not me." She stepped closer to Avery, bringing the scent of decay and earth with her, as well as the stench of death. She looked into her eyes. "Break your bonds, I will not interfere. That which you seek is beneath your feet. You have the power to find it."

Hecate vanished in the blink of an eye, as if she had never been there at all, and relief washed through Avery. She'd been terrified that Hecate would stop her, or try to kill her, but she hadn't. She slowed her breathing, and at the same time eased her grip on the standing stone magic, slowly lowering herself to the earth.

Caspian looked up at her. He was still prostrate on the ground, his face whiter than before. "Well, that was something else."

"Did I imagine that?"

"Nope." He gestured to the centre of the crossroads. "Time to get the ring."

Avery looked down. The fey magic still affected her vision. The earth seemed to shimmer and move, as if there was another Earth just out of sight. She smiled. There probably was, she just couldn't normally see it.

She held her hands out, cupping her palms, and said the spell to find the ring. Within seconds, the earth writhed and buckled, and a small box rocketed upwards, as if it had been spat out. It landed in her outstretched hands and she opened it cautiously. There, on a bed of black velvet, was an elaborately designed silver ring with a deep red stone set within it. Next to it was a bundle of feathers, and a bundle of twigs and leaves. *The totems of the Raven King and the Green Man.*

She grinned at Caspian. "Got them. Shall I destroy it?"

"I think you should try, after all this."

She dropped to her knees, pulled the knife from her belt, and then placed the ring on the grass. She brought the knife down on the ring, gently at first, but nothing happened. Then she raised it above her head and brought it down quickly, stabbing the metal. Sparks flew outwards, sending Avery backwards in shock.

"Damn it!" She looked at Caspian. "Harlan was right."

"It seems the sorcerer knew his stuff."

"We're going to have to go back and get that ring off her finger after all. Are you better?" she asked, concerned.

"I can fight, the tonic has helped, but I can't fly."

A horrible thought struck Avery. "What if the time thing works against us? We could have been gone for hours." Her heart almost stopped. "They could all be dead!"

Caspian rolled to his knees and looked around. "Tricky to say. The boundary magic is making everything weird. But, you have got fey magic, temporarily at least. Use it. Think of the place *and* the time you want to return to."

The screech of the raven shattered the night and sent the sound of the drums fleeing, and at that Avery stood, pulled her boots on, and held her hand out to pull Caspian up. "Time to go. I'm strong enough now to take both of us."

He looked up at her for a moment, his expression deadly serious. "You're extraordinary, do you know that? I don't think you've ever looked more beautiful."

Avery felt incredibly self-conscious, and her voice faltered. "I'm not extraordinary or beautiful. It's the fey magic."

"No, it's not. You always are. I wish I had found you sooner, Avery."

Caspian looked suddenly lost, defeated, and with horrible clarity, Avery realised the depth of his feelings for her.

She started to speak, fumbling for her words, "Caspian, I'm sorry, but—"

"I know. You love Alex."

"I really do." She smiled at him, tears threatening to fall. "But thank you. You're quite extraordinary, too. I couldn't have done this without you."

"We're not done yet." He took her outstretched hand, and she pulled him to his feet.

"True. But when we get back and this is all over, because we *are* going to kick Caitlin's butt, I'm going to find you a girlfriend."

He stood behind her, sliding his arms around her waist, and said softly in her ear, "She won't be you."

"But she'll be amazing. Trust me. I'm a witch."

Twenty-Three

T he fey magic was strong, and Avery and Caspian arrived back in the madness and chaos of the area around Caitlin's gypsy caravan. Caspian reluctantly released her.

The wood that had appeared out of nowhere was thick and rustling with life, and from somewhere in its dark confines, Avery heard the *clang* of steel on steel, and the *zing* of magic and spells. A figure appeared just at the edge of her peripheral vision, and Avery turned, catching the briefest glimpse of a strange, green-skinned, almost ethereal creature before it stepped back into the trunk of tree, disappearing from sight.

Avery blinked, doubting what she'd seen, but this was not the time to think. It was time to act.

She and Caspian ran towards the noise, and it seemed as if they had arrived only minutes after they left.

Reuben and Newton were fighting with Rafe and Mairi, Newton trading punches with Rafe, while Reuben ensnared Mairi with magic. El and Shadow were fighting furiously with the Empusa. Shadow was moving so quickly that Avery could barely follow her, but El ran forward when she could, making quick jabbing thrusts and flinging fireballs at the Empusa when there was no danger of hitting Shadow. Briar and the Raven King were everywhere all at once. Tree roots and branches were tearing through Caitlin's home, and the fire in front of her van had reignited, fed by chunks of wood that fell onto it. Overhead, ravens screeched, wheeling through the branches above them.

Avery left Caspian to help El fight the Empusa and ran to the hedge, just in time to see Alex break free, leaves exploding outwards as he spelled his way out. She launched herself at him, wrapping him in a hug. "You're okay!"

He plucked twigs and leaves from his hair. "I'm fine, if half-crushed by a crazed hedge. What happened to you? You're sort of glowing."

"Am I?" She looked down at herself properly, and saw that she shimmered, as if she was covered in gold dust. She grinned at him. "Fey magic. I'll tell you later. Take this. I found it at the crossroads. It has the ring and the talismans in it. I can't destroy the ring—Harlan was right. We have to take it off her. Can you break her bonds with the Raven King and Green Man?"

He looked bewildered. "Sure, but—" He looked around. "I think they're doing just fine!"

"But they can't attack her. This is as much as they can do. That's why the ravens are overhead."

He nodded. "That makes sense. What are you doing?"

"Getting the ring, of course. Keep that half safe."

Avery ran to where the Empusa was fighting, and skidded to a halt. El and Caspian arrived next to her, breathless. El was exasperated. "Nothing works! I've tried spell after spell, but nothing gets through! If it weren't for Shadow keeping her pre-occupied, we'd all be dead."

Caspian nodded. "I've tried, too. She's impervious."

For a few seconds they watched them fight, and Avery felt breathless just watching. Although Shadow was quick, the Empusa always seemed to have the edge, but Shadow wasn't backing down. Both had cuts to their arms, and the Empusa had a long wound down her side, but it didn't slow her down as she relentlessly advanced on Shadow. In turn, she rolled, slashed and parried, while they both darted around trees and jumped over tree roots.

"I bet she's not impervious to this," Avery said, raising her hands. "Let's see how she likes being on the *punishing* end of boundary magic."

Avery summoned the wild fey magic that still coursed through her, and although it was not as strong as it had been, she sent a tendril of magic across the ground. It writhed over roots until it reached the Empusa's feet, and it started to wrap around them.

Realising what was happening, the Empusa slashed at the magic, slicing through it with ease, but the distraction meant that Shadow could get closer, and the Empusa couldn't fight both, not successfully. With renewed enthusiasm, Avery whipped magic at the Empusa again, and it snagged around her limbs, tangling her feet and arms in bonds she couldn't get to quick enough. With a snap of her fingers, Avery dragged her to the ground, and Shadow kicked the swords from her hands and stood over her, her blade to the Empusa's throat.

Screams and a skirmish behind them made Avery turn briefly to see Reuben and Newton dragging Rafe and Mairi into the small clearing. Both Newton and Rafe were bleeding, but Rafe had a black eye and appeared unconscious. Mairi, mute with anger, was next to him.

As Avery turned back to Shadow and the Empusa, a *boom* resounded across the newly grown wood as Alex broke the bonds tying the Green Man and Raven King. If the wood was impressive before, it was nothing compared to what was happening there now. The trees soared higher, their trunks growing broader, becoming alive with a mysterious Otherness, and already feeling ancient, even though they had appeared only minutes before.

Alex skidded to Avery's side, the box in his hands.

Through the tangled branches, ravens cawed and dived earthwards, until they coalesced in the shape of the Raven King. He brought his own luminescence with him, illuminating the space around him with a soft white light, and throwing the Empusa's figure into sharp relief. He watched her writhing furiously on the ground, his face impassive.

Avery tightened her fingers and the fey magic tightened too, until the

Empusa could barely move, allowing Shadow to stand back, breathless and bleeding, her eyes alive with curiosity.

Corbin had vanished, and in his place stood the Raven King alone. He was taller, his shoulders broader, and he had long black hair, as glossy as a raven's plumage, and shot through with midnight blue. He wore a long black cloak, black clothes, and black boots, his eyes were as dark as night, and his white face was square jawed. A raven perched on his shoulder, rustling his wings and looked around imperiously.

"You desire the ring?" the Raven King asked Shadow, his voice deep and melodious.

Shadow nodded, unusually silent for once.

"Take it."

Shadow leaned forward, stepping on the Empusa's closest hand to keep her immobile, and not knowing which ring to choose, tried to pull them all free, but they were trapped on the larger fingers of the creature, far larger than Caitlin's hands. With a grim smile Shadow raised her sword and brought it down quickly, severing the hand.

The Empusa screamed, and behind her scratchy voice, Avery heard Caitlin's. "Hecate will make you pay for that!"

Avery's voice carried across the rustles and scurries that filled the night. "No, she won't. She told me your deal had nothing to do with her."

Avery felt all heads turn to look at her, but none so swiftly as the Raven King's. His black eyes met hers. "You met her?"

"Briefly."

"You carry fey magic. You finally understand what soul-yoked means."

Avery nodded, feeling the power of his words trembling though her. "I did, finally. Thanks to you."

He looked at Shadow holding the Empusa's hand. "You have the ring?"

Shadow grimaced as she pulled one free. "I do now." She held it up. "Is this it?"

Alex walked over and took it from her, holding it next to the one he held.

"That's the one." He looked around at the others and then hesitantly at the Raven King. "Shall I?"

"Wait. Where's Briar?" Avery said. "She should be here."

"She's here," the Raven King said, gesturing around him. "She's everywhere!"

Alex looked at them hesitantly, and then pushed both rings together. They clicked as they joined, and with it came an audible *snap* as the power of the ring released, throwing them to the ground or crushing them against tree trunks. Alex loosed his grip on the ring in shock and it flew into the air, but Shadow and her lightning-fast reflexes recovered quickly, and she leapt forward and grabbed it, squeezing her palm around it tightly.

With a frustrated scream, the Empusa disappeared, leaving Caitlin in her wake, blood pouring from the end of her arm. Within seconds, her youth ebbed away, and she was left an old woman, her face deeply wrinkled, her hair grey, and her frame withered. Her eyes, however, burned with fierce hatred as she glared at Avery, but if she was going to say anything, it stalled on her lips as the Raven King stood over her.

"What should I do with her?" he asked. "I can take her with me."

Newton looked anguished. At his feet, Rafe and Mairi were bound with magic, lips sealed, but their faces were furious. "I have no idea if I can ever prove what they've done. There's no evidence, nothing that I can hold them with! They could do this again, and more could die."

The King cocked his head, birdlike, as he looked at Caitlin. "Was it all to be young again?"

"You will never know the frustration of age, and the loss of power and beauty. When I found the Ring of Callanish, I saw a way to save myself, and I took it!"

He looked at her with distaste, then turned to Reuben, and pointed to Rafe and Mairi. "Let them speak. I would like to know what they wanted."

Reuben eased his spell, watching them dispassionately.

"Tell me," the King prompted. "What should I do with you?"

Neither answered, their fury burning away into fear as seconds ticked by.

"You're right," the King finally said to Newton. "They will never get the justice they deserve, so I will take them all."

Shadow was trembling, too. "You will take them to the Otherworld? Take me with you! Take me home!"

He shook his head. "I shall take these somewhere far worse. They will go to the Underworld to answer for their crimes."

"But you *could* take me home," she said, almost pleading. "It is within your power."

"Child, your destiny lies here, at least for now. I cannot take you." His voice was gentle, but firm.

She jerked her chin up, eyes flashing, and her hand gripped her sword tightly. "What destiny? You lie!"

"Do not challenge me; it is a fight you shall lose. You must trust me. Your path is long and varied. It is for you to discover."

Shadow fell silent, but Avery saw her swallow and blink, as if to chase away the tears.

He turned to the witches, looking at each one in turn, and dropping his head in acknowledgement. "I thank you for releasing me from my bonds. We may meet again, one day, when the worlds turn and boundaries collide. Until then, some of my friends will stay here, in this place of ancient magic." The raven flew from his shoulder to the tree above them, settling on a branch, as the King dragged Caitlin to her feet, looking more like a bundle of rags than a person. He then marched over to Rafe and Mairi. They cowered, but he didn't care. He swirled his cloak around his shoulders, covering all of them, and then with a rustle of feathers and a snap of air he was gone, taking them with him, and leaving Corbin behind, his body spent as he collapsed on the ground.

Avery ran to his side, and felt for his pulse, relieved to find it was there, unexpectedly steady. Corbin's eyelids fluttered and Avery gripped his hands. "Corbin, wake up! You did it!"

He groaned. "Am I dead?"

Reuben laughed. "No mate, you are most definitely alive."

He struggled to sit up, and he looked around, confused. "Where am I?"

"At the campsite—sort of," Avery said gently. "Do you remember anything?"

"Flashes of things, and *him*, I remember him." His eyes came into sharp focus. "Was it real? Did it work?"

"It did. You saved your circus, and us."

"I did? You'll have to tell me how." And then he fell back on the ground and looked up through the branches to the night sky above.

Avery realised she was shaking, and she sat on the rich soil, feeling Alex's hand grip her nape, and then his warmth as he sat next to her, his arm sliding across her shoulders. He murmured, "What the hell just happened?"

"We have had the most extraordinary moment," Reuben said softly, and he patted Newton on the arm, and pulled El into a hug.

Shadow's voice was almost a whisper. "He left me. I am stuck here!" She couldn't help herself as tears poured down her cheeks. "I could taste home, it was so close."

Caspian did the most unexpected thing. He gathered her into his arms and held her as she shook and trembled. His eyes met Avery's and he smiled, his face full of sorrow.

"Where's Briar?" Newton asked, as he pulled himself together. "She must be here somewhere!"

"I'm here," she called as she emerged from the darkness. Her hair cascaded down her back, and she wore a crown of leaves, a certain wildness emanating from her eyes. "The Green Man has gone."

Newton held the tops of her arms as he examined her. "Are you okay? You look..." He struggled for words. "Different."

She cupped his face in her hands. "I'm not sure I'll ever be the same again. And I don't think you will be, either."

239

"We need a fire," El declared, easing herself out of Reuben's hug. "And I want to sit here while we can, in this amazing wood. Can we?"

"I should think so," Alex answered, "before we have to go back to reality. I'm not even sure what that is anymore."

The fire in front of Caitlin's smashed home was still smouldering, so El reignited it with a word, and they dragged chairs and wood from the remnants and sat around it, the flames throwing shapes onto the wildness of their surroundings.

"What is this place, Briar?" Avery asked. "It can't last, surely?"

Briar laughed. "Oh, I'm afraid it can. This isn't going anywhere!"

"You have got to be kidding!" Reuben said, looking at her as if she'd gone mad. "How do we explain how a bloody great wood grew overnight?"

"We don't." She grinned impishly. "It's nothing to do with us. He called it his gift to us, and White Haven."

"No, no, no!" Newton said, appalled. "This place can't get any weirder! You have to keep the magic here that hides it. It is hidden now, right Reuben?"

Reuben nodded. "Yep, my giant wall of mist is still there. We're hidden for now, but it will be a hell of spell to hide it forever."

Briar's voice was sharp. "It is not meant to be hidden. He said that no one would question it. It would be as if it had been here forever."

There was a universal, "*What?*" expressed by the group.

"It's his magic, not mine," she explained. "I think it was more for you, Shadow, than anyone. To bring you closer to home," she said gently.

Shadow sighed as she stared into the fire. "So be it, then. I will be glad of it. It will be a long life so far from home."

"Have you still got the ring?" Alex asked.

She patted her pocket. "Right here." And then she took a sharp intake of breath. "Harlan! I left him outside by my horse."

"I knew it!" Alex said accusingly. "You double-crossing, fey-blooded—" He spluttered as he tried to find words.

She just looked at him. "I'm here, aren't I? Did I leave you to die at her hands? No. I risked my life for you!"

Avery placed a hand on his arm. "It's true, Alex. Thank you, Shadow. And I'm sorry you're still here, but if I'm honest, I quite like you, and am glad you're staying."

"So am I, sister," El said, winking at her across the fire.

"What are we going to do about Harlan?" Reuben asked. "Shall we go fetch him?"

"I think you should," Newton said, ominously. "I'd like to know more about him. Planning on giving him the ring, Shadow?"

She looked shifty. "Maybe."

"I'd like some assurances, first," Alex said.

Shadow jumped to her feet. "Come on then, Reuben. Let's introduce Harlan to the team."

Newton held his hand out. "Hand it over first."

She glared at him. "Don't trust me?"

"No."

She reluctantly pulled the ring from her pocket and placed it on his palm, before turning her back and marching away.

Twenty-Four

W hen Reuben finally returned with Harlan, he had a wry smile on his face.

"The Green Man has outdone himself!"

"What do you mean?" Alex asked, suspiciously.

"This wood covers the entire field behind this one, right up to the lane that runs across the back. We had a bit of trouble finding Harlan."

"I wondered what was taking you so long," Newton said. He had the shotgun on the ground next to him, in easy reach in case anything else happened, and he still looked on edge.

Shadow was grinning from ear to ear. "It's amazing. It's like the woods from home! It's tangled and ancient and mysterious and I love it!"

Harlan, however, looked in shock as he stepped into their circle. "This is quite some trick you've pulled off."

"It ain't no trick," Reuben drawled as he pointed to a salvaged bench. "Take a seat." He quickly made introductions as they settled themselves down.

"Hi, Harlan," Avery said, with a mischievous smile. "Fancy meeting you again."

"Yes, fancy that. You're very resourceful."

"I know."

He leaned forward to rub his hands over the fire. "It's cold out there. How have you managed all of this?" He lifted his chin to indicate the trees around them.

"We didn't, the Green Man did," Briar told him.

For a moment Harlan didn't answer as he looked at them all, examining each face as though to memorise them. He stared a little longer at Corbin in his Raven King costume. "I've seen many strange things in my life, but nothing as strange as this."

Newton frowned. "What *did* you see? We've received reassurances that no one would notice—incredible though that sounds. And yet, you have."

"I was at the edge of the field, on Shadow's horse, when I saw the mist thicken until I couldn't see a thing. And then all of a sudden, I was surrounded by an ancient forest. It just appeared—literally in the blink of an eye. It gave me quite a shock, but the horse was completely fine with it."

"That's because he's from the Otherworld," Shadow explained. "He has his own magic, like me. That's why you remember it happening." She shrugged. "At least I think so. Otherwise, the Green Man is wrong and there'll be a lot of questions tomorrow."

"Makes sense," Caspian said, nodding. He narrowed his eyes at Harlan. "Avery and Shadow tell us that you want that ring. We need some assurances first. Who are you, and what will you do with it?"

"And make it good," Newton added. "Or it stays with me."

"I work for The Orphic Guild. We acquire unusual things for buyers for their private collections. Sometimes these objects have magical or mythical histories, sometimes not. And that's it. It's nothing dodgy. You can look it up. We have a website and contact numbers."

Newton leaned forward, his arms on his knees. "I did. It tells me very little."

Harlan's expression was as steely as Newton's. "We like to keep things private, that's why. Our clients pay a lot for our services and discretion."

"Will someone be paying a lot for this?" Newton laid the ring on the palm of his hand.

"Yes. It will be placed somewhere as an object of art, for appreciation only."

Newton snorted. "I doubt that."

Harlan straightened his shoulders. "Have you ever found anything of a criminal nature about us?"

"No. And believe me, I checked. You haven't even had a parking ticket."

Harlan smiled tightly. "Well, there you go then."

Avery watched Harlan carefully. He had recovered his composure, but he still looked wary, glancing nervously over his shoulder from time to time. She couldn't blame him. She was doing the same herself, they all were. There were strange rustlings from behind them, and the feeling that something was watching them, something maybe like the strange, green-skinned creature she had seen so briefly before it vanished into the tree. The feeling of age that came from these trees was unnatural, as if it had not just grown there, but had been pulled from somewhere else.

Perhaps the firelight was playing tricks on her. It cast the branches' shadows into strange, contorted shapes, and the rich smell of loam beneath their feet was heady, making her almost giddy, but maybe that was just tiredness as the events caught up with her.

Newton's voice was sharp, and she focused on the conversation again. "What's your role in this, Shadow?"

"Are you interrogating me?" she asked, her hand on her sword hilt.

"Yes," he said bluntly.

She scowled at him like a child. "I'm stuck here, and I need to make a life, and money. Harlan offered me a finder's fee for my help when Avery refused."

Newton looked between Shadow and Harlan. "And how did you two become acquainted?"

Harlan answered. "I make it my business to know about unusual things and places. This town has been on my radar for a while, and *she* is noticeable."

Shadow smirked. "I am fey."

"I think we know," Alex said, wearily.

Newton ignored her, focusing on Harlan. "Who's your buyer for this?"

"I can't tell you that, but I can tell you that it will be far safer with the buyer than anywhere else."

Newton looked at the other witches. "What do you think?"

"It caused a lot of trouble," Caspian said, taking it from Newton and holding it close to the firelight. "It seems so innocuous now, if it weren't for the power it exudes." He looked at Harlan. "How old is it?"

"It was made sometime in the twelfth century. It's impossible to say exactly when."

"And the sorcerer's name?"

Harlan rubbed his jaw and looked up at the sky before saying, "It escapes me right now."

"Of course it does," Caspian said.

"May I?" El asked. Caspian passed it to her, and she examined it. "It's been made with great skill. The design is intricate and unusual, and the metal feels different."

"Your knife wouldn't work on it," Avery told her.

El's head jerked up. "Really? Damn it. I thought I'd covered everything."

Harlan's tone was even, but impatience was creeping in. "Like I said, it's very special."

Newton persisted. "Are you sure it won't be used again?"

"As sure as I can be." Harlan looked at his watch. "It's late, and I need to go. The ring?" He held his hand out.

Newton nodded, and El placed it on his palm. Harlan immediately put it into a small box he pulled from an inside pocket and tucked it away safely. "Excellent, and now I must leave. Shadow, will you escort me?"

Shadow had spent the last few minutes polishing her sword and cleaning the blood from it, and she slid it into her scabbard, and then picked up one of the Empusa's swords that lay at her feet. She examined its finely wrought blade and unusual hilt. "This is made of bronze. I'll take these if no one has any objections?"

El reached forward and picked the other one up, running her finger down its blade. "Actually, I'd like one. Don't ask me why, but I'd feel happier if they were separated."

Shadow looked as if she might complain, but then she rose to her feet. "You might be right."

Harlan's stared at the one that Shadow held, but he didn't say a word, and Avery wondered if another transaction was about to take place. He stood and made a short bow. "I'm sure we'll meet again sometime. Meanwhile, it's been a pleasure."

Shadow merely smiled enigmatically as she led him away.

Reuben waited a few moments until he was sure they had left. "Is it me, or have we just witnessed the start of an unholy relationship?"

Caspian picked up a stick and poked the fire. "She needs something. She's stuck here, and it might be just what she's looking for."

"I'm just glad it's all over for now," Newton said. "I'll worry about it another time. Are you all right, Corbin?"

Corbin had sat quietly for a long time, staring almost vacantly into the fire. Avery had almost forgotten he was there. He'd edged back from the others, and his cloak of feathers was pulled closely around him. He dragged his gaze from the fire. "It's been a long night. It's been a long few months, actually. A nightmare."

Briar patted his arm. "You have your circus back now, and memories to last a lifetime."

"How do I move on from this? I feel...*different*."

"That's magic for you. And you did become the Raven King," she pointed out. "That's something to treasure, surely?"

"But what about my circus?" His eyes were wild. "Will it be as successful without magic? How do I explain Rafe and Mairi just disappearing? And this forest! We're so close—what if they noticed something?"

"We'll see soon enough," Alex said. "In the meantime, let's enjoy the peace and quiet, and I'd like to know what happened at the crossroads."

He nudged Avery with his shoulder. "Fey magic?"

Avery laughed. "Things got very weird."

"I admit, it was bit strange there for a while," Caspian said, leaning back in the old deckchair he'd found. "You tell them what happened, Avery. I was a mere spectator!"

"Not true," she remonstrated. "But I'll start."

Between them they told the others about Hecate and the standing stones, and then Briar talked about her experience with the Green Man, but it wasn't long before Avery's head started to nod.

"You're tired. We need to go home," Alex said.

Reuben jumped to his feet. "Bed sounds good. Let's get rid of my magic wall of mist and we'll see what's happening out there. Give me a moment." He disappeared into the trees and within minutes they heard shouts, laughter, and music. Lights appeared at the edge of the wood as the campsite reappeared. There was a gap where Rafe and Mairi's van had been parked a few meters away from Caitlin's destroyed van, but Corbin's was still there, looking completely untouched.

Corbin walked away from the fire as Alex quickly doused it. "Their van! Where is it?"

"All gone! Maybe you won't have much explaining to do after all," El said.

One of the performers walked towards Corbin, the greasepaint now wiped from his face. "Corbin! There you are. We've been looking for you. It was another good night. Are you coming for a drink?" He looked beyond him. "Who are your friends?"

"Just some locals, they're heading home now," Corbin explained, and he raised his hand to them. "I'll see you soon."

They watched him leave, and it was clear the performer had no concerns about the wood that had suddenly materialised.

"That answers that, then," Reuben noted, and he slung his arms around El's shoulders as he led the way across the castle grounds.

Twenty-Five

The following day, the five White Haven witches met in the early afternoon in front of Hawk House, El's old family home, and they walked to the edge of the hill to look down on the castle and the circus.

Alex let out a short laugh. "Look at the size of that!"

"I don't think I'm ever going to get used to it," El said, as they stared at the newly created wood below them.

Reuben whistled. "That is quite unexpected. It's bigger than I thought."

The wood stretched from the back of the campsite, starting more or less by the hedge, cutting over the corner where Caitlin's van had been, and spread to the entire field beyond it. It finally stopped at the roads that bordered it to the top and the side, and ran to the cliff's edge on the other end. Most of the castle was unaffected, other than the remnants of the wall at the rear corner.

"Unbelievable," Avery said, taking it all in. "If you hadn't had your magic wall of mist up, sealing the area off, it might have spread the other way, too, Reuben."

"Maybe. I did have to work really hard to keep it going once the Green Man did his thing."

They all watched Briar, who stood quietly taking in the scene below her.

"Are you okay?" El asked her.

She nodded and finally looked at them, her eyes haunted. "I'm fine. I think I have a Green Man hangover. I've barely slept, even though I'm exhausted. I had the weirdest dreams."

"Like what?" Avery asked.

"I was still in the wood, and I saw strange things—dryads, satyrs, sprites, and other things I can't explain. Maybe it was like when you kept seeing the crossroads, Avery?"

Avery nodded. "Maybe. Although, I'm glad to say that did not happen for me last night, and I slept like the dead."

"Is the mark still on your hand?" El asked.

"All gone," she said, showing them her unmarked palm. "Which is quite a relief. I thought being soul-yoked might mean forever."

"Come on," Reuben prompted them. "I want to get down there and walk in it."

Fifteen minutes later, after they had navigated the lanes, they pulled up next to a gate in the hedge and walked into the newly formed ancient woodland. As soon as they were beneath its broad branches, a deep, dreamy silence enveloped them, broken only by birdsong.

"It really does feel old," Alex said, as they walked along a barely there path, which was more of an animal track than anything made by humans.

Thick moss covered patches of ground and the occasional fallen branch lay rotting in deep shadow. Shafts of sunlight pierced the canopy, and the farther in they walked, the quieter the wood became.

"This is insane," Reuben murmured, as he pushed back overhanging branches. "You really outdid yourself, Briar."

"It's got nothing to do with me."

"Not true," Avery said. "You allowed him to do this. You helped him break free."

"We all did," she replied. "He was using our White Haven magic. That's why the spring came early. I just gave him a nudge in the right direction."

El swatted another branch away. "Has anyone said anything to you guys about this?"

"No one!" Alex said. "Just like we were promised."

They paused in a small clearing, enjoying the pale rays of the sun, and

Avery asked, "Has this place got a name?"

Reuben laughed. "It sure has. I Googled it earlier. It's called Ravens' Wood."

"No way!" Avery said, astonished.

"It's there, on the map, just like it's been here forever."

Avery turned slowly, squinting as she peered into the wood's murky depths. "I thought I saw a dryad last night."

"You probably did," Briar told her. "That fey magic you channelled for a while allowed that to happen. I think there are more of them, too—although I doubt we'll ever see them."

El's eyes were shining, and she was almost bouncing with excitement. "We were part of something astonishing last night. This is where we should have our solstice celebrations from now on. What do you think?"

"I think that's a brilliant idea," Reuben said. "But I have a feeling it's going to be popular with everyone."

A shimmer of movement disturbed them, and they turned swiftly, hands raised, but it was only Shadow doing her usual fey appearance trick. She leaned against the trunk of the closest tree, grinning at them.

"This is officially my favourite place in White Haven. How are you all?"

"Pretty good," Avery admitted. "What about you?"

"I'm aching a little. I haven't had such a good fight in a long time—even against Gabe."

El walked over and hugged her. "Thanks for last night, Shadow. We couldn't have done this without you."

Although Shadow looked uncomfortable at first, she eventually responded, giving El a quick hug in return. "Thank you, sister."

"Things go well with Harlan?" Reuben asked, a wry smile on his face.

Shadow looked impish. "Very well, thank you. He's a very generous man."

"Of course he is," Alex said. "I'm sure you'll have a beautiful friendship."

Shadow pushed away from the tree. "A girl's got to keep herself busy, and that's all I have to say on that."

"Fair enough," Avery said laughing, and then quickly sobered. "I'm sorry you're stuck here, though. I can't imagine how that must feel."

Shadow's eyes darkened to a stormy blue. "I'll survive. At least now I have this place—a taste of home."

"Is it really?" Briar asked. "It feels magical to us, but does it to you, too?"

"It does." She spread her arms wide and turned slowly. "The Green Man will always be strong here, a little oasis of fey magic. Something to feed my soul if there are dark days ahead. I have a feeling there are things hidden here that only I can find." Her eyes lit up again.

She was irrepressible, Avery thought, feeling a flood of affection for her.

"Well, this is great," Reuben declared, "but now I'm starving. Let's head to the pub for a late lunch. Magic is hungry work."

+ + +

Early on the following Saturday, the final night of the circus's stay in White Haven, Avery entered the back room of Happenstance Books. However, she didn't beat Sally, who was already there and putting the coffee machine on.

"Have you moved in and I don't know about it?" Avery asked, watching her work.

Sally laughed. "Not likely. You know me, the kids wake early and I've abandoned them to Sam. He gets the joy of sorting them out on a Saturday. Has Alex moved in yet?"

Avery grinned sheepishly. "His sofa arrives today. Reuben's going to help him load mine into the back of my van, and then take mine to his place and do a swap. But he's already moved his clothes, and toiletries, and books and stuff. They're picking up more boxes today."

Sally hugged her. "That's fantastic. I'm so pleased for you. I like Alex, I always have, but I've told you that before."

"I know. All those months ago, and you were right."

Sally gave her a final squeeze before releasing her. "I always am. Heard anything else from Shadow?"

"She's been suspiciously quiet, probably setting up some new business venture with Harlan."

"The American?" Sally asked, as she finished preparing the coffee.

"Yeah, and I haven't seen him, either."

"Maybe he left as soon as he'd got the ring."

Avery nodded. "He probably did. If it was so precious, his buyer wouldn't want to wait."

Sally leaned against the counter, her expression thoughtful. "And what about Caspian?"

"Nothing all week. I guess he's busy. We asked him if he wanted to come with us tonight, but he says he'll be away on business for a while."

"Good. I think he needs to get away."

Avery mulled over what she was thinking, but in the end said it anyway. "I feel guilty, like I've led him on, and that it's my fault he developed these feelings for me."

"Don't be ridiculous. You've done no such thing. It's very obvious that you love Alex, and that he loves you, and you two moving in together makes that very clear. Caspian's a grown man, Avery, not a kid. He'll move on. This is his way of doing that."

Avery nodded. "I guess so. I feel I've driven him away."

Sally rolled her eyes. "Stop being a drama queen. How's Alex doing?"

"Being calm and rational as usual, and very pleased about moving in. He's up there right now reorganising the kitchen, which is why I'm here. He says my cupboards are as disorderly as my mind. Cheeky sod."

Sally sniggered. "It's part of your charm."

"Oh, don't you start!"

"Start what?" Dan said, catching the end of the conversation as he barrelled through the door.

"Criticising my organisation skills."

"They are legendary for their nonexistence," Dan admitted. "But it's okay, that's why you have us."

Avery folded her arms. "Don't you start, either. I'm not a child!"

"That is not what we're saying. It's what allows you to be such a creative witch," he said as he took his jacket off. "Anything you can do about the cold?"

"No. It's February, suck it up."

Sally poured them all coffees and passed one to each of them. "I miss the Green Man. Do you think he'll come back?"

Avery sipped her drink, enjoying its sweet warmth. "I doubt it, not like that again, anyway. All the green shoots in my garden have got frost damage, and the early spring warmth has gone. Every now and again, I feel he's here, looking over my shoulder."

"What about Briar? How's she doing?" Sally asked.

Both she and Dan knew that Briar had become the Green Man for a few hours over a week ago.

"It's changed her. She sort of carries this Otherness now, and her magic is even stronger. You should see her garden, and her allotment! She showed me a few days ago. The other gardeners think she has magical compost. They're not wrong, but not quite in the way they think! Hunter arrived last night. I think she needs him now more than ever. He's good for her."

"So he's going tonight, too?" Dan asked.

Avery nodded. "We all are. Corbin has given us free tickets. I can't wait."

Sally said, "Caitlin's disappearance doesn't seem to have ruined the show. Everyone still loves it, from what I've heard."

"You're right, and the performers are happier, too, although I don't think they actually remember her anyway. Or Rafe and Mairi."

"I must admit, I have trouble remembering them," Dan said, his forehead wrinkling with concentration. "If you didn't keep telling me, I wouldn't give them a second thought. I can't even picture what they look like."

Avery stared at them both, as she prepared to ask the question she'd been repeating all week. "And you're sure that wood has been there, next to the castle, all along?"

Sally and Dan exchanged a glance, and Sally said, "One hundred percent. You can't magic an entire wood overnight, not ancient woodland!"

"But the Green Man did!" Avery insisted. "You know about him, you can remember that much."

Dan grabbed a biscuit to dunk into his coffee. "Of course. We're not idiots." He winked at Avery. "But I like the fact that you're trying to tell us it just appeared overnight. Another layer of mystery to White Haven. But trust me, it has enough already."

Unbelievable. The Raven King had effectively made three people disappear, and the Green Man had spelled an entire wood into existence. Their magic was insanely powerful. No one had questioned the appearance of the ancient wood. No one. Not the locals, the visitors, the circus folk, or the news. If they weren't there during the spell, it hadn't happened.

She nodded, giving up. "You're right, it has. I'm just messing with you."

"You look better, though," Dan continued. "You've finally caught up on your sleep."

"I have. The crossroads no longer appear in my head every time I close my eyes, and my magic is back to its normal self."

"And your fey magic has gone?" Sally asked.

"Completely, which is probably a good thing. It was very odd," Avery reflected, remembering how she could feel and see things that weren't really there—not in her world, anyway. "I'm enjoying normality. Speaking of which, I'm going to open up and refresh my spells." She left them to walk through her shop, enjoying its peace and security as she mulled over the latest crazy happenings in White Haven.

✝ ✝ ✝

It was dark when Avery arrived at the circus with Alex, and they parked at the normal car park rather than down the lane behind the hedge.

"This is already feeling weird," Avery told him.

Alex laughed. "We can walk across the fields if you prefer."

"The car park is just fine," she said as she exited the car. "I'm hoping we can enjoy the show like ordinary people."

"Got the tickets?"

She patted her bag. "In my purse. I gave the others theirs earlier, so we'll meet them in there."

As they walked up the path to the castle and the entrance of the circus, it was clear that the circus hadn't suffered from losing the magic of the Raven King and The Green Man. There were as many people milling around as on the first night. A few circus performers were entertaining the crowds—a juggler sent balls whirling in a bewildering show of skill as he balanced on a unicycle, a young man was walking on his hands, and a female acrobat dressed as a dryad cart-wheeled and back-flipped at the edge of the crowd.

They made their way under the arched entrance at the beginning of the path, the fake standing stones looking over them like guards. There were still ravens at the castle, and one was perched on top of one of the stones, cawing loudly as they passed by. Avery gave an involuntary jump.

"Bad memories?" Alex asked, pulling her close.

She shook her head. "It was the raven at the crossroads that made me act so quickly. It was like the Raven King himself was watching over me."

Alex kissed her forehead. "He probably was. He's very resourceful."

"Speaking of which." Avery pointed to the entrance of the Big Top, where the tent sides were pulled back, revealing a glimpse of a shadowy interior. To the side, welcoming the crowd, stood Corbin as the Raven

King. His costume still looked amazing, and when he saw them, he lifted his caped and feathered arms, shouting, "Welcome to the Crossroads Circus!"

The screeching sound of hundreds of ravens filled the air, and the light show flashed images of dark wings across the tent behind him. They smiled at him as they passed, but didn't speak. There were too many people around, and it would have ruined the illusion, but he looked their way, and for the briefest of moments, Avery thought his eyes turned inky black, before people came between them, obscuring him from view. She strained to look back. Did his eyes change for a moment, or did she imagine it?

As soon as Avery entered the tent, she knew for certain. The Raven King was still there, and it was still his circus. She felt like an excited child again as she made her way to her seat, Alex's warm hand in her own, to watch the old myths come to life.

$$+ \quad + \quad +$$

Thanks for reading *Crossroads Magic*. Please make an author happy and leave a review at Happenstance Books! Thank you.

Crown of Magic: White Haven Witches #7 is available now at Happenstance Books.

Newsletter

If you enjoyed this book and would like to read more of my stories, please subscribe to my newsletter at tjgreenauthor.com. You will get two free short stories, *Excalibur Rises* and *Jack's Encounter,* and will also receive free character sheets for all of the main White Haven witches.

By staying on my mailing list you'll receive free excerpts of my new books, as well as short stories, news of giveaways, and a chance to join my launch team. I'll also be sharing information about other books in this genre you might enjoy.

Ream

I have started my own subscription service called Happenstance Book Club. I know what you're thinking! What is Ream? It's a bit like Patreon, which you may be more familiar with, and it allows you to support me and read my books before anyone else.

There is a monthly fee for this, and a few different tiers, so you can choose what tier suits you. All tiers come with plenty of other bonuses, including merchandise, but the one thing common to all is that you can read my latest books while I'm writing them – so they're a rough draft. I will post a few chapters each week, and you can read them at your leisure, as well as comment in them. You can also choose to be a follower for free.

You can comment on my books, chat about spoilers, and be part of a community. I will also post polls, character art, share rituals and spells, share the background to the myths and legends in my books, and some of my earlier books are available to read for free.

Interested? Head to Happenstance Book Club.

https://reamstories.com/happenstancebookclub

Happenstance Book Shop

I also now have a fabulous online shop called Happenstance Books where you can buy eBooks, audiobooks, and paperbacks, many bundled up at great prices, as well as fabulous merchandise. I know that you'll love it! Check it out here: https://happenstancebookshop.com/

YouTube

If you love audiobooks, you can listen for free on YouTube, as I have uploaded all of my audiobooks there. Please subscribe if you do. Thank you. https://www.youtube.com/@tjgreenauthor

Read on for a list of my other books.

Author's Note

T hank you for reading *Crossroads Magic,* the sixth book in the White Haven Witches series.

After the crazy evil of the vampires in the last book, I fancied turning to the old myths again, specifically the Raven King and the Green Man. I had an idea for a circus with a twist, and thought this was a great way to bring these myths to White Haven. The Green Man and the Raven King have special places in English mythology, and are familiar and beloved figures. I couldn't wait to have them interact with White Haven magic.

As usual, my characters continue to grow and change, and I thought it was only natural that Alex and Avery's relationship should evolve, but of course Caspian did, too. I'm sure there'll be more to come of his story!

I'm very fond of my new character, Shadow, and I think Harlan Beckett could become a new favourite, too. These two, and the Nephilim of course, will get their own spin-off series, called White Haven Hunters.

I hope you enjoyed our new enemy, Caitlin. The Empusa is a real myth as well, and I love crossroads magic, so what a perfect fit!

I'll keep you updated on the release information. Join my readers' group by going to https://tjgreenauthor.com to keep up to date, or follow my Facebook page. I post there reasonably frequently.

Thanks again to Fiona Jayde Media for my awesome cover, and thanks to Kyla Stein at Missed Period Editing for applying her fabulous editing skills.

Thanks also to my beta readers, glad you enjoyed it; your feedback, as always, is very helpful!

Finally, thank you to my launch team, who give valuable feedback on typos and are happy to review on release. It's lovely to hear from them—you know who you are! You're amazing! I love hearing from all my readers, so I welcome you to get in touch.

If you'd like to read a bit more background to the stories, please head to my , where I blog about the books I've read and the research I've done on the series—in fact, there's lots of stuff on there about my other series, Rise of the King and White Haven Hunters, too.

If you'd like to read more of my writing, please join my mailing list. You can get a free short story called *Jack's Encounter*, describing how Jack met Fahey—a longer version of the prologue in Call of the King—by subscribing to my newsletter. You'll also get a FREE copy of *Excalibur Rises*, a short story prequel.

You will also receive free character sheets on all of my main characters in White Haven Witches and White Haven Hunters—exclusive to my email list!

By staying on my mailing list you'll receive free excerpts of my new books, as well as short stories and news of giveaways. I'll also be sharing information about other books in this genre you might enjoy.

Give me my FREE short stories!

I look forward to you joining my readers' group.

About the Author

I was born in England, in the Black Country, but moved to New Zealand in 2006. I lived near Wellington with my partner Jase, and my cats Sacha and Leia. However, in April 2022 we moved again! Yes, I like making my life complicated... I'm now living in the Algarve in Portugal, and loving the fabulous weather and people. When I'm not busy writing I read lots, indulge in gardening and shopping, and I love yoga.

Confession time! I'm a Star Trek geek – old and new – and love urban fantasy and detective shows. Secret passion – Columbo! Favourite Star Trek film is the Wrath of Khan, the original! Other top films – Predator, the original, and Aliens.

In a previous life I was a singer in a band, and used to do some acting with a theatre company. For more on me, check out a couple of my blog posts. I'm an old grunge queen, so you can read about my love of that here. For more random news, read this.

If you'd like to follow me on social media, you'll find me here:

f   facebook.com/tjgreenauthor/

P   pinterest.pt/tjgreenauthor/

♪   tiktok.com/@tjgreenauthor

▶   youtube.com/@tjgreenauthor

g   goodreads.com/author/show/15099365.T_J_Green

instagram.com/tjgreenauthor/

bookbub.com/authors/tj-green

https://reamstories.com/happenstancebookclub

Other Books by T J Green

Rise of the King Series

Call of the King

The Silver Tower

The Cursed Sword

✦ ✦ ✦

White Haven Witches Series

Buried Magic

Magic Unbound

Magic Unleashed

All Hallows' Magic

Undying Magic

Crossroads Magic

Crown of Magic

Vengeful Magic

Chaos Magic

Stormcrossed Magic

Wyrd Magic

Midwinter Magic

White Haven and the Lord of Misrule Novella

✦ ✦ ✦

White Haven Hunters
Spirit of the Fallen
Shadow's Edge
Dark Star
Hunter's Dawn
Midnight Fire
Immortal Dusk
Brotherhood of the Fallen

✦ ✦ ✦

Storm Moon Shifters
Paranormal Mysteries set around the wolf shifter pack, Storm Moon.

Storm Moon Rising
Dark Heart

✦ ✦ ✦

Moonfell Witches
This series features the mysterious and magical witches who live in Moonfell, the sprawling Gothic mansion in London. They first appeared in Storm Moon Rising, Storm Moon Shifters Book 1, and then in Immortal Dusk, White Haven Hunters Book 6, and features characters from both

series. However, this series can be read as a standalone.
If you love witches and magic, you will love the Moonfell Witches.

The First Yule: Novella
Triple Moon #1

Printed in Great Britain
by Amazon

4c3761c1-7713-4f21-b527-d8ed4b07bc38R01